Still GRINDIN'

KENDALL BANKS

THE ANTICIPATED SEQUEL TO WELFARE GRIND

Life Changing Books in conjunction with Power Play Media
Published by Life Changing Books
P.O. Box 423 Brandywine, MD 20613

Library of Congress Cataloging-in-Publication Data;

www.lifechangingbooks.net
13 Digit: 978-1934230411
10 Digit: 1-934230413

Acknowledgements

All the things which have made my life worthwhile, not only those of which I know, but also those of which I'm unaware, every one of them has been a loving gift from God, which makes me enormously grateful for all of His blessings.

It's still hard to believe that I'm on book #5. I honestly didn't think I would get past the first book, so I'm still in shock a little bit. It's amazing what you can accomplish, and there's definitely no limit to what you can achieve.

To all my family and friends, thank you from the bottom of my heart for all your support. I also want to thank you for your generosity in allowing me the time to devote to this project, as well as your patience and diligence in proof reading my newest work. I love each one of you dearly.

To my publisher, Azarel I truly appreciate your support, and guidance. I also can't thank you enough for all the attention you've given to each one of my novels, and for your invaluable input. Thanks for giving me the break that so many deserving authors never get, and for that I'm forever grateful.

Special thanks go to author, Tonya Ridley who always delivers intensive line-by-line critiques of my drafts and notable suggestions. I always benefit from our numerous discussions on how my book can be improved, and I'm thankful for your time.

To the LCB fam…Tasha, Kellie, Tony, Shannon, Cheryl,

the entire author roster, editors, and all the test readers, thanks for all you do. Each one of you are truly an asset. #TEAMLCB!!

Thanks to all the bookstores that support me by selling my books and hosting signings. You all are truly invaluable.

And finally, many thanks to the readers who purchase my books. I can't thank you all enough for the numerous uplifting emails, or messages on Facebook and Twitter. It's beyond flattering to hear how much a reader enjoys my work. Knowing I have motivated a person to a point where they're willing to put forth the effort and time to contact me is gratifying. As always, I hope you enjoy this book just like all the others. Until next time…

Smooches,

Kendall Banks
www.facebook.com/authorkendallb
Follow me on Twitter @authorkendallb

1

Prison is *everything* they say it is. Muthafuckas get their heads split wide open with mop ringers. They get stabbed in the neck with homemade shanks and left for dead, on the chow hall floor, bleeding like stuffed pigs. They get raped in the shower and some get sold like cattle for Little Debbie snacks or boxes of cigarettes. The place is nothing short of hell on Earth. Thank God I was just visiting. The place still gave me the damn heebie jeebies though.

Dressed in a royal blue, off the shoulder maxi dress and flip flops, I turned from the bathroom mirror and watched the last bitch walk out. I'd finished checking my make-up, but the bathroom was filled with several other women doing the same, wanting to look their best for their pussy starved baby daddies and boyfriends. After quickly glancing underneath the row of stalls to make sure everyone was gone, I knocked on the one I'd been watching through the mirror for the past fifteen minutes.

"What?" Treasure asked from behind the door as if she didn't appreciate being interrupted.

"Don't *what* me, girl," I said, glaring at the stall, but glancing quickly towards the door, hoping no one, especially a guard, walked in. "Are you ready?"

"Yeah, I been ready," she responded sassily.

The stall opened.

Treasure stepped out dressed in a mini skirt, a graphic t-shirt that said TOO FLY and silver gladiator sandals. Even though she'd turned twelve just days ago she was filling out nicely, slowly beginning to gain a shape. Even her titties were beginning to grow wildly. More importantly her pre-teen hormones had her starting to smell her own piss.

"So, is it in?" I asked.

"Yeah,"

"Are you sure?"

She rolled her eyes. "I said yeah, dang."

"Bitch, don't roll your damn eyes at me. Are you sure that sack won't slip out?"

She sucked her teeth annoyed at my persistence.

"Look, damn it!" I took a step towards her. "That shit has to be stuffed deep so it can't fall out. If it falls out your damn pussy while we're out there, do you know how much time you're looking at?"

She rolled her eyes again. "Mom, I got this. You drilled me enough already."

"Are you wearing the panties I bought you, the extra tight ones?"

"Yes. I told you that before we left the house."

"You sure? They should keep it from slipping."

"I told you I got 'em on."

"Alright, let me see you walk," I said, glancing at the door again.

I had to be sure she was all the way ready. One mistake could get us jammed up. Treasure rolled her eyes again and began to walk. Immediately, I noticed she was walking slightly wide legged.

"Why are you walking like that?"

"It hurts."

"Girl, I don't give a damn. Them guards out there ain't stupid. They're trained to notice shit like that. Now straighten that shit out."

She sighed but walked back and forth from the door

again. This time her stride was the way it was supposed to be.

"That's better. Now, when we get out there, act normal. Don't do anything stupid, alright?"

Treasure nodded.

I stared at the door and took a deep breath. It was show-time. Although I'd done this several times before, I still got nervous each time. Now was even more stressful because Treasure was with me. Having my own pussy stuffed with a plastic sack of weed and rocks was one thing. But having Treasure's stuffed with it was another.

My heart pumped as I watched the door, gaining the composure to walk out into the lobby. Damn, I was nervous. But after realizing I had to get this money, I finally walked out of the bathroom proudly.

The prison's intake lobby was filled with wall to wall bitches waiting to get called back to see their men. It reminded me of the fucking welfare office. There were mostly young girls all over the place talking on their cell phones, dressed in tight hoochie-mama shit. Nearly each one of them had kids with them. Shit, some of them had three or four.

Moments later, Treasure and me found a chair and sat down. Still worried, I glanced at my watch. The guard would be calling us any minute for our visit. Sure enough, minutes later, he did. Both me and Treasure stood and walked across the room to the desk.

"Do you have anything metal on you?" the guard behind the desk asked. "Any money or keys?"

"No," I said in the sweetest voice I could muster.

I'd left my purse in a locker because you weren't allowed to bring anything into the visiting room so him asking me a bunch of questions would annoy me if he continued.

"Alright, head on through the metal detectors over there," he said quickly.

A burly looking dark-skinned broad standing on the other end of the metal detector signaled me to come through. I walked through the detector without making it beep. Knowing the procedure, I raised my arms and let her search me. I always hated having this particular guard's hands on me. It was obvious she liked women. Touching up the cute ones like me proved to be the highlight of her day. After the inappropriate search was over, I stepped to the side and watched as Treasure went through the same process.

As the dyke broad began to pat Treasure down, I couldn't help but feel my heart beating crazy again. I was scared to death that the sack was going to fall out from underneath her skirt. If it did, I didn't have any idea what I would do. Plan A was to play dumb, like I didn't know she had it. She was a minor and would get less time than me. Playing innocent worked a year ago with Shane when the police ran up in my spot so I'd try it again if anything kicked off. Plan B was to have Treasure say they planted that shit on her. I just prayed everything would go okay.

"Dang," Treasure said, annoyed at the female guard's callous filled hands. "Do you gotta grab on me like that? I'm a minor."

I wanted to smack the shit out of her. I looked at her little narrow ass like she'd lost her mind. We'd had the talk about being nice to the guards hundreds of times. This was not the time or place to be getting smart. The last thing we needed right now was to give them a reason to give either of us a more thorough search. I gave Treasure a stern look that said, "Bitch, are you crazy?"

Ignoring my stare, she snatched away from the guard. "That's why I hate coming up here. Y'all always touching on people real nasty-like and stuff."

Her neck jerked. Her eyes rolled. The attitude she gave was super nasty. Her voice was loud and snobbish, and the way she glared at the guard's shaved sides and Mohawk disturbed me. All eyes in the lobby were directly on her. That attention was exactly what the fuck we didn't need.

I could see from the look on the female guard's face that she wanted to be a bigger bitch than she already was. Without hesitation, I grabbed Treasure, told the lady thank you and headed for the door. When we reached the door, the lock popped and it opened. As soon as we walked down the long path leading to the visiting room and passed another guard, I snatched Treasure's dumb ass by the shoulder.

"What the fuck is wrong with you?" I whispered angrily. "Don't ever do that shit again. You want to get us caught?"

Treasure pulled away. "Whatever," she said dismissively. "She shouldn't have been grabbing on me like that. That was nasty."

"Look, chill out with that little attitude. This not the time or the place for it. We gotta be about business."

The little bitch rolled her eyes again and sighed as if my advice was getting on her nerves. All I could do was shake my head. *God, please give me the strength to hold back from knocking her fast ass out in front of these people.*

The two of us finally walked inside the actual visiting room and made our way to an empty table and sat down. As Treasure looked around the room at everyone talking and laughing, I looked down at my bronzed looking legs and pedicured feet to be sure I was on point. I also looked down at my perky breasts and exposed shoulders. My eyes immediately took in the scar on my right shoulder. It was my skin's only blemish. But as much as I hated it, I loved it. It was my war wound; the wound that always reminded me that getting greedy and not properly thinking a plan out could be fatal.

As usual, the sight of the scar always took me back to that dreadful day just one year ago when me and Treasure witnessed so much bloodshed. It always reminded me of how close I was to death. I could still feel the blood seeping from my body. My ears could still hear the shot from Paco's gun. My eyes could still see the flash from the nozzle, but even more, my heart could still feel the fear and disbelief I had while laid out on the floor staring up at Treasure as she held those two guns on me.

Behind her, Paco's dead body was sprawled out on the floor lying in blood. I remembered Rick's wounded body against the wall while his life slowly left him. Just to see someone take

5

their last breath must've scarred my baby for life. I felt terrible for surrounding her with so much tragedy, but there was no turning back. Too much had been done.

It was obvious that I'd fucked things up. It was because of me that her brother and grandmother were dead. It was because of me that we were on the run from so many people. It was all because of me that we could never go back to the only home Treasure knew, McCulloh Homes. I'd shattered our life and family so I couldn't blame her for wanting to kill me.

Thankfully Shane, of *all* people, was able to talk some sense into her. The moment had really made him come out of his shell in a way that I never imagined he was capable of. It was like he had truly become a man that day. But it wasn't just his words that saved me. Lucky also played a part.

As Lucky laid on the floor bleeding from the hole Paco's gun had ripped through his stomach, he also spoke sense into Treasure's ears. He let her know that despite her anger for me, enough blood had been shed. He promised her that killing her own mother would give her nightmares and regrets she would never be able to escape. Those words combined with Deniro charging out of the kitchen and planting himself in my arms as I lay bleeding eventually made her put the guns down.

Several moments later, police sirens were heard approaching in the distance. The sound of them made me realize that I had to get our story straight. While I plotted on what I would say, Lucky and Treasure had a plan of their own. That day I realized he really did love her and felt that she'd been through enough.

By the time the police entered the house, Treasure had wiped her finger prints off of the guns with her shirt and placed Paco's gun back into his hand. Lucky then took my gun so his own fingerprints were on it. *How heroic and stupid,* I thought, all at the same time.

When the police arrived he took the wrap for shooting Paco, but in self defense after Paco had shot Rick. Treasure corroborated Lucky's story like a pro, no hesitations at all. She was

6

a thorough little bitch, who was far more mature than what I gave her credit for most times.

Before we left Arizona, Lucky had begun to treat me slightly better during his time spent in the hospital. Maybe that was a sign of forgiveness. Each time we talked, the conversations mainly revolved around Treasure. I hated that and wanted him to show interest in me, but he never really did. He couldn't really be blamed. I did feel guilty for putting him in the middle of the Paco and Rick bullshit. He'd looked out for me and I'd fucked him over. But despite my betrayal, he still cared enough about my daughter to put her before himself. That was some real nigga shit.

Returning back to reality and placing the memory behind me, I stuffed my mirror back into my purse as I saw Treasure's father walking across the visiting room towards us. He was dressed in blue, state-issued Dickie pants with sharp creases. He was also wearing a light blue short-sleeved button down, and tan colored work boots. Years of working out had given him what I called a penitentiary build; buffed and chiseled in the upper body, but slim in the legs.

Drake was still as fine as he was ten years ago though. He was the color of ground cinnamon and his head was shaved down to the scalp. His goatee was neatly trimmed and his eyes were a lighter brown than I remembered. His arms were also covered with a few tattoos that he told me he'd gotten from some white boy up in here for a few boxes of cigarettes. They looked as good as the work of any professional artist on the outside, especially the cross that took up most of the space on his right arm. At least I knew he believed in Jesus.

Drake leaned in and hugged me as soon as he reached the table. I hugged him back. Tightly. He held me for a little longer than I would've liked. I was here for business, nothing else. When he let me go, he hugged Treasure next. But instead of being happy to see her father, she rolled her eyes and puckered her lips to the side. Even though she was only two when he went down, visiting him still never seemed to make her the slightest

7

bit happy. Besides, she hadn't been to see him in over three years.

"How you doin', Princess?" Drake asked as he let her go and looked at her oddly.

Treasure folded her arms, took an annoying sounding deep breath and said, "I'm good." She refused to look at him. No eye contact at all. She began to survey the room as if he wasn't standing in front of her.

Seeing how aggravated she looked, Drake asked, "What's up, baby? You ain't happy to see your old man?"

She looked down at her manicured finger nails like the sound of his voice was getting on her nerves. "Yeah," she spoke halfheartedly.

Drake looked at me as if to say, "What's up with her?"

"You know she's almost a teenager," I told him. "You know how they are at that age. She wanna be grown."

Treasure sighed.

Drake laughed. "Yeah, you right," he said jokingly, then sat down.

"I gotta go to the bathroom," Treasure said just before getting up and walking off.

Drake shook his head then shot me the sexy, googly eyes.

He placed a hand over mine. "You lookin' good in that dress, Keema. Damn, girl, you give a nigga a hard on every time you come up here."

"Thank you," I replied, not really liking the feel of his rough hand on mine. I didn't want to give him the wrong impression. I had just one dude that I was willing to give all my pussy to lately.

"Nah, I'm serious, Keema. You really lookin' good. You got a man yet?"

I took my hand from underneath his. "Why, Drake?"

He smiled. "Because I wanna know."

"Drake, look, I can already tell by the way you're looking at me and talking that you wanna hit this, but those days are over."

"Come on, Keema. Why you actin' like that? You know I'm gettin' out in just two more months."

"Drake, what we got is business only. I'm only fucking with you because of our deal."

Drake had been down ten years for bank robbery. I'd never really fucked with him or given him the time of day since the judge sentenced him. Shit, the nigga couldn't do anything for me but run up my damn phone bill. But that was before he called a few months ago and asked me if I was interested in making some money. Of course at the sound of the word *money* my antennas went up. He told me he needed someone on the outside to bring him in some weed and sometimes crack every couple of weeks. The shit was big business behind the fences. He told me that I would be paid five hundred dollars per trip.

I took the job.

Gladly.

I even recruited Treasure. Drake didn't know it, but her pussy was just as stuffed with work as mine was. That's why she'd just gone to the bathroom.

"Come on, Keema," Drake pleaded, looking me in my eyes. "I need a wife. I ain't gettin' any younger. Besides, you know I still love you. You're the mother of my seed. I never stopped lovin' you."

I wasn't stupid. He talked that same shit all penitentiary niggas talked when they were behind bars. They all say they love you, they don't eat pork any more, and that they've changed their lives forever.

"Keema," Drake continued, taking my hand in his own, glaring at me with sincerity. "I know you don't have a reason to believe me. I know I was a cold dog ten years ago. I know I was. But these ten years taught me a lot."

The look on his face was the sincerest I'd ever seen it.

"I've learned that nothing in life is worth more than family. And, baby, you and Treasure are the only family I got. I want to make it right for being out of your lives. I swear I do."

I was tuned in. He sounded genuine.

9

"That's why I asked you to bring this stuff in for me. You're the only person I trust. And when I get home, I wanna marry you."

I was still a little skeptical, but he was breaking down my walls.

"I'm serious about this, Keema. I want to do this right this time...share everything I own with you. Everything I got on the outside."

Damn, my pussy was starting to grow moist. Shit, I had to close my legs tightly to keep the sack of drugs from sliding out.

"I'm ready to be yours," Drake told me with sincerity.

He had me giving it some thought. He had me thinking about giving him a chance.

Drake looked around quickly and pressed closer to me. "Look," he whispered, "that paper you makin' each trip ain't shit compared to what I got set up when I get out of here."

I looked at him intently. "What do you mean by that?"

He looked around again. "I mean, the Feds didn't find all the money from the robbery."

"What?"

My heart skipped a beat.

Chill bumps spread across my entire body. The sound of money always did that to me.

"Yeah, I stashed some."

"How much?" I leaned in closer to him.

He smiled. "Enough."

"No, really. How much?"

"I said enough."

"Why didn't you tell me?"

"I didn't know if I could trust you. But after seeing how you've been getting that work up in here for me, I know you got me."

I smiled widely.

"But look, though." Drake reached into the pocket of his pants and pulled out a small piece of paper and handed it to me.

10

"I need you to call this dude for me Friday. He got something for me."

"What is it?"

"You'll see when you call him. I can't call because these phones are monitored. But it's real important, Keema. I can't get the money without it. He's been holding something for me for safe keeping ever since I got in here."

My curiosity was peeked.

"I need you to do this, Keema. It's for us."

"I got you," I assured him.

Moments later, I got up and headed for the bathroom to get the package out. As I walked across the visiting room, all I could wonder was what Drake's friend was holding for him and how much money Drake had stashed. As I approached the bathroom door it opened. A female guard stepped out. She gawked at me suspiciously.

"Can't let you go in," she stated firmly.

"But I have to use the bathroom."

"No one can go in right now."

She then pulled her radio from her waist, pressed a button on the side of it and said, "We've got a situation in the female bathroom. I'm going to need assistance."

My heart dropped to my stomach as I looked over her shoulder to see Treasure standing in the bathroom with a scared and nervous look on her face.

Damn it, Treasure!

2

Seeing Treasure come walking out of that bathroom was like a breath of fresh air. I'd immediately thought the worse when the guard told me I couldn't go in. I thought for sure Treasure had gotten caught. Come to find out, one of the toilets had overflowed.

Thank God!

Within fifteen minutes I handled my business, handed the goods over to Drake and left the prison with a smile on my face. As usual, his brother met me off of Liberty Road to pay me for my services. I hit Treasure off with a crisp twenty dollar bill even though I got double the money for double product delivered. The little ungrateful bitch just rolled her eyes never even saying thank you.

It was a little after four o'clock by the time we pulled into our driveway after the two hour drive from the prison back to Baltimore. I turned off the engine of my platinum Camero and climbed out. Its spinning chrome rims were still chopping like windmills and shining hard underneath the August sun. Along with the rims it was also laced with small TV's in the headrests for the kids and an expensive sound system that I couldn't pronounce. The name on the plates read #1 Hustla so no one would think I was fronting. My shit belonged to *me*, not my baby daddy or a boyfriend. I hated when chicks fronted.

My mother had willed me her Cadillac. It wasn't really my style, so I traded it in for my Camero the day I heard she'd left me everything. I liked muscle and speed. I liked shit that growled and ate up the highway. That was the shit I looked good in. Cadillacs were for old folks and people who had shit to prove. My mom also left me her house and thirty thousand dollars in the bank. It surprised the hell out of me since we weren't on good terms just before she died. We hadn't really been on good terms my entire life, so the last thing I expected was for her to leave me the shit she'd worked her ass off to buy.

The money definitely came in handy given that I was still waiting on the millions from Frenchie, Dupree and Rick's estate. Rick was the last man standing of the three brothers, so after that nigga got shot up and died, the empire was left to Shane and Deniro. And since I was their loving mother and guardian, it would all come to me. I would have control of all the money and businesses myself, at least until Deniro turned eighteen. Shane would be under my care forever until the day he died or got a new brain, so that shit worked in my favor. Thank God the state required him to be mentally stable and able to care for himself to collect the money.

Since Dupree and Rick both died in separate homicides, the money was tied up in a lot of red tape, prolonging things even more than the usual time needed to handle an estate. So basically, until the money came through, I had to do what I knew best...

Hustle.

Hustle Hard.

Since I'd gotten back from Phoenix, I had been laying low. I knew there were a few lingering enemies out there, so being out and about wasn't a good idea. I still had a few people who wanted to blow my head off, possibly Cee-Lo or some of Dupree and Rick's family. The only reason I'd come back in the first place was because of my mother's money. The only people who knew I was back was my cousin Raven and some new bitch I was fucking with named Shy who lived four doors down from my mom's house. Raven told me that since word got out Paco was dead, the streets weren't mentioning my name too much anymore, but I still wasn't going to chance it.

I figured the state still had a score to settle with me, too. They had a warrant out for my arrest for welfare fraud, but that shit didn't stop me though. Welfare grinding had always been my best hustle, so leaving it completely alone was impossible. I simply drove out to Delaware two weeks ago and applied for benefits out there with a fake ID, Social Security number, and an address. The whole process cost me two thousand dollars but I got it done and now had new connections in Delaware. Now, I was just waiting for all my paper work to go through. I'd even used Cash, my dead son's information to get money off of him, too.

"The more kids to claim, the better...chi chang," I said to myself hearing the cash register sound go off in my head.

Treasure and I headed up the walkway to the house still not saying anything to each other. When we walked in, our ears were bombarded with the loud volume of the plasma television. *Bad Girls Club* was on and both Deniro and Shane were posted on the floor in front of it. They were stacking up gift cards from Lowes, Walmart, Target, Best Buy, and a few other department stores.

One thing I'd learned in life was that it was never good to have only one hustle. It was always best to have as many as possible. That way, if one dried up, money could pour in from other directions. The gift card hustle was a new one to me. Raven had put me onto it. Through her *get money* male associate, I had a hook up that could get me gift cards in bulk at a super cheap price. I was selling them for half the retail price. Sometimes I'd even sell them for a third of the price to sell them off quickly. Either way, it was bringing me good clientele. I was making five to six hundred dollars a day off that hustle.

I rushed over and kissed Shane and Deniro on the cheek after seeing Raven and Shy sitting near the back of the house at the dining room table babbling like gossiping hoes. "Did y'all

15

eat yet?" I asked.

"Nah," Deniro answered.

"Did y'all eat yet?" Shane chimed in. "You mad at us, Keema?"

"No, I'm not mad, boy. Why didn't y'all eat?"

Shane shrugged, grinned widely for no reason at all then continued stacking the cards.

"I'll order pizza," I told both of them.

"Alright," Shane responded.

Shockingly, he didn't just repeat things anymore. He now answered questions more reasonably from time to time. *My boy was maturing*, I thought looking at how big he'd gotten. Then I frowned. I didn't want him getting too much sense though. I needed him to stay dumb, under my influence for life.

"Did y'all work on the box of cards I told you to pull from the bedroom?" Treasure asked her brothers.

Shane shrugged which meant, 'no'.

"Y'all been here all day," Treasure blasted.

Deniro didn't say anything. He kept on sorting the cards.

Treasure turned to me. "Mom, they should've been had those cards done. They get on my nerves with that. They do it all the time."

"They're good," I said, "It's really your job to do that."

"But that's not fair. They're lazy and you let them get away with it," she quickly shot back.

"Treasure, I said they're good. Don't tell me how to run my business."

She was really starting to get on my nerves with her attitude.

Treasure sucked her teeth, said something underneath her breath, and sat on the couch, rolling her eyes like she paid the bills. I didn't appreciate her trying to tell me how to run my hustle, but I also didn't feel like arguing.

Raven walked out of the dining room area blazing a blunt and talking on her cell phone. My cousin was a beast, beauty wise; I had to admit. She inherited it from her mother, Charise,

my mother's sister. All the women in my family had killer bodies. I didn't go for women, but if I did, she could definitely get it.

I watched her sashay through the living room with the
phone clutched tightly to her ear. Someone must've been telling
her something good as she ran her fingers through her jet black,
long hair. It was all hers, no fake shit, so that was a plus, too. Her
walnut colored eyes were big and complemented her golden skin
tone perfectly. She also rocked a natural beauty mark just over
the corner of her right lip. She always rocked the hottest shit,
too. Nothing was fake or knockoff. She had a boosting hustle
going on that kept her in Prada, Gucci, Chanel, and numerous
other designers. She even had a few dope boys lacing her with
new clothes on the regular, but mostly she lived off her boosting
hustle.

"I'm sayin' Keema, you can't get money with me?" Shy,
my next door neighbor asked out of the blue as she walked toward me.

With a wide smile, thick eyebrows and eyes that didn't
seem to blink too often, Shy's features were striking, but not
drop dead gorgeous. She also rocked nice clothes, but nowhere
near as expensive as Raven or even me. As usual she wanted in
on one of our hustles. Evidently, getting paid to deliver the gifts
cards wasn't enough.

I chuckled. "Girl, stop begging. It makes you look bad."

"Fuck you Keema. I just wanna make good money, not
this weak ass loot I'm gettin' now."

"Beggers can't be choosey, bitch." I followed up the
statement with a wild laugh. "Just give it some time. Your day is
coming."

Shy shook her head. "Y'all always say that. I'm gonna be
an old bitch with dry ass pussy and a house full of cats by the
time it happens."

"Shy, we got you. Just chill," I added.

She sighed, not truly convinced. "Anyway, why didn't
you come with us to the club last night?"

"Because I didn't feel like it," I responded.

17

In all actuality, I wasn't hitting any clubs until I was sure it was safe for me in these streets again. I'd even used my fake ID to switch all the utilities in the house from my mother's name to Trina Douglas, my fake-me-out identity. Nobody could be trusted. So clubs were out.

"You shoulda been there. It was mad niggas up in that bitch." Shy got hyped as she began to explain.

Unfortunately, her boasting ended all too soon. Raven ended her cell phone conversation and interrupted us seconds later.

"Guess what?" Raven asked me with her hands on her hips.

"What?"

"You know that nigga I fuck with on the East Side with the Phantom?"

"Dollar? Yeah, what about him?"

"You'll never guess what he just told me."

"What?"

"He found Peppi."

I instantly sat forward on the couch at the news.

Treasure did the same.

"Where?" I asked.

"He opened a bar on Euclid Avenue."

I was pissed. "With my muthafuckin' money, I'll bet."

I couldn't believe that after fucking me out of thousands of dollars he actually had the nerve to show his face in Baltimore again. That nigga tricked me out of my money, telling me that he was investing in my own personal spa. Lies…all lies.

"He must really think I'm a weak bitch. How much would your homeboy charge to body that muthafucka?"

"Why you can't kill him yourself?" Treasure asked with a straight face.

This was something I didn't want Treasure involved in. "Treasure, shut up and stay out of this."

"No, why you want to get someone else?" she snapped. "He stole from you, so *you* need to handle him."

"Treasure, I said stay out of this."

With a quick smack of the lips she ripped into me. "No wonder he took advantage of you. You're weak."

Immediately, all the blood in my face scattered. I was now pale from hearing those words. "Didn't I just tell you about telling me how to run my shit?"

"Well, maybe if you would do it right, I wouldn't have to tell you," she countered.

Without hesitation, I slapped Treasure so hard her knees buckled and she dropped to the floor. I was fed up. I couldn't take another second of her smart ass mouth.

The entire room fell totally silent.

All eyes were on us.

"Don't you *ever* talk to me like that again! Do you understand me?"

Treasure held the side of her face as she looked up at me with tears in her eyes. For a second she looked at me with surprise. But soon the look changed. It grew dark and evil. I could see spite in her eyes.

Immediately, despite my anger, I felt terrible. My mother whipped me viciously when I was younger, sometimes so bad the authorities needed to come. But I'd vowed to never whip my children. Sure...I threatened them, cursed at them, but I never hit them. Treasure had pushed me too damn far. She'd gotten too grown and her mouth had gotten too smart.

Treasure finally stood from the floor and stared at me. The spiteful look in her eyes hadn't changed. I felt bad, but wouldn't dare apologize. She had to be put in her place. She'd been talking foul out the mouth for three years now.

Seeing the awkwardness of the situation, Shy told Shane to gather the gift cards so they could drop them off to my clients. She then placed an arm around Treasure. "Come on," she said, "let's go get this money."

Treasure gave me a final look as she, Shane and Shy headed for the door. She obviously wanted to say something, but thought against it.

"And bring back *all* my damn loot!" I shouted to her as she headed out the door.

I didn't give a fuck about her attitude. I also wouldn't advise her to use that as an excuse to short me. Playing games with my money would get her slapped again, or possibly pistol whipped with my gun.

"You alright?" Raven asked as soon as the door shut.

I nodded. "I'm good. I'm just sick and tired of her damn mouth."

"That's understandable. So, what you wanna do about Peppi?"

"I wanna get at that slimy muthufucka."

"So, let's do it," Raven commented deviously.

Suddenly, my cell phone rang interrupting us. The ring tone surprised me. It was Lucky so I answered. Quickly.

"Hey, Keema."

I smiled at the sound of his voice. "Hey, baby."

"Treasure around?"

Hearing Lucky ask for her made my smile fade immediately.

"Nah."

"Well, how is she doing?"

I rolled my eyes. The last thing I wanted to talk about was Treasure. "She alright," I answered with attitude evident in my tone.

"Well, I got some business in Baltimore. Is it alright if I come see her? It'll be in a couple of weeks?"

Unable to bite my tongue, jealously invaded my veins. "Is *she* all you want to see?"

Hearing my attitude, Lucky responded, "Keema, I appreciate you sticking by my side at the hospital when I was fighting for my life. But don't get it twisted. Let's not forget that it was *your* fault I was in there in the first place."

He was right. All the shit that went down in Phoenix was definitely my fault. If I could only turn back the hands of time, I would've never put Lucky in harm's way.

20

"What we had is over," he continued, "but I still want to do for Treasure. She's a good kid. And you know I see her like a daughter. Did she get the money I sent last week?"

"Yeah," I answered dryly as I slumped down on the couch.

"Alright, well tell her I'll be there soon. I'll let you know the exact date later. I'm going to take her shopping."

With that said the phone went dead.

I took the phone from my ear and dropped it on the couch. I couldn't help being jealous of my own daughter. Treasure was getting what I wanted…Lucky's love. I also couldn't help being mad at her for that as I stared down at the white Tahitian Michele watch around my right wrist that I'd bought with the thousand dollars he'd sent for Treasure. Just like I hadn't told her about the money, I wasn't sure if I was going to tell her about the upcoming visit.

3

"Damn, Keema, what the fuck?" Drake asked. "You ain't hooked up with 'ole boy yet? What's goin' on?"

"He never answers the phone," I said with major attitude.

In all honesty I'd been calling the nigga. Shit, I called him several times, but he never answered. I had no idea what was up with him. I was beginning to wonder if maybe it was a wrong number or maybe he was somehow playing Drake.

"What do you mean he ain't been answerin'?"

"I mean just what I said. I've called him eight or nine times and he never answers."

"That don't sound right."

"What, you think I'm lying? Drake, don't call me with that bullshit. I'm not going to argue with your simple ass."

"I ain't arguin'. I'm just sayin' the shit sound fishy."

"Well, I can't force the nigga to pick up the damn phone."

"Shit," he whispered.

There was silence.

I could hear the chattering of surrounding convicts in the background.

"Did you leave him any voice mail messages?" Drake questioned.

"Yeah, each and every time."

"Did you tell him you're my baby mama?"

"Yeah. I told him that, Drake."

"I'm serious, Keema. He don't fuck with people he don't know. So, it's real important that you let him know who you are."

"Nigga, I told you that I let him know who I was. Shit, I even texted him. The nigga ain't got back yet."

"And why didn't you come see me this weekend? It's been two weeks since the last visit."

He was getting on my nerves with the questions. I wasn't really in the mood. My mind was on something a whole lot more serious. As soon as Raven got here, I was going to handle some business that I'd been waiting a long time for.

"I've been busy," I told him.

I really had been. I'd been hustling hard body for the past couple of weeks selling over three hundred gift cards in the process. I also had to take a trip back down to Delaware to finalize my welfare benefits. The last thing I felt like doing was taking that long ass trip to the prison. The money he was hitting me off with failed in comparison to what I was getting off of the gift card hustle. Taking a chance on getting caught smuggling drugs into a prison just wasn't worth it.

"Too busy to get this money?" Drake asked. "Shit, Keema, I've got a business to run up in here. Niggas is dependin' on me. I really need you to step it up. My competition is makin' me look bad."

My eyes rolled.

"For real, Keema. I called you a couple of days ago. You didn't even answer. What's up with that?"

I saw the number on the house phone's caller ID. It came through as *Restricted,* but knew it was a prison call. He was the only person who called my house from a restricted number.

"I didn't know you called. No one told me."

"Damn, Keema. Haven't you thought about what I told you when you came to visit? I was real about my feelings for you. I meant that shit."

"I know."

"Then make me know that shit then. I need you to handle that business."

"Look, I got you."

"You sure?"

"Yeah, nigga. And what's up with this dude anyway? What exactly does he have for you?"

"You'll see."

"Why can't you just tell me? Why is the shit such a big ass secret?"

"Because this phone isn't safe to talk on. I told you these damn white folks monitor shit."

My curiosity was definitely sparked since the visit, but at the same time, I didn't like walking blind folded into a situation. I'd ducked enough bullets and wasn't in too much of a hurry to duck anymore. But knowing that Drake had money stashed would keep me fucking with him temporarily, just until I got my share.

"This call is about to be disconnected in sixty seconds," an automated voice suddenly spoke.

"Alright, Keema, I gotta go. But make sure you get on that business."

"I got you, Drake."

"And get down here this weekend. I need some of that as soon as possible."

"Un huh," I mumbled nonchalantly.

He hung up.

I immediately tried the number he'd given me again. As usual, all I got was a voicemail. Once again I left a message explaining that I was Drake's baby mama and that I'd been told to call. After hanging up, I texted the number and left the same message. Soon as I sat the phone on the couch, a car horn blasted from outside. I got up, looked out of the window and saw a silver Lincoln Navigator sitting in the driveway. The passenger side window was down and Raven was sitting in the seat, her lipstick glistening in the darkness. When she signaled for me to come out side, I grabbed my phone and walked out of the house.

"What's up?" I greeted, smelling weed as I approached the SUV and hopped into the backseat. The interior was flooded with thick weed smoke as Damian Marley's, *Welcome to Jamrock* blasted from the speakers.

In the driver's seat sat Dollar, Raven's boyfriend for the month of August. He was tall, slim, and had dark blotches spread across his pale colored face. His hair was twisted into thick dreads that hung past his shoulders. Dollar wasn't the most attractive guy in the hood, but his eyes were a sexy shade of green and his pockets were fat...making him fine as hell in my book.

"What's up, girl?" Raven asked, turning to look me in the eye. "You ready?"

"Hell yeah," I told her, admiring the new diamond studs in her ear. They appeared to be at least two carats.

She passed me the blunt just as Dollar spoke to me without turning around.

I leaned forward, hit him on the shoulder and spoke sexily. "What's up, Dollar? Good looking out."

I couldn't help but notice the two gleaming, platinum chains dangling from his neck and the white wife beater he wore, exposing his thick biceps and barbed wire tattoo. The nigga was sexy, but since he was Raven's pick of the month, I'd fall back.

"You sure all you want to do is talk to the nigga first?" Dollar questioned as we pulled off. "I told you my price for taking care of him for you."

"I should be good. Once I let the nigga know what it is, everything should be straight. He better have all my cash. Payable on the spot."

"A'ight," Dollar said, speeding down the block. "I can gut the nigga for that small fee."

"Nah, it's cool. I know he'll pay me all my money. All of it!" I replied.

I finally hit the blunt and leaned back. I couldn't wait to see the look on Peppi's face when I walked up in the club on his ass. The shit was still amazing to me that he actually had the heart to open up a club here in Baltimore like he had no worries at all about being found.

That was the crazy thing about people from B-more, we didn't give a fuck about consequences. That thought had me thinking more and more about pressing up on Dollar. The nigga's scent filled the back seat and had me wet as Raven kept rubbing her hands through his dreads. The shit had me wanting to pull over for some threesome type shit.

Thankfully, we finally reached the club before I was crazy enough to act on my thoughts. Dollar pulled straight to the front and slammed on brakes. The parking lot was half filled maybe because the evening was still early. It was just after eight, so I figured most people hadn't come out yet.

"You want me to come in with you?" Raven asked. "I wanna be there when he sees your face."

I hopped out the truck then agreed to let her come in.

Dollar simply shook his head giving me a look of pity as if I had no idea how to handle shit. I winked at his ass real quick then turned to head inside. As we entered, some sort of Mexican music played from the speakers. Dozens of people, either Mexican or Puerto Rican danced throughout; all them muthafuckas looked alike to me. I stopped at the door and let my eyes scour the room for Peppi.

"There he is," Raven said, tapping me on the arm and pointing towards the bar.

I let my eyes focus on the area of the bar she was pointing to. Within seconds, they caught sight of Peppi. His back was towards me, but there was no doubt, it was him. He was being his normal jovial animated self as he macked to some young Latin broad. The son of a bitch was probably right in the middle of talking her out of her money just like he'd done to me. I sure as hell wasn't going to let that happen. Quickly, I took off with speed headed straight for the slimy taco-eating muthufucka. When both me and Raven reached him, I tapped him on the shoulder. He took a sip of his drink and turned around with a huge smile on his face. But once he laid his eyes on me, the smile abruptly disappeared and he nearly choked on his drink.

"Uh-uh-uh," he stuttered nervously. "Keema, my little chocolate butter cup."

"Where's my damn money, Peppi?" I asked sternly.

"Money?" He pretended to have no idea of what I was talking about. He quickly glanced at the woman he'd been talking to and then back to me trying to make me look stupid.

"Don't fucking play with me, you piece of shit! Where's my damn money?"

"My precious mocha colored flower, Peppi does not know of such thing. What money do you speak of?"

"Peppi, quit fucking playing with me, damn it!" I roared.

People began to take notice. They began to stare at us.

Seeing that we were drawing attention, Peppi said, "Princess, I'm afraid that you have me confused with someone else. I know nothing of money. In fact, I know nothing of you. Do we even know each other?"

My eyes widened. "You cruddy muthafucka, I want my money right now! I don't care how you get it or where the fuck you get it from! All I know is I want my damn money!"

"Boss, is there a problem?" a tall heavy-set Mexican dude asked Peppi. He was built like a brick wall.

"Yes," Peppi told him, gaining confidence now that his bouncer was standing beside him. "It seems this *person* has me mistaken for someone else."

He spoke like he was royalty and I was garbage off the damn street.

"Muthafucka, I'm not just some damn *person*, you banana boat riding son of a bitch! You know who the fuck I am! Now, go get my money right now, Peppi!"

"Oh my, such foul language. Please remove this bad influence from my establishment," Peppi instructed.

I quickly snatched the collar of his shirt. "You taco eating, bastard!"

At that moment the bouncer grabbed me.

"Get the fuck off of her!" Raven screamed as she began to hit the bouncer in the back of the head. As the man shielded his head from the blows he kept hold of me.

Peppi broke my grip and quickly dashed around the bar to place a distance between us. "Go back to the ghetto that you come from!" he yelled.

"I want my damn money, Peppi!" I yelled as I screamed and kicked to get to him.

I couldn't break the bouncer's grip. The bouncer was so tall and strong that he'd lifted my feet right up off the floor like I was as light as a feather. I found myself kicking in mid-air the entire time he carried me towards the door.

My cousin was so down for me, willing to do whatever. She kept screaming, cursing, kicking over chairs, and willing to do whatever to help me.

"Put her down!" Raven screamed as she followed us. "Put her the fuck down!"

Peppi finally came out from behind the bar and began to follow us. "I do not want to see you in my establishment ever again!"

"Fuck you! I want my money you piece of shit!" I belted.

The bouncer carried me out to the parking lot, then dropped me like I was a bag of trash. When he let me go, Peppi stood in the doorway.

"I do not allow peasants in my place of business! Do not come back!"

I was heated as I headed out of the lot back to the SUV, which was parked two buildings away. My mind couldn't think straight as I rushed down the block emotional and defeated.

Dollar quickly hopped out of the Navigator. "Y'all good?" he asked.

"Hell fucking no!" Raven yelled at him. "That bitch ass nigga was all the way out of pocket! He actually thinks he can get away with that foul shit!"

Dollar looked at me. "What's good, Keema? You want me to handle him? Like I told you before, for two grand the nigga will die tonight."

I turned around one final time to see Peppi and his

bouncer standing in front of the club. Seeing that crooked snake ass son of a bitch standing in front of a club that *my* money paid for was something I couldn't take. I reached in my pocket and pulled out a thousand dollars, half of the money I'd promised Dollar if it came to this.

"This is half. I'll hit you off with the rest later. Do that shit," I said, handing him the money.

Dollar looked at me with dead seriousness. His eyes didn't blink or stray. "Are you sure this is what you want? 'Cause once I go deal with him, that's it, no turning back."

For a brief second Cash's body appeared in my mind. My mother's appeared, too. Then the flashbacks began, reminding me that I was the cause of their deaths. Those thoughts were followed by Imani's, Paco's, Dupree's, and Rick's faces. My pulse raced at the memories. Damn, I'd wanted to leave the dead bodies behind me, but Peppi had to be dealt with.

He *had* to be.

"Kill his ass," I instructed.

"I got you," Dollar said, accepting the money.

Both me and Raven hopped into the truck still mad as hell.

Dollar stuffed the money in his back pocket and headed up the street towards the club.

I turned in the backseat to look out the window. With each step Dollar took, my heart thumped. He strutted like a trained soldier ready to amputate a muthufucka on contact. The closer he got, the more my own adrenalin rushed.

"I hope he shoots him in the fucking face," Raven said with spite. "I hate snake type muthufuckas with no integrity. He deserves to die."

She'd taken Peppi's deceit just as serious as I had.

Before long, Dollar walked into the lot and headed directly towards Peppi and the bouncer. Peppi was now on his cell phone, his mouth moving a mile a minute. I had no idea if he was calling the police, so I sat with my face pressed against the window like a toddler. When Dollar reached both men, he said

30

something. We were too far away to hear what it was. We could only see both Peppi and the bouncer saying something back to him.

"What are they talking about?" Raven asked real antsy like.

I had no idea.

Seconds later, Dollar turned to walk away like he had a change of heart.

"What the fuck is he doing?" Raven questioned.

This time I just shrugged.

Peppi and the bouncer turned to go back in the club.

Suddenly, Dollar reached underneath his clothes, pulled out his gun, and turned. In a split second he raised his hand and squeezed the trigger. The spark from the barrel appeared and disappeared in the blink of an eye. The shots sounded like fire crackers on the Fourth of July, scaring the shit out of me. Even from the distance I could see a huge chunk of Peppi's forehead tear away from his face as a bullet ripped through the back of his skull.

"That's what the fuck I'm talking about!" Raven shouted.

Peppi's body dropped to the ground immediately. Dollar then squeezed the trigger again.

Then again.

Then again.

 The bouncer's head exploded just like Peppi's. His body dropped directly beside his boss'. With the mission fulfilled, Dollar tucked the gun back into his shorts and jogged back toward us. He hopped inside, started the truck, and pulled away from the curb like he hadn't just murked two dudes in cold blood.

"Spark that blunt," Dollar told Raven as he leaned back into his seat and turned on the music nonchalantly like killing a muthafucka was no big deal.

As Raven put a lighter to the blunt and handed it to him, I sat silently. Although I wanted Peppi dead, I wasn't sure if I had acted too quickly. I reacted out of anger. Now, I hoped it wouldn't come back to haunt me. As my eyes stared out of my window at the passing houses, my cell phone beeped, letting me know I had a text. Grabbing the phone from my pocket and looking at the screen, I was surprised to see the number and message. It was the number I'd been trying to reach for Drake along with an address and a time to meet tomorrow.

Damn, what a night.

4

The headboard banged against the wall and the bed-springs shrieked loudly in my ears as my hips repeatedly dug themselves deeply into the mattress with each stroke of Trent's muscular body. The nigga was *punishing* the pussy. He had one of my legs over his shoulder while he held me down in a position that wouldn't allow me to move or maneuver. When it came to fucking I'd always been used to having control. I normally had the ability to make a nigga buss when *I* wanted him to, not when *he* wanted to. This time was different though. The nigga was definitely in charge as he guerrilla fucked me with no mercy. The shit felt good. But he was so long and thick, I was scared he would shift my damn uterus. I mean the nigga was digging *that* fucking deep.

Moans escaped my mouth over and over again. Some of them were from pain. Others were from pleasure. A few screams belted out as well. I couldn't contain them even if I wanted to. I was going to probably walk away from this session with a headache since my head kept ramming against the headboard.

As he grinded inside me like a wild beast, I dug my nails into his back and even bit him a few times. I couldn't help it. He was working my pussy just that damn wild and good, causing me to buss twice in the last ten minutes. It had been a long time since a nigga had fucked me like that.

I liked being caressed at times just like any other bitch. I liked to be kissed. I liked to be held. I liked to be made love to. But sometimes I just needed to be *fucked*! And right now that's just what I was getting.

I honestly hadn't planned on fucking Trent. I had only come to the block he'd told me to meet him on through that text he'd sent the night before. When I pulled up, I saw several young niggas, all in white tees, posted in front of a liquor store hustling.

Since I had no idea who I was looking for or how he looked, I just parked and waited. Ten minutes later, an older dude who looked to be in his early thirties pulled up in a white Tahoe. He headed into the store and came out a moment later with a bag of salt & vinegar potato chips. He leaned against the wall and began to stare at me. Finally he nodded. I rolled down the window and asked him if he was the guy I was there to meet. He nodded again.

The two of us walked around his hood as he asked me how Drake was doing and if it was a guarantee that he was finally coming home. I had no idea what any of that had to do with me. I didn't really care. I just wanted to get down to the business at hand. All I wanted to do was get whatever the fuck it was I was supposed to get and go on about my damn business.

Before I knew it we were in some hole in the wall bar. As we talked he gave me a key. There was nothing written on it or engraved in it. I wasn't sure if it was a P.O. Box key or a safety deposit key. When I asked him what kind of a key it was, Trent said it was proprietary information, and that I'd have to ask Drake.

We sat and had a few more drinks over more conversation. That's where I think I fucked up. Everything from that moment was either a blur or I simply couldn't remember it. I was now sure he'd slipped something into my drink. He had to. I couldn't even remember leaving the bar or how we'd gotten to his house. All I know is when I came to about an hour ago, he was on top of me and fucking my pussy like I'd stole something.

34

I had to admit the shit was good though. That was the only reason why I hadn't pushed him off of me.

"You like this dick?" Trent said into my ear.

"Yeah, baby," I replied. "Hit that shit, nigga."

He continued to grind hard, digging deep with each and every stroke. My pussy was soaking wet, causing a puddle underneath my ass cheeks.

"Damn, you got good pussy," he groaned into my ear while never missing a beat. His rhythm stayed vicious and continuous.

"Ohhhhh, shit," I moaned, clamping my thighs around his waist like a vice grip and locking my ankles.

He began to pound so hard the legs of the bed began to repeatedly slide across the floor back and forth towards the wall. I thought the bed and headboard was going to knock a hole through it. The force seemed like it had the entire room shaking. The nigga was trying to dismantle my pussy.

"Fuckkkk!" I screamed just before biting into his shoulder and closing my eyes tightly. I could feel him up in parts of my insides I wasn't sure he belonged.

"Take that dick, bitch!" he yelled. "Take that shit!"

I moaned and groaned loudly as my body took his punishment. My hands reached downward to grab a hold of his thighs. Trent finally let out a growling like sound. He was getting ready to cum. I squeezed him tighter and dug my nails deeper into his skin.

He finally bussed off and collapsed beside me. I laid there for several moments until he fell asleep and began to snore. He sounded just like a fucking grizzly bear when I finally slid out of the bed and got dressed. After getting my clothes on, I noticed his pants lying on the floor and came up with an idea. I looked at him to make sure he was still asleep then dug into his pockets.

The son of a bitch was a damn rapist. He'd basically taken my pussy without asking. The way I saw it, he owed me. He was lucky I wasn't calling the fucking cops. When my hand reached into his pocket, I felt a fat roll of money. After glancing at his ass quickly, I pulled the roll out and squinted attempting to see clearly in the dark. Benjamin Franklin's face came into view. It wasn't totally clear, but even in the dark, I knew those facial features anywhere.

Trent had at least sixty. I took just three of them, since having more niggas after me didn't sound too good. My thieving days were over for now unless there was some big payoff. Besides, Trent would never notice three bills gone. So, I stuffed the money in my pocket and headed out the door. When I got outside I had no idea where I was. I didn't recognize the street at all. I could only tell it was a side street. Seeing busy traffic at the upper end, I headed that way immediately. I was trying to get the fuck away before Trent woke up and realized I'd jetted.

As I walked, I finally remembered the key he'd given me at the bar. I reached into my pocket to be sure it was still there. It was. As I held it in the palm of my hand my thoughts scrambled for what secret it held. It *had* to be the money Drake had stashed. It had to be. But how much though? He'd robbed the bank for over seven hundred thousand dollars. When the cops finally caught him, he'd gone through a lot of it. Or at least that's what everyone thought. Maybe he hadn't gone through the money they thought he had. Maybe he'd stashed all of it. My pussy instantly got wet.

Damn, I couldn't wait for Drake to call me again. The suspense was now killing me. He most likely wouldn't tell me over the phone though. He'd already made it clear that he didn't like talking on the phone. I was gonna have to make a trip up to see him. Fuck waiting for his ass to get out. I wanted to know exactly how much money was stashed.

As I reached the busy street, I finally recognized something familiar. I knew I had to hop on a bus to get back to my car. While waiting at the bus stop, the thought of crossing Drake's ass out of the picture completely filled my thoughts. If I could somehow get him to tell me where the money was, I would be able to get it and be long gone by the time he finally got out of prison. I wouldn't have to deal with his ass at all.

A bus finally pulled up with large letters across the side that read Charm City. I couldn't help but smile. My city always had some shit popping. I hopped on, paid and took a seat way in the back. As I stared out of the window at the passing streets, the thought of crossing Drake wouldn't leave me. I wouldn't have to hustle anymore if I could get my hands on that cash. That money would hold me until Dinero and Shane's insurance money finally came through.

After getting off the bus several minutes later, I finally got back to the block I'd left my car on. Thankfully it hadn't been touched. Before I unlocked the door, my eyes glanced up the street to see a black Impala sitting at the curb. Its windows were so tinted, I wasn't sure if someone was inside. Thinking nothing of it, I hopped in my car and pulled off. As I stopped at a red light with my mind still on the key in my pocket and figuring out a way to talk Drake into giving me the info I needed, my phone rang. Treasure's cell number appeared on the screen. Lucky had given it to her before we left Phoenix.

"What's up?" I answered.

Loud noise clamored in the background. It sounded like glass shattering, shit being throwing around, somebody getting their ass beat.

What the hell?

"Mom!" Treasure shouted.

The noise grew even louder. It sounded like a table was being flipped over. Then there was growling.

"Yeah, what the fuck is going on? What's all that noise?"

"It's Shane, mom!" she yelled over the noise.

"What do you mean Shane?"

"He's flipping out!"

"What are you talking about?"

"He's yelling and screaming. He's throwing stuff! He's tearing up the house!" Treasure belted.

"What did you guys do to him?"

"We didn't do anything! He just started acting crazy for no reason!"

"How long has he been acting like that?"

"It just started! You really need to get here right now! He's going off and I can't do anything with him!"

"Alright, I'm on my way. Call Shy right now! Tell her to come over 'til I get there."

"I got you!"

We hung up with my thoughts spiraling out of control. What had gotten into Shane? This was definitely not like him. He'd never done anything like this before. I headed straight for the highway. As I hit my blinker and attempted to merge with traffic my eyes looked in the rearview and noticed the same Impala I'd seen earlier. It was now directly behind me. Something inside told me to be careful.

As I drove, it stayed a couple car lengths behind me. Something about it made me believe it wasn't a coincidence though. I had a strange feeling about it. But to be sure, I began to gain speed and switch lanes while keeping a close eye on the rearview mirror. The Impala did the same each time. A lump formed in my throat then I sat straight up, turning off the music. I began to dip in and out of traffic. When I looked in the mirror the Impala was doing the same.

"Shit," I whispered. I really was being followed. Fuck!

Who the fuck was it, I wondered. I quickly imagined the worst. My heart began to speed like crazy as I realized just how many people in Baltimore could possibly want me dead. A member of Paco's crew could be out for revenge. After all, I'd robbed him and he was soon found dead in Arizona. Or maybe one of Peppi's friends wanted some get back. Damn, that had to be it! The Mexican muthafuckas were after me. Both my hands gripped the steering wheel so hard my knuckles pressed tightly against my skin. My body trembled convulsively at the thought of dying on the highway tonight, possibly in a car wreck or a hail of bullets.

I kept my foot on the gas pedal, going eighty refusing to let up, although knowing the Impala was purposely staying at least two car lengths behind me. If it wanted to catch up or make an attempt at catching up, it could. Whoever they were, if they had intentions of getting at me tonight, they were biding their time. My eyes darted from the windshield to the rearview mirror to the side view mirror over and over again, but the car was too far behind for me to see inside of it. I couldn't make out even exactly how many people were inside.

What the fuck did they want? Did they have guns? Question after question filled my head and racked my nerves but there were no answers. Suddenly, I found myself going down a dead-end street.

"Fuck!" I shouted to myself.

I reached the end of the street and had no other choice but to stop. Nervously I began to ring out my hands like wet rags, realizing I was trapped. I let my eyes rise to the overhead mirror as my ears were filled with the calmed growl of my car's engine. The Impala had stopped. It was a distance behind me. I still couldn't make out who was inside it. All I could see was its bright shining headlights.

"What do you want from me?" I whispered to the car as if its driver could hear me. "What the fuck do you want?"

My heart was beating viciously against the inside of my chest as I was forced to realize I was nothing more than a sitting duck. Through the mirror, I watched the Impala, expecting its doors to open at any moment. Each passing second that I stared at it seemed like forever.

Finally, not knowing what else to do and realizing that if I planned on surviving tonight, I had to explore any and every chance available, I placed the car in reverse and slammed my foot down on the gas pedal. My engine came to life loudly as its sleek monstrous frame sped backwards.

"It's me and you, muthafucka!" I screamed into the mirror at the Impala. "It's me and you!"

The tires of the Impala squealed as it began to back up quickly also, trying to avoid me. I gripped the steering wheel tightly, never letting my eyes leave the mirror or allowing my adrenaline to slow.

The Impala finally reached the end of the street and spun out. A second later, I did the same. Immediately, I threw the car in drive and slammed on the gas pedal once again. Before I knew it, we were on a busy street darting in and out of traffic.

"Who the hell are you!" I screamed into my mirror. "What do you want?"

Both of our engines were roaring as we shot through traffic lights, causing other cars to slam on their brakes and skid out to avoid hitting us.

"Damn it!" I yelled in frustration as I slammed my fists against the steering wheel. No matter what I did, I couldn't seem to shake the Impala. With every turn, it was on my ass. That was it. I'd decided to give up. If it was my time to die- it was my time.

5

I *had* to be seeing things. I just *had* to be.

"There's no way the person I saw in the Impala last night could've been him," I told myself peeping out the window for the seventh time in just two minutes.

That shit seemed impossible. My hand trembled nervously as I placed my cigarette to my lips and inhaled deeply. That face had my nerves wrecked. It was all I could envision. I hadn't slept at all, and it was like I had actually seen a ghost.

When I pulled off the highway last night and stopped at the red light, my heart was beating a mile a minute. I watched my rearview as the Impala approached speedily from behind. My eyes wouldn't blink. It was as if someone or something held my body captive. I had no idea what to expect, but knew something bad was coming. My pistol was at home so I was basically fucked.

When the Impala finally reached me, it slowly pulled up to my passenger side in the right lane, but didn't come to a complete stop. The window was rolled down halfway. Just as it pulled up on me, so did the police. It was clear they wanted me to pull over and not the Impala. Just before the Impala made a right turn, the driver looked directly at me with a glare that was cold as ice. I remembered letting out a loud gasp. The inside of the car was too dark to see him clearly, but I saw enough of his eyes and facial features to send chills down my spine.

I hadn't told anyone what I saw. Not a single person. Everyone would think I was crazy. They'd probably think I was a damn nut. Shit, was I? Could I be losing my damn mind? Maybe this was a sign of one of those nervous breakdowns that older folks have. I'd heard that stress could cause them. After what I'd been through over these past few years, maybe it was possible for my mind to be playing tricks on me. Maybe I really was losing it.

No matter how much I tried to tell myself that what I'd seen was merely my imagination running wild with me, I couldn't feel at ease, so I kept my Ruger .380 Pistol close, ready to blast off if necessary. I kept thinking back to the last time I saw his face. The memory horrified me. But not more than possibly thinking about what he'd do to me if he were really alive.

I took another hit of the cigarette. I had been blazing Newport after Newport since last night like a chain smoker. The shit just wouldn't let me rest. I just couldn't get it out of my head. Damn, I needed to get a hold of myself.

Suddenly, my house phone rang causing my body to jump. My attention was so buried in my worries and nervousness the unexpected ringing scared me back into reality. Without looking at the caller ID, I snatched it from the cracked cocktail table, compliments of Shane, and answered.

"You have a collect call from…" an automated voice said from the other end of the line.

"Ughhhhhhhhhh."

Drake said his name.

"Who is an inmate at a correctional facility," the automated voice continued. "Do you wish to accept the charges?"

I didn't want to. The last thing I wanted to do was talk to his incarcerated ass or anyone else. My nerves were too bad right now. But realizing I had the key Trent gave me, I accepted.

"What's good?" Drake asked.

"Nothing," I responded dryly.

As usual, the sounds of loud convicts in the background

filled the phone.

Shane walked out of his bedroom and came into the living room. He sat down in a chair and just stared into one of those distances he was known to disappear into every once in a while. I wanted to shout and tell him to clean up all this shit he threw around the house, but I didn't want to incite another riot.

When I got home last night, he'd already calmed down. A few dishes were broken and a few chairs were over turned, but he was back to being his normal self. Treasure told me that she had no idea what set him off. Since the day Rick had taken custody, Shane had been good. He seemed to be coming along really well. He was even laughing a lot. He was playful. He didn't drift off into his own world as much, and was beginning to take care of himself a little better than before. He'd definitely come out of the shell he'd been trapped inside of for so long. So, last night was completely out of character for him.

"Damn, you don't sound too happy to hear from me?" Drake commented.

That would be correct, I thought to myself. "I saw your boy yesterday." I quickly wanted to get off that subject.

"I heard."

I wondered exactly what he heard, but didn't bother to ask.

Treasure came out of the kitchen, grabbed the remote, and sat down beside me on the couch. When she turned on the television, BET was showing the movie, *Baby Boy* for the millionth time. I swear, my kids seemed to have an infatuation with that movie.

"So, you got that for me?" Drake inquired.

"Yeah, now are you going to tell me what it's for?"

"You know I don't do phones, Keema. But you'll find out soon enough. Guess what?"

"What?" I asked.

Shane wrapped his arms around himself and began to rock back and forth. He also started to talk to himself. Both me and Treasure looked at him and then ourselves, but didn't say anything. When we looked at him again, he was scratching his forearms.

"I got good news," Drake said. "I'm getting out Friday."

That shit caught me by surprise. "What?" I asked in disbelief.

"Yeah," he said happily. "They're cuttin' me loose this Friday."

Fuck, I thought to myself. I needed his dumb ass to stay locked up until I could figure out how I could use this key to take everything the nigga owned. I was even thinking about fucking Trent's ass again to see if maybe he would tell me. I wasn't going to mention anything to him about knowing that he drugged me to get the pussy.

"Why are they letting you out so damn early?" I asked angrily.

"Damn, lil mama, you sound like you want me to stay in here. What the fuck?"

I hadn't realized my anger had shown so clearly. I quickly changed the tone in my voice. "Nah, it's not like that. You know that. I'm just surprised. That's all."

"The prison's overcrowded so they lettin' out the ones who got parole or who are real short timers."

My eyes rolled. I wanted to start cursing, letting Drake know that as a taxpayer, I didn't like the government letting muthafuckas out early. Just the sound of his voice now had me aggravated and pissed off. What type of justice system would let a no good ass muthafucka like him out early? Are you serious? That's why there's so much crime and shit in the hood. The courts keep letting muthafuckas like him out of prison.

Drake hadn't learned his lesson. I knew he hadn't. No matter how much money he had stashed, I knew he was going back to his old ways. He'd rob another bank for sure. Eventually he would either end up dead or back in prison. That's just the way he was built. That's why I hadn't given the shit he was talking about during my last visit any real thought. That shit was nothing but game. All I wanted to do was get his money and kick

44

his bum ass to the curb.

"Keema, you gonna come get me, right?"

I rolled my eyes again. "Yeah," I told him. Unable to take anymore of his voice, I said, "Look, Drake, I got another call, I gotta go."

Hearing me mention her father's name, Treasure sucked her teeth.

"Damn, I was hopin'…"

"I'm busy, Drake," I told him, cutting his ass off in mid sentence. "I gotta go."

"Keema…"

CLICK!

I tossed the phone to the side and rushed back over to the window, making sure no new cars had parked on the block. I sighed after seeing no sign of anyone. With Drake's surprising news, I could feel a headache coming on. As I sat back on the couch, I heard Shane muttering something under his breath. That wasn't like him. I stared at him for a moment. Treasure did the same. He began to scratch his arms again like something was crawling on them.

"Shane, you okay?" I asked.

He stopped muttering, but didn't answer me. He just kept scratching.

"Shane, what's up? Why are you scratching yourself?"

"He said he's coming to get me."

"Who?" I asked Shane. "Who are you talking about, boy?"

He didn't give an answer.

I looked at Treasure.

She looked me up and down like she was trying to size me up or like I had something to hide. "Why are you looking at me like that?" I questioned.

"Because something's not right with him. Don't you think you should take him to a doctor or something? Y'all be smoking so much weed around him, that's probably what's wrong. He's probably having a reaction to it."

45

Her little ass thought she had all the answers.

"You can't be serious. You know how much weed you in-haled as a child?"

"This shit isn't funny! He needs to go to the doctor!" Treasure spat.

"Watch your damn mouth."

She sucked her teeth and rolled her eyes again.

"Roll them shits at me again and I'm gonna slap them right out of your damn head."

"I'm just saying, he should see somebody."

The last thing I wanted to do was take Shane to a doctor or a psychiatrist. They asked too many questions. He'd seen too much and he knew too much. He could possibly let the wrong shit slip out of his mouth to the wrong person and get a bunch of nosey muthafuckas all up in my business. That's something I didn't need. There was no way I could take a chance on him pos-sibly discussing the gift cards, Rick's and Paco's deaths, or any-thing else he'd seen. Besides, I was rolling under an alias.

"He's alright," I told her.

"You just think him going to see somebody is going to af-fect the insurance money, don't you?"

My eyes locked on Treasure sharply. I wanted to slap fire out of her ass. She was getting too fucking nosey and grown. The insurance company representative had called a few hours ago to ask a few questions, nothing major. They still weren't giv-ing me a specific time on when I would get the money. They just said that until the investigation was over, there was nothing else they could tell me. As I talked to them, Treasure came into the kitchen and fixed herself a bowl of cereal. I should've known the little fast ass heifer was ear hustling. The last thing the lil' sneaky bitch was thinking about was a bowl of Captain Crunch.

"Treasure, let me tell your lil' punk ass something," I said, snatching her frail body towards me, and looking directly in her eyes. After gripping her chin, our faces were so close we could smell each other's breath. "I'm the momma and *you're* the daughter. You came out of *my* pussy. I didn't come out of *yours*.

That means you are to stay the fuck out of my damn business."

Spite and anger boiled in her eyes. She wanted to say something, but knew it was in her best interest to just shut the fuck up.

"The next time you question me about *my* shit, I'm gonna lock these doors and me and you are gonna tear this fucking house up." I gripped her chin even tighter. "I'm the queen of this castle. I run everything all up and through here. *You* just live here. Do you understand me?"

She didn't speak, and managed to keep a stone face.

"Treasure, I asked you a question. Do you understand me?"

She nodded and jerked her head away from me.

"Little wannabe grown ass bitch," I muttered to myself as I hit my cigarette. She was really pushing me to kick her ass like a nigga in the streets. I swear she was. It was taking everything in me to keep from doing so.

Suddenly, the doorbell rang sending me racing to grab my gun. I tripped in the process, but still made it over to the window in record time. My breaths became stronger and stronger as I thought of a repeat of what went down in Phoenix. My chest tightened even more after not seeing any strange cars on the block. Shy hadn't said she was coming over, so I wondered who the fuck it was.

My head pounded even more and my eyes grew to the size of watermelons as the doorbell rang again.

Damn it! My car was parked in the driveway so whoever was knocking knew I was home. They would probably keep ringing until a bitch answered.

FUCK!

"Answer the damn door," I told Treasure, cocking the gun back.

She jumped up from the couch wanting so desperately to say something smart but didn't. She knew she was skating on thin ice with me at the moment. Without even looking out the window or asking who it was, she opened the door. I had my gun

47

cocked, loaded and ready. The next thing I knew, Treasure began screaming at the top of her lungs so loud that it startled the shit out of me. I looked at the door and saw the figure, just in time to see her rush Lucky and jump into his arms. He lifted her off of the floor so high she wrapped her legs around his waist and locked her ankles.

I'd forgotten that Lucky was supposed to come today. He was a sight for sore eyes, so I quickly lowered my gun and breathed a heavy sigh. I was happy to see him, of course, but as I watched Treasure's legs wrapped around him and her arms holding him tightly, all I could think about was how over exaggerated her happiness seemed. It wasn't necessary. It was as if she was putting on a show to make me angry or jealous.

She was succeeding, too.

"Lil bitch," I mumbled to myself.

6

The next day rolled around with me feeling like a boss bitch.

"That's a five star chick. That's a five star chick," I repeated, singing along with Yo Gotti's old song as he blasted loudly from the speakers of my car.

That was my fucking theme song. It fit me to a tee. None of these bitches out here could fuck with me. Their swag game was bummy and stank compared to mine.

As the whip made its way down my street towards my house, I realized just how much my nerves had chilled since thinking I saw my worst nightmare on the highway the other night. That night, I thought his face would never leave my mind. I thought it would stay forever. Thankfully it eased up. I'd come to the conclusion that I was tripping, too much weed. Besides, the fact that I was about to come into a fat ass pay day real soon took my mind off of anything that had the possibility of stressing me.

"I'm rich, bitch!" I screamed in my Dave Chapelle voice over the music.

The passenger seat of my car was filled with bags of freshly cooked seafood from my favorite spot. Lucky had a taste for crabs and spice shrimp, so he sent me out to grab enough to feed the whole house. He peeled off four hundred dollars like it wasn't shit. He didn't even stipulate that I should bring his change back. So, I didn't.

On my way to the spot, I stopped off to meet Trent first. I wasn't sure if he'd noticed the money I'd took, and if so, if he was angry about it. But since the perverted muthafucka raped me, I figured if he knew I'd gotten him, he would be willing to just take it as a loss and keep it moving. I turned out to be right. When I knocked on his door, he greeted me with a massive smile. The two of us ended up fucking again.

When the sex session was over, we laid in his bed and talked. It felt weird since he was Drake's man, but I chopped it up with him anyway. As it turned out, he was on the same shit I was on. He wanted Drake's money, too. He asked if I had the key he'd given me. I told him yes, but felt real funny about it. I thought the nigga was gonna rob me for it, the same way I'd robbed him.

Within minutes he had me up, dressed, and following him to a Public Storage on York Road. When I asked him why, he said it was real important and he'd tell me when we got there. By the time we got to the entrance of the storage place my wheels were spinning. I'd become overly antsy.

"Look, you gotta tell me why we're here?" I asked getting out of the car.

"This is where the money is," Trent said matter-of-factly.

My eyes glistened like new money at those words. "How much is it?"

"Your boy told me two hundred thousand."

"Well, let's go get it," I said sassily.

My pussy instantly got wet as I realized I was about to be two hundred thousand dollars richer.

"Alright," I told Trent. "Which storage unit is it?"

He looked at me strangely.

"Well, which one, nigga?" I asked impatiently.

"That's what I was about to ask you."

"What?"

"Drake never gave me the unit number. I thought since

you was his girl, he'd given it to you."

My stomach dropped.

Seeing my disappointment, Trent quickly grabbed my shoulders. "Don't trip, baby girl," he stated reassuringly.

"What the hell you mean don't trip? What did you bring me down here for if you didn't know the damn unit number? What the fuck were you expecting us to be…psychic?"

I was ready to walk off. I hated a stupid muthafucka. I snatched away from his grip and headed back towards my car.

"Keema!" Trent called from behind me.

Ignoring his dumb ass, I kept right on walking. He pissed me all the way off. I'd already been missing from my house for over two and a half hours now. And now there was nothing to show for it. I was starting to seriously think about pressing charges against his ass for rape.

"Keema!" Trent called again.

I continued to ignore him.

"Keema!" he shouted one last time as he grabbed my shoulder from behind and spun me around.

"What?"

"Will you stop for a second and listen?"

"What? What do you want me to listen to?"

"First of all, lower your voice," he said, then quickly looked around.

I placed my hands on my hips and shifted my body's weight to one foot as I waited for him to talk.

"We can still get the money," Trent told me.

"How?"

"We still have three days before Drake comes home. We've just got to figure out how to either keep him in there or how to get him to give us the storage unit number. That's where you come in."

"What do you mean?"

"You're a woman, Keema. I'm pretty sure you know how to be persuasive."

He had a point. I wasn't sure how to make it work

though. It was going to take a little thought. But for two hundred stacks, shit, I was definitely up for it.

I pulled into my driveway forty minutes later, still thinking about a way to get the info out of Drake. I snatched a couple of bags from the passenger seat and quickly headed up the walkway to my front door. When I walked inside, the gang was all there. Shy and Raven sat comfortably on the futon together blazing a blunt. Of course, Raven had the phone glued to her ear as usual. Deniro and Shane were sitting in the middle of the floor watching a movie.

"What took you so long, Ma?" Deniro shouted. "Me hungry."

"Look boy, I took my time making sure I got your ass the best crabs in the state of Maryland so stop complaining."

"I want scrimps," he whined.

I couldn't even correct my son good before Raven interrupted.

"Yo, Dollar said he needs to get that loot from you this week."

"Tell 'em, I'll have it on Friday."

"He said no later," she warned with a stern look that I easily ignored.

Little did they know, I wasn't paying shit. My eyes immediately locked on Treasure's fast ass. For a moment I froze as I looked at her sitting on Lucky's lap while he talked on his cell phone. What pissed me off most about it was I could've sworn the little heifer gave me a quick smirk before turning her head like she didn't see me. I couldn't be sure because she turned so quickly, but I still could've sworn I saw what the fuck I saw.

Since Lucky had gotten to Baltimore, he'd been throwing me shade. He wouldn't give me no dick or too much conversation. I asked him to at least sleep in my bed with me, just one night. He refused. Instead, he preferred to sleep on the couch. I even surprised him with a big breakfast yesterday morning when he woke up. He merely took two bites, said he wasn't hungry, and got dressed to go handle some business. He headed out the door without saying two words to me. When he left, I sat on the couch pissed off and sexually frustrated.

Treasure on the other hand, was getting treated like a queen. He was giving her money like she was his bitch. He took her out for a pedicure and manicure, took her shopping for clothes and sneakers, and even took her out to a movie. He was spoiling her ass rotten. From what I saw as my eyes looked beside the couch, he'd taken her shopping again. There were Foot Locker and Nordstrom bags sitting at their feet. I glanced at Deniro. Even he was rocking the new Jordans; courtesy of Lucky. Ain't that a bitch? The nigga was spoiling my kids, but wasn't giving me any play whatsoever. The shit made me see red.

Aggravated, I shouted, "Treasure, you see me at the fucking door with these bags! Get your ass the fuck up, go outside and make yourself useful."

Treasure let out a heavy breath in annoyance. She then climbed off of Lucky and rolled her eyes at me as she strutted by me.

"I've already warned you about rolling your fucking eyes at me, girl! Roll 'em one more time and I'm going to knock them out of your muthafuckin' head."

She didn't say anything.

"Keep playing with me," I invited her, hoping she had something she wanted to get off of her chest.

"Damn, Keema. You gotta talk to her like that? She's only twelve. You talking to her like she's grown," Lucky chimed in.

This nigga had his nerve.

"Hell yeah," I told him. "I was out here in these streets looking for a good batch of crabs for her and everybody else up in here to eat. That's what took me so long. The least she could do is get up and help me carry the shit in. She saw me standing here."

Lucky shook his head and went back to his phone conversation.

I lugged the bags to the dining room. When I came out, I looked at Shane. Although he was sitting in front of the television, he wasn't watching it. He seemed to be somewhere else. He was also occasionally scratching his forearms again. I wanted to smile but kept it hidden. Everything with him was going as well as planned. Although I felt bad about having to do him that way, it had to be done.

The lawyer, Mr. Hyde representing me in the inheritance investigation had called me the night before and wanted to meet me tomorrow over lunch. He said things were getting ironed out and getting close to some closure. Shane and Dinero were looking at inheriting over two million dollars in cash and property. When he saw me, he would discuss it more.

Shane would be eighteen in five more months. If he could prove that he was capable of taking care of himself and managing his life, he would be able to get his half of the money and do with it as he pleased. But as long as he came off crazy, at least his share of the money would remain under my control. To ensure that, I had to keep him drugged. It was fucked up. I felt bad about doing it to him, but I needed that money. Besides, what would he do with a million dollars anyway? He'd waste it. The people around him would use him up, take advantage of him, and milk his dumb ass dry. In all actuality I was a blessing, his fairy Godmother. As long as I had control of his money, he'd have a roof over his head and food to eat.

I was being careful not to beam his ass up too high. After doing research on the internet, I was only giving Shane enough PCP to keep him off balance. I didn't want to turn him into a vegetable or have him walking around the house licking windows and drooling at the mouth, although I was surprised when he tore up the house the other night. I wasn't expecting him to get violent.

As Treasure walked back into the house carrying bags I

told her to take them to the dining room. When she walked past me I followed her. I had some words for her little fast ass. As soon as she placed the bags on the table, I noticed the gift cards sitting there. It was only one stack. When I left there were four.

"Where's the other stacks of gift cards?" I asked Treasure.

She hunched her shoulders. "I don't know."

"Treasure, don't play with me." My tone attested to my seriousness. "Where are the other gift cards?"

"I don't know. I ain't seen no gift cards but the ones here right now."

I turned on my heels and headed back to the living room. Not asking or looking at anyone in particular, I spat fire.

"Where are the gifts cards that were in the dining room when I left?" No one seemed to be paying me any attention. *These bitches must think this is a game*, I thought. "I don't play about my fucking money." I walked across the room, turned off the television, and took center stage. "Where are the fucking gift cards I left on the table this morning?" I asked louder than before.

Everyone looked around at each other and muttered, "I don't know."

My eyes focused in on Raven and Shy. They were still smoking and Raven was still on the phone like losing three stacks of gift cards wasn't important.

"Oh, so y'all bitches don't know shit?"

"First of all," Raven said as she took the phone from her ear and placed it to her chest so the caller couldn't hear. "Watch your damn tone when you come at me, Keema. I'm not a child. Second, I don't know shit about no gift cards."

"So, they just sprouted legs and walked?" I placed my hands on my hips and eye-balled her down for several seconds then switched my scrutinizing gaze to Shy. "There was four muthafuckin' stacks on the table this morning. Now there's only one. So, where the fuck are the cards?"

"Well, I ain't got 'em," Raven replied defensively.

"Maybe Shy got 'em."

"So, what are you sayin', Raven?" Shy asked. "How you gon' incriminate me? I wouldn't do that!"

"I said what I said. It's clear by my gear and the shit I got, I don't need to steal and especially from my own cousin."

At that moment, Treasure made her way out of the dining room. She was watching the confrontation silently.

"Oh hell naw!" I yelled angrily, fed up with what I was hearing. "I don't tolerate shit just getting up and walking out of my house! I don't like that shit!"

"Well, I didn't take shit!" Raven yelled erratically.

"Me neither!" Shy hollered, her face losing color by the second.

I knew they were lying. It *had* to be one of them. I could feel it. Lucky had money so he would have no reason to steal some punk ass gift cards. The only muthafuckas with a reason to take my shit was Raven and Shy. They were jealous of me and wanted to see me fail.

"Mom," Treasure said with suspicion in her tone, "I told you this would happen. I told you that you weren't watching your business close enough."

"Stay out of this, Treasure!" Raven yelled. "Get out of grown folks business!"

"Bitch, watch your damn mouth when you talk to my daughter! She's just telling the truth! She's right! I should've been watching your damn asses!" I roared.

"You never know who you can trust," Treasure added.

"Will everybody just calm down?" Shy yelled, seeing where the situation was going. "Let's all calm down and search for the cards. They gotta be here somewhere."

"They're gone. One of you took them," Treasure sounded again.

"Fuck that!" I screamed as I took off my earrings. Those cards equaled over seven thousand dollars in would-be profit. "I want my muthafuckin' cards right now!"

Raven stood up from the futon.

56

"Damn, chill out," Lucky finally said. "Treasure, take the kids upstairs," he instructed.

Treasure did as she was told. No hesitation whenever Lucky spoke to her.

"I said I ain't got your damn cards!" Raven yelled.

"We'll see, bitches. I want y'all thieving muthufuckas to strip right now. All I wanna see are tits and ass." My face tightened and my fists were clenched. I meant every word I'd spoken. "Take everything off!" I shouted. "Now!"

Raven shook her head back and forth. "You're on crack if you think I'm about to degrade myself and take my clothes off in front of your dumb ass. Shy can do that shit, but I'm not."

Before I knew it, I'd flipped, and snatched Raven's Gucci purse from the floor causing all of her shit to fall out. That started World War II. She went ballistic and I was all over her ass, yanking her clothes wildly, attempting to make her strip down to nothing. I knew she had my shit. I just knew it. If those cards were stuck in the crack of her ass, I'd find them.

I rushed her towards the futon, causing her to trip and fall flat on her back. Shy immediately got out of the way saying it was all a mistake. "The cards gotta be somewhere," she kept saying. "Stop y'all! Stop!"

In my heart I believed that Shy was innocent. I just wasn't willing to let her leave without stripping down first.

"Where's my shit?" I screamed sending a right punch which connected to Raven's jaw so hard it jerked her head to the side. Raven tried to reach up and grab me by the hair, but I swatted her hand to the side and caught her with another right cross.

"I want my shit!" I screamed.

Raven tried to block her face, but I kept swinging for it.

"Keema, chill out!" Lucky shouted as he grabbed a hold of me from behind and pulled me off of her.

Raven kicked at me from the floor.

I jolted, scratched, and punched back to get at her but Lucky was too strong. I couldn't break his grip.

"Bitch!" Raven shouted as she got up from the floor with

57

her hair all over her head and her lip busted. "You just crossed the wrong hoe! I swear on my momma! Your ass just crossed the wrong hoe!"

"Fuck you! I want my damn money, bitch!"

Raven headed for the door.

"I want my money, Raven!" I hollered as my hands tried to grab a hold of her. "I swear I'll kill your ass if I don't get it, cousin or not."

"Your ass is in trouble!" Raven shouted as she scurried out the door in rage.

"Go home," Lucky told Shy.

"Oh, hell naw, I gotta check her pussy for my shit!"

"Go home, now," Lucky said to Shy again.

When he knew Raven was somewhere at a safe distance, Lucky finally let me go, but not in enough time to catch Shy before she waltzed out the door.

"So, you're just gonna let the two suspects waltz outta here with my damn livelihood?"

"Whoahhhhh, what the fuck?" Luckly kept mumbling to himself. "You're crazy," he kept repeating.

For at least ten minutes I ranted and raved as I walked back and forth across the living room over and over again. My temper hadn't been that hot in years. I literally wanted to kill that bitch. Even Lucky couldn't calm me down. Eventually, I headed to the kitchen to pour me a drink. While I was in there, I fumed to myself. As moments passed, the anger subsided. As I leaned against the sink taking sips of Peach Ciroc from the glass, my heart couldn't help but feel the hurt.

I felt betrayed. Betrayed by my own cousin, someone I trusted, not only with money, but with my life. I'd shared so many secrets with her and now this. The betrayal began to outweigh my anger. Besides the kids, Raven was the only family I had in the Baltimore area. She was the closest thing I had to a sister. Now, we were enemies.

"Damn," I whispered to myself as I dropped my head.

7

Smoking had always been a favorite past time of mine. I'd been doing it since the age of fourteen. Instead of picking it up from friends, I picked it up from my mother. She was one of those, at least, one pack a day smokers. She'd been doing it for as long as I could remember. That was a habit we both shared. We also took smoking to a whole new level whenever excited or nervous. During those moments, that one pack a day habit could easily turn into two. Right now was one of those moments.

In between each hit of the cigarette, I bit my nails. I couldn't help it. That was a habit I swore I would one day break. But it was easier said than done. My life was complicated. And those complications *kept* me chewing on my nails and spitting slivers of them on the concrete.

As I hit the cigarette and chewed my nails, I stood at the end of my mother's walkway staring up and down the street, still dressed in my t-shirt and pajama shorts that ran up into the crack of my ass. I paced back and forth occasionally like an expecting parent in a hospital lobby. My eyes repeatedly glanced down at my watch and then back towards both directions of the street looking for the mailman like a drug starved crack head.

Vincent, my hook up out in Delaware, said he'd mailed my EBT cards yesterday Express mail, which meant they would be arriving today. He'd just gotten them yesterday at the address we'd agreed on. He said the cash was already on them so I was good to go. It was nine hundred and fifty between available funds and food to be exact. The shit was music to my ears. Just the thought of it made me want to cum. I needed money fast to help me with my big come-up plan.

The clock was ticking. Drake would be home in only two more days, and I still hadn't had any success in trying to talk him into giving me the locker number. The shit was easier said than done. I tried to run game on him this morning using the Trust Factor; "What, baby? Don't you trust me?" I asked him while trying to sound innocent. But it didn't work. He just said it was best for everyone involved if he just kept it to himself.

"I'll be home in just two more days," he told me.

Shit, I thought to myself.

It looked like I was gonna have to share the money with his ass after all. But then again, I was also thinking about maybe setting his ass up. I was thinking about putting both him and Trent against each other; maybe having Trent take him out. It was a sure bet that my pussy game was fire enough to make Trent down for it. Afterward, when the job was done, I would cross Trent out of the picture and keep all the money for myself.

The mailman's jeep finally turned onto my street causing me to raise my body straight as a board. He parked at the corner. I was too anxious to wait for him to sort the mail and then make his way down the street to my house, so I headed straight up the block to his truck, batted my eyes, smiled like butter wouldn't melt in my mouth and asked for my shit. As soon as he took it from his mail bag, I snatched it and headed back to the house.

While ripping the envelope open and walking, my mind began to calculate numbers, decimals, and percentages like a calculator or a cash register. The card had nine hundred and fifty dollars on it and I had thirty-two hundred dollars worth of gift cards sitting on my bedroom dresser waiting to go later today. A bitch no longer just left them sitting around the house anymore after the Raven episode. Fuck that shit. Those types of losses hurt. Anyway, I also had three thousand left in the bank from the

60

money my mother had left.

Damn, I thought to myself as the numbers ran through my head. My spending habits definitely needed to slow the fuck down. The money was going out just as quickly as it was coming in. I couldn't help it though. I'd grown accustomed to a certain lifestyle. I liked nice clothes, nice cars, and good weed. All that shit cost. Besides, when I first started spending, I thought the money from Frenchie's estate was going to come through as soon as I signed my signature to the paperwork. I had no idea the shit was going to take this fucking long, or that Mr. Hyde would cancel our appointment today. That call damn near devastated me this morning. What was the fucking hold up?

As I headed up the walkway, the numbers in my head put my mind in a position where it couldn't help but think about what Raven had done. That treacherous bitch! The seven thousand in cards she'd gotten me for had placed a hurting on my pockets. Those seven stacks could have gone to good use.

"Fuck," I said. *If there's one thing I hate in this world, it's losing money.*

That shit gave me a headache. Money just had that type of effect on me. And to know Raven was the culprit hurt me pretty bad.

I also thought about the threats Raven made just before leaving. There was a part of me that wondered if she was truly serious about making good on them. I wasn't scared or anything. Never that. There wasn't a bitch alive and walking around on two feet who could pump fear in my heart. She just wasn't a good enemy to have. I knew about all the treacherous shit she'd done to bitches before. A nigga sure as hell didn't want or need any surprises. My life lately had been filled with enough of them. Shit, one too many could probably drive my ass crazy.

As I began to walk up the stairs, I mumbled, "Fuck it."

I would just ask Lucky for some money before he left tomorrow. He could definitely spare it. He'd been pulling out knot after knot since he'd arrived. I don't know exactly what type of business he was handling down here. But whatever it was, it was keeping a whole lot of paper in his pocket. And I could use some. If worse came to worse, I'd just tell him I needed it for Treasure. He couldn't say 'no' then.

It felt terrible to have to lie to Lucky yesterday. I told him that me and the kids were going out of town tomorrow and I didn't feel comfortable leaving anyone in my house while I was gone. He was good with it though. He said he'd spend the rest of his trip in a hotel room. *Thank God*, I thought to myself relieved. Drake was getting out in two more days. The last thing I needed was Lucky being at my house to complicate shit.

My eyes were staring down at the EBT card when I opened the door of my house and walked in. When I focused, I couldn't believe what I was seeing. Lucky was sitting on the couch. Treasure was straddling his lap and kissing him on the lips.

"What the fuck?" I gasped in total shock.

Immediately, Lucky pushed her away, causing Treasure to tumble slightly to the floor. He looked just as shocked as I did, but I wasn't sure if his reaction was genuine or fake. All I knew was Treasure was a child and he was a grown ass man. On top of that, Treasure was *my* child.

"Treasure, you okay?" Lucky asked with a surprised look on his face. His eyes quickly darted from Treasure to me.

Treasure didn't say anything.

"What the fuck is going on in here?" I screamed again.

Lucky quickly jumped to his feet. "Keema, it ain't what it looks like," he responded. "I swear to God it's not like that."

"Then what the fuck is it like? I just walked in and caught you kissing my fucking twelve year old daughter!"

"Keema, I…I…I," he stuttered nervously. "I wasn't kissing her. She kissed *me*."

"What?"

"I know it doesn't look that way, but I swear it's true! I ain't no fucking punk ass child molester. I don't get down like that!"

I looked at Treasure. She was standing in silence with a

frightened look on her face. A part of me believed Lucky because Treasure truly *had* been getting out of hand lately. She truly *had* been trying to act older than she really was.

"Treasure, what happened?" I asked her, noticing that she had on my pink-colored Mac lipstick.

She dropped her eyes to the floor as if she was ashamed.

"Treasure!" I yelled.

"Damn, Keema, quit hollering at her," Lucky interjected. "That's her problem. You're always talking *at* her instead of *to* her."

"Lucky, don't tell me how to fucking talk to my child, especially after what I just walked in on! I should call the cops!"

He took a deep breath, shook his head, and stayed quiet.

Turning my attention back to Treasure, I asked her again what happened.

Treasure kept her eyes on the floor but answered. "I kissed him," she said innocently.

"What do you mean *you* kissed him?"

She raised her eyes to me.

"Did he make you?"

"No, he didn't make me," Treasure said as if offended. "I love him." She looked at me like I was crazy. "What, do you think I have to *make* someone kiss me? Do you think I'm too ugly for someone to kiss me?"

"Treasure, Lucky is a grown man. He doesn't want your lil' scrawny ass. He wants to suck on big titties like these," I told her, pulling out my right tit and flossing it in her face. Luckily, my huge nipples were hard, and looked her in the eye.

She rolled her eyes.

"You need to apologize, and after that I'ma beat your ass."

"She's good," Lucky said. "She ain't got to do that."

"Yes, she does. She needs to know that shit ain't right."

"Look, Keema, no disrespect, but I don't blame her. I blame you."

I looked at him like he'd lost his damn mind. "What the

63

fuck do you mean you blame *me*?"

"It is what it is, Keema. You're making her grow up before her time. You got her around shit she shouldn't be seeing on a daily basis."

"Nigga, don't judge me. You're a damn drug dealer. What right do you have to tell me anything?"

"Yeah, I am a drug dealer. But my decision is something that only affects *me*. Keema, *your* decisions affect her and the rest of your children. They learn from you."

He was right, but I really wasn't trying to hear it. The truth hurts.

"She also needs a good father figure in her life, Keema. A child should have both parents around."

Treasure folded her arms, shifted all her weight to one foot and stared at the floor.

"Look Keema, I might've over stepped my boundaries, but I took her to see her father yesterday."

"What?" I asked, completely caught off guard by the news.

"Yeah," Lucky confirmed. "I took her to see him."

"Why?"

"Because she asked. She said she wanted to see him before she started school in a couple weeks after Labor Day."

My eyes went from him to her growing larger by the second. I carefully watched her body language. "When did she ask you?" I inquired while still keeping my eye shiftily on Treasure.

"Yesterday morning. She came to me crying and saying that she missed her father. She said she'd been wanting to go see him, but you said no."

That was it. I couldn't take anymore. It was obvious that Treasure was running game. The bitch definitely had something up her sleeve.

"Get out!" I told Lucky while still keeping my eyes locked on Treasure.

"Keema," he attempted.

"I said get the fuck out!" I hollered at him. "Get your ass

64

out of my house right now!"

He sighed in defeat, headed toward the door.

"And don't bother calling," I said without turning to face him. "I'll put your shit outside so you can take it with you. You're not welcomed here anymore. And you're definitely not welcomed around my daughter."

Treasure finally looked up from the floor. Obviously she didn't like those words at all. "But it's not his fault!" she cried, "I told you I love him."

All I could do was stare at her. "You're joking, right?"

Lucky said nothing. He simply opened the door and walked out.

"Why did you tell him that?" Treasure asked pleadingly. Her heart was clearly broken. "He didn't do anything!"

"You were kissing him, Treasure," I reminded her angrily.

"And I'm sorry," she replied. "Don't take him out of my life for something I did."

"Fuck all that, Treasure! Why did you tell him that you wanted to see your father?"

She didn't answer.

"Why, Treasure?"

"Because I just did, okay? I guess I was really missing him more than I thought."

She folded her arms again and dropped her eyes to the floor. Tears began to fall from her eyes. Seconds later, she turned, ran up the stairs, and slammed her bedroom door.

I stood in the living room by myself. A piece of me was willing to take some of the blame. I knew that what Lucky said was right. I really had been placing Treasure in situations that were causing her to grow up too quick. I really had been allowing her to see things a child her age shouldn't. Shit, she had even killed a man. All of that had to be traumatic for a child to deal with and comprehend.

I understood all of that. But despite how badly I felt for her, something else was pulling my thoughts and pulling me in another direction, over riding my compassion and sympathy for

65

Treasure's position. I couldn't help but wonder why exactly she went to see her father. My curiosity wouldn't allow me to let that go. Something about it wasn't sitting right with me. She never wanted to see him before, so why now? And on top of that, why would she wait until only a few days before he was scheduled to come home? It also dawned on me that Drake hadn't called in a few days.

Something just wasn't right.

Obviously Treasure was wise beyond her years. She could be sneaky when she wanted to. Knowing that, had me on pins and needles.

Something was up.

8

Somehow giving great head just came naturally to me. The taste of a dick had always made me want to do my best on it, even if I wasn't too crazy about the nigga I was giving head to. Shit, every nigga who'd gotten it from me said my mouth was off the chain. I'd never gotten even one complaint about it, but lately I'd decided to step my game up a little.

When we were still cool, Raven had once told me there was some new head out. I didn't know what the hell she was talking about. She said it was white girl head. I still had no idea what she was talking about so she explained to me that white girls give head differently than black girls. She said that white girls really get into choking and gagging on a dick. The shit drives a nigga *crazy*.

I later rented a porn movie to check it out for myself. Sure enough Raven was right. White girls go hard on the dick, choking and gagging on the dick, acting like savages. I don't have gag reflexes and my tonsils were taken out when I was a kid so deep throating came easy. It had always been in my repertoire. I just never got too extreme with it…

Until now.

The room was dark and I was down on my knees going to work on Dollar's dick. My head bobbed back and forth furiously.

With each bob of my head, I swallowed him whole. My mouth made wet smacking sounds. He loved it so much that he grabbed a hold of the back of my head and began to fuck my face like a mad man. The entire time, I kept my mouth open enough to take in air so I wouldn't suffocate.

"Oh shit, Keema," he moaned looking down at me devouring his pole. "Do that shit, girl."

I took the dick out for a second, gave him a freaky look, and began to smack his dick against my tongue. Raven's face appeared in my mind. Jealousy filled me. I'd be willing to bet the bitch didn't have head skills like mine. Deep down I really wanted to take Dollar from her ass just to prove to the bitch that she wasn't on my level. I didn't actually *want* the nigga. I just wanted to show him off in places where I knew Raven would either see us or hear about us. That would be the ultimate get back since she wanted to steal from me.

Bitch you take my money, I take your man, I thought wickedly.

"Keema, you're a damn freak," Dollar moaned, enjoying my skills.

Immediately, I shoved the dick right back into my mouth and began to make slurping sounds on it.

Don't get me wrong. I don't just suck *every* nigga's dick. What I was doing right now was just business. Dollar was only getting some head because it was a down payment on the money I still owed him for murking Peppi's crooked ass. I still owed a thousand. Since my pockets had been taking such a huge hit lately, I suggested he give me a discount in exchange for some fire ass head. I'm a bad bitch, so it was no wonder that he would say yes. What nigga wouldn't want to see his dick shoved in my mouth? Dollar damn near tripped over his words to say yes.

"Fuck, Keema!" he shouted as I began to stroke the shaft of his cock and lick his balls. His knees began to buckle.

"Cum for me, daddy," I said innocently as I took his dick back into my mouth and looked up into his eyes.

The nigga couldn't take anymore. His pipe shot off like a

water hose. His entire body locked up as I stroked his shaft harder and sucked like a vacuum, draining him completely. He went weak and plopped down onto my bed. I got up off of my knees, went to the bathroom, and spit his babies in the toilet. Nah, nigga, I don't do no swallowing unless I'm in love or some shit.

Dollar was buckling his belt when I got back to the bedroom from brushing my teeth. "You good?" I asked.

"Yeah. But we need to talk, though."

Uh-oh, I thought to myself. Usually when someone says we need to talk, it doesn't turn out to good. My face twisted. "Talk about what?"

He finished buttoning up his pants, then pulled his dreads into a tight ponytail just above his neckline. He gawked at me for a few seconds before speaking. " Look, you gon' have to come up off a little more cheese," he said.

"What the fuck do you mean?" I asked, looking at him like he was insane.

"I mean the streets are starting to talk. My name is being mentioned. Somehow, someone recognized my truck that night."

"Who?"

"I don't know."

"Well, just find out and get rid of their ass," I told him as thoughts of police cars surrounding my house suddenly appeared in my mind.

"I'm on the job."

"But I don't see what the fuck that has to do with me. You and me made a deal."

He shook his head. "It has *everything* to do with you. Why the fuck didn't you tell me that Peppi has connections to them damn MS-13 muthafuckas?"

"What?" I took a step back as my eyes tripled in size. I knew who MS-13 was, but I had no idea that Peppi was connected to them.

"Those muthafuckas are like the damn mafia, Keema. They're even worse. They bury muthufuckas alive. Now, they're looking for my ass."

Oh shit.

If they were looking for him, eventually my name could come up. Fuck the damn police. Fuck doing time. I was more worried about them MS-13 muthafuckas. I saw a special episode of *Gangland* about them. Those dudes were known for torturing folks who crossed them. The thought made me grab my head stressfully.

"Now, you see why I need more money, Keema. Having those muthafuckas on my ass wasn't part of the deal."

"Shit," I responded, knowing Dollar wouldn't even get the remaining balance that we agreed on.

Things were starting to bother me. Both Raven and the fact that someone had seen Dollar's truck crossed my mind. Dollar had killed Peppi in a Mexican neighborhood. Who could've recognized him? Raven's threats just before leaving my house filled my ears.

"So Dollar, have you talked to Raven?"

"Yeah."

"And?"

"And what?"

"What the fuck was she talking about, nigga?"

His eyebrows wrinkled. "What do you mean?"

"Do you think the bitch may be the one who put the word out about your damn truck?"

Dollar looked at me like that was ridiculous. "Hell naw."

"How do you know?"

"Because Raven has just as much to lose as me and you. She planned it with us and she was there."

He was right, but it did little to comfort me. I wasn't absolutely convinced.

Suddenly, someone knocked at my bedroom door. The knock startled both of us. No one was home but us. We both looked at the door.

"Keema," Shy's voice came from out in the hallway. "You ready?"

Ready for what, I thought to myself.

Then it came to me. I immediately remembered that Drake was getting out today. I looked at the clock to see that I was supposed to have been on the highway ten minutes ago. Shy had taken Treasure and the kids with her to drop off the latest batch of cards. As soon as they got back Shy was going to ride with me to the prison.

"Yeah, Shy, give me a second," I said through the door, then hurried to grab my purse. "Look, Dollar, I gotta go."

"What about my money?"

"Nigga, I got you. You just find out who the fuck saw your damn truck and lullaby their ass."

"When am I going to get my money though?"

Snatching the bedroom door open, I said, "Soon, nigga, damn. Now get out. I gotta go."

Shy looked at Dollar with complete surprise. She knew he was Raven's dude. Obviously she was wondering what he was doing in my bedroom. She was a bigger fool than I thought if she couldn't figure it out.

"I'm ready. Let's go," I said, ignoring her.

Drake had told me that as soon as I came and got him, we were headed straight to the storage place to get the money. I'd let Trent know and me and him came up with a plan to get the money and erase Drake from the picture. All I had to do was go pick Drake up, and Trent would handle everything else. I would be a paid bitch by midnight.

The kids were sitting in the living room eating Taco Bell and watching television as me, Shy, and Dollar quickly made our way down the stairs.

"Treasure, I'm going to be gone for a few hours," I told her. "Hold shit down."

Without even waiting for a response, I was out the door. All I could think about was the money I was getting ready to come into. The thought made me forget about MS-13, the police, Peppi, Raven and everything else.

Dollar hopped into his truck, backed out of the driveway,

and pulled off as me and Shy headed to my car. As we walked across the grass to the driveway, I looked in my purse for the keys. As soon as I found them and raised my head, my heart plunged to my stomach. My feet froze in the center of the lawn. Shivers ran down my spine.

Stopping ahead of me and turning, Shy looked at me, wondering what was going on. "Keema, what's up?"

Words wouldn't leave my mouth.

"Keema?"

I couldn't speak. I couldn't even blink. All I could do was stare fearfully at the Impala sitting parked across the street from my house. It was the same car I'd seen on the highway that night.

My body shook.

Shy looked at the car and then back at me. "Keema, what's wrong?"

Nothing else around me existed. I couldn't even hear Shy. The only thing I could focus on was the car, even more importantly, the wonder of who was possibly inside it. Just like that night when I exited the highway and saw his face, I was now terrified. Could it be him, I wondered? It *had* to be. This shit wasn't a coincidence. Why else would he follow me here?

My blood ran cold.

"Keema, what's going on?" Shy asked once again. "Who's in that car?"

Words still wouldn't escape my lips.

Suddenly, out of nowhere two Mercury undercover cars screeched to a an abrupt stop directly in front of my house, taking my eyes off the Impala.

"What the fuck?" Shy said, looking at the cars.

Within seconds, several white cops leapt out of them each storming my lawn. I had no idea what to say or how to react. I'd been caught totally off guard.

Shy took a step back.

"Keema Newell?" one of the cops asked as they approached me.

"Why?" I wasn't quite ready to volunteer any information to the cops unless I knew what was going on.

"Keema Newell," he said again. "Are you Keema Newell?"

"Why? What's this all about?" I kept asking.

One of the cops pulled a photo from his pocket and looked at it. He looked at me and said, "Yeah, it's definitely her."

The other cop grabbed my arm, turned me around, and pulled out a set of handcuffs. "Ms. Newell, you're under arrest," he informed.

"What the fuck are you talking about?" I screamed. "I'm not Keema Newell! My name is Trina Douglas! Get the fuck off of me!"

"What are y'all doing?" Shy questioned. "She's not Keema Newell! Her name is Trina Douglas!"

"Step back and stay out of this ma'am," they told her.

My front door opened and my kids stepped out onto the porch.

"Mommy!" Deniro shouted. He tried to run to me but Treasure grabbed him.

"Let me go!" he screamed. "Mommy!"

"Look," I told the older, bald cop as he locked the cuffs around my wrists. "I swear I'm not Keema Newell. All you've got to do is check my ID in my purse. Check the name on the house."

"Ma'am, I'd advise you to stop talking. We already know about how good you are at stealing and using other people's identification. That's what we're here for. You're being arrested for welfare fraud."

Damn it, I thought to myself. They were on to me finally.

The cop wearing the badge that read Campbell began to drag me to the car.

"Shy!" I turned and yelled to her. "Get my bail money ready!"

"I got you!" she yelled back.

My eyes then looked at Treasure. She was kneeling and

73

holding Deniro in her arms as he cried. For a moment I could've sworn I saw that same smirk on her face that I'd seen that day I walked in with the seafood and saw her sitting on Lucky's lap, or better yet, the day Rick and Paco got killed. She gave me that same smirk when Lucky knocked on the door that day and everything went fatally haywire.

Treasure's smirk disappeared, but her expression became like stone.

"Treasure, Shy is going to hold everything down 'till I get out. She's in charge, you hear me?"

Treasure didn't answer. She just nodded.

Before I knew it, I was sitting in the back of the vice car. Suddenly, I remembered the Impala. Quickly, my eyes darted towards it, but there was nothing there. The Impala had disappeared. With my hands cuffed behind my back, I jerked my head around frantically looking for it, but it was nowhere in sight. My eyes continued to search desperately for it; not paying attention to anything else, not even the cop who'd slid in the backseat beside me and began reading me my rights.

"They're gonna love you where you're going," he told me sarcastically.

I closed my eyes thinking of a way out of all of this.

9

"What the fuck!" I spat angrily. The phone was now on its sixth ring and my blood boiled ferociously. My ears listened to each ring intently, hoping and expecting someone to answer.

"Sorry," the automated voice spoke. "The party you are trying to reach is not available. Please hang up and try your call again."

The line went dead.

"Damn it!" I shouted.

I slammed the pay phone back into the cradle so hard and loud the C.O. looked at me from the desk with a glare that silently said, "Bitch, you better calm your ass down before I call the goon squad in here."

Several other inmates looked at me also. Some laughed and whispered to each other, finding my misfortune funny. Ignoring all of them I took the phone from the cradle again and made another collect call to my house. Once again after telling the automated operator my name, I leaned a shoulder against the wall and listened as the phone rang over and over again. Just like the last twenty or thirty times I had called today, no one answered.

"Shit!" I slammed the phone back into the cradle again.

"Slam that phone again and your phone privileges are gonna be taken away!" the C.O yelled to me from her desk.

Ignoring her overweight ass, I grabbed the phone again and dialed Lucky's number. Even though the last conversation wasn't a good one, I was hoping against the odds he'd answer. After three rings my wishes came true. I perked up and listened anxiously as the operator told him he had a collect call from me. I couldn't wait to talk to him. Shit, fuck that! What I really couldn't wait for was to tell him to come pay my damn bond and get me the hell up out of this hot bucket of piss these damn white folks had me locked up in. I was already set to give him a sob story and tell him I was sorry for everything when suddenly he hung up right after the operator said my name.

"What the fuck?" I said to myself in disbelief. "No he didn't."

"We're sorry," the operator chimed in. "The party you have reached has refused the charges for this call. Please hang up, and try your call again later."

"Fuck!" I screamed, pissed all the way off. "I didn't want to talk to your faggot ass anyway," I said into the phone as if Lucky could hear me and slammed the phone down again.

The C.O looked at me with an evil glare.

"What the fuck ever," I told her as I rolled my eyes, walked away from the phone and took a seat at a table in front of the overhanging television.

An old episode of Jerry Springer was on. One by one, I nervously began to bite my nails and spit slivers of them onto the floor. The huge crowded dorm felt tiny and closed in.

What the fuck was going on, I wondered? Why wasn't anybody answering the damn phone? They knew I was locked up and needed them to come bail me out. What the fuck was taking so long? The shit had me wanting to pull my damn hair out.

I'd been sitting in County for the past four days without a visit or word from anyone. I'd been calling the house over and over again, but got no answer. I'd also tried calling Treasure's, Shy's and even Trent's cell phones, but found out that cells couldn't accept collect calls. Basically, I was in here stuck and ready to go crazy.

Over the past four days my mind ran through scenarios and possibilities of what may have happened. Something was definitely wrong. The memory of the Impala and the nigga who could possibly be driving it materialized in my mind several times. Could he have possibly done something to Shy? Could he have maybe even killed her? The thought sent chills down my spine each time I thought about it. After what I'd done to him, there was a strong possibility that he would be willing to kill a bitch just to get to me or back at me. That thought brought the faces of my kids to me. Worriedly, I wondered about them. Were they okay? Maybe Child Protective Services took the kids. Maybe Lucky somehow found out what happened and came by to get the kids himself.

Drake was also on my mind. I wondered if he knew I was locked up. If so, why hadn't he come to get me out? Why hadn't he even visited? Did Trent go ahead with the plan without me? Was he successful at it? Shit, that nigga was probably somewhere out of state chilling with Drake's money. The shit wasn't fair. The money from Frenchie's will was also on my mind. I hoped like hell this wouldn't affect it. I was certain the insurance and inheritance agent, Mr. Hyde had called me back by now.

So many thoughts. So many questions. So many scary possibilities. They bombarded my thoughts and overwhelmed me so hard that I jumped up from the table and walked over to a window. I couldn't sit down. Shit, I couldn't even sit still. I wanted out of this place so badly I wanted to scream. This shit was for the fucking birds.

As I stared through the window down at the busy downtown traffic, several dozen bitches sat behind me at scattered steel tables playing cards or dominoes while they talked loudly. They were each wearing baggy orange jumpsuits, rubber sandals, and white sox. I didn't like them and for damn sure didn't trust them. My guard was up at all times and I wasn't going to take no shit from any of them, no matter what size.

Although I wasn't too familiar with jail life, I knew the best way to keep bitches off of me was to punish the ass of the very first muthafucka who talked shit. The worse the ass whipping, the more the rest of the bitches in here knew I wasn't to be fucked with. Busting a bitch's head open would mean nothing to me, especially right now as pissed off as I was about not being able to reach anyone on the outside. Any of these funky cock bitches could get it.

My arms were wrapped around my body as someone coughed so terribly I thought they were coughing up a damn lung. I cringed. The place was unsanitary as fuck. The vents blew out recycled air nonstop, which meant germs were constantly in flight. The bitches were nasty, too. They ate each other's pussy in the shower while the C.O's weren't looking and some of them didn't take a shower at all. My celly even left blood on the toilet of our cell while on her period this morning. I made her shameless nasty ass clean that mess up immediately because I wasn't having that trifling shit.

This place was driving me crazy. I couldn't take it too much longer. It was only a matter of time before I would lose my muthafuckin' mind. These bitches were built for this shit. They acted like it was their life. They acted as if they were used to it. Not me though. Hell no! I wanted out. I had shit to do, money to make, dick to get. Before I knew it, I was back on the phone again calling my house. Once again no one answered.

"Son of a bitch!" I yelled slamming the phone onto the cradle.

"That's it!" the C.O yelled from her desk. "Your phone privileges are taken away for the rest of the day!"

"You think I give a fuck?" I yelled back to her.

She stood slowly, allowing her fat to jiggle all over her body. She looked me directly in my face and placed her hand on the radio strapped to her hip, prepared to hit the panic button.

"Be easy, girl," a dark skinned woman said from a nearby table.

"What?" I asked her, not liking the fact that she was sticking her nose in my business. The bitch didn't know me. None of these off brand ass bitches knew me.

78

"I don't want no beef with you," she said seeing the look on my face and hearing the tone of my voice. She stood from the table and walked over to me. "I'm just saying that if you don't, she's gonna hit that button. If she does that, the goon squad is gonna run up in here and beat you so bad your own momma won't be able to recognize you. Trust me on that one. I've seen it happen."

"Don't tell her ass nothing," another girl at the table added. "Let her hard headed ass find out for herself. C.O Bradley got some shit for her. Might do her some good."

Although I looked at the C.O again, hearing the words of the dark skinned woman calmed me down. I was pissed, but not enough to fight with a bunch of burly C.O's who would get a kick out of breaking half the bones in my body. Knowing there was nothing I could do to change my situation, I turned around in frustration and headed back to the window. I would've gone back to my cell, but being in that tiny space would only piss me off even more. My eyes stared down at the downtown traffic again, making me wish I could be out there among it as people got off of work and headed home. Half of me was angry. The other half wanted to cry.

"That phone ain't nothin' but a headache," the dark skinned woman added.

"What?" I asked, not quite understanding what she meant. My tone was also defensive. I didn't trust her. Besides, the many war marks that covered her face troubled me.

"I said that phone can be a headache up in here," she repeated. "That's why I stay away from it. As she scratched her scalp, I eyed her old-school zig-zag corn rolls. "I haven't been on it in over a month. Every time I used to get on it, all I got was bad news and a bunch of disappointment. When you're in here, the outside world's attitude towards you is out of sight, out of mind. They ain't thinkin' about you. You ain't got shit to offer 'em in here."

I exhaled deeply, knowing she was right.

She turned, headed back to her table, and grabbed a pack

of cigarettes. She came back to me and offered me one. Not wanting to owe the bitch something later on, I turned it down, although my lungs were in dying need of a cigarette.

Seeing my reluctance but recognizing a fellow smoker, she smiled. "I don't get down like that," she said. "I'm strictly dickly. There's nothin' a bitch can *ever* do for me."

I had to chuckle at that one.

"Go ahead and get you one," she told me, still offering the pack to me. "I can see it in your eyes. You know you want one."

Fuck it. I couldn't hold out anymore. Besides, she wasn't any bigger than me, same height, same build, she just looked like a rough neck. So, if she came back later on trying to say I owed her, she wouldn't be too hard to handle. After grabbing one, she lit it for me. The smoke filled my lungs better than it had ever done before. I never knew a cigarette could taste so good.

After lighting herself one, hitting it and exhaling the smoke the girl introduced herself. "I'm Stormy."

"Keema."

We gave each other dap.

"What you in here for?" she asked.

"I don't want to talk about it," I replied, not feeling comfortable discussing my business with someone I'd just met. She came off cool, but I wasn't sure.

"I understand."

I took another heavy hit of the cigarette, raised my head, and released the smoke to the ceiling. My kids filled my mind. Shy filled my mind. The Impala filled my mind. Each thought made me feel like the entire world was on my shoulders.

"I need to get the fuck up out of here," I told Stormy. "I got shit to do, money to make."

She looked at me thoughtfully. "You a hustla, ain't you?"

"Yeah, how you know?"

"Credit cards?" she guessed.

Knowing she meant credit card fraud, I said, "Nah, but something like that."

80

She smiled. "Real recognize real. I see it in you."

I looked at her kind of skeptically. "What you in for?"

"Drug traffickin'," she stated nonchalantly.

"What they get you with?"

"A brick and a half?"

My eyes widened slightly. I'd fucked with plenty of niggas who moved that kind of weight. But I never knew a bitch who was getting it in like that.

"How much time you looking at?"

"The prosecutor saying ten years."

Stormy was still nonchalant and worry free as if ten years was small time.

"Ten years?" I asked in disbelief. There's no way I could be as nonchalant if I was looking at ten years. I'd be a fucking basket case.

She took another hit of her cigarette and shook her head. "I ain't worried about that shit," she told me as cigarette smoke disintegrated in front of her face.

"Why not?"

"I've been in the game for fifteen years. You don't stay in the game for that long without realizin' how important it is to keep a few important people paid off. Muthafuckas owe me favors."

Damn, this is a boss bitch for real, I thought to myself.

"This right here is just a vacation in a crappy hotel," she continued. "I ain't doing nothin' in here but chillin' and stackin' money. These muthafuckas can't stop that."

My curiosity was peeked. How the hell was she stacking money in here?

Seeing the curiosity on my face, she continued. "Baby, hustle doesn't stop just because you're in jail. You simply switch it up a little bit. There's countless ways to get money up in here."

My mind immediately began to race. Stormy was someone I needed to get cool with and fast.

With those words said, I knew I would be sticking to her from that point forward. Just one issue irked me. There was something shady about her that I just couldn't put my finger on. But I knew she was about making paper so whatever her issues were, I'd deal with them.

10

Six more days had gone by and still no word from back home; not a letter or a visit. The shit was stressing me to no damn end. Every time a C.O. yelled for visits, I would listen, hoping my name would be on the list. Every time someone yelled "Mail call" I would rush to the desk, hoping I had gotten something. Each time, I was greeted with disappointment. I'd also been continuing to call home. Through Stormy and her boyfriend on the outside, I was able to make three-way calls directly to Shy, Treasure, Lucky, and Trent. I never got an answer. It also surprised me to discover that Treasure's phone was off. The number had been disconnected.

Being in the dark didn't feel good at all. No one had shown up to my bond hearing. I knew it for sure because I spent damn near the entire hearing twisting and turning on that hard ass wooden bench looking for a familiar face but saw no one. I was then forced to accept a punk ass public defender. That shit pissed me off. I *hated* public defenders. The sons of bitches were poor excuses for lawyers. They didn't give a damn about their clients. They just wanted to get a case over as soon as possible with the least amount of work, even if that meant talking their client into taking a plea that would send them to prison. Fuck that shit! I wasn't copping to nothing. I didn't give a damn what my public defender tried to tell me. If there was any way possible for me to weasel my way up out of this shit, I'd find it.

I wasn't quite sure if I had been left out to dry by my family. A part of me was angry and felt betrayed. But the other part of me felt there had to be a good explanation. There just *had* to be. I couldn't see them leaving me stranded. Something they couldn't control must've happened. Something they had no power over had to be keeping them from coming to see me and getting me out of here.

The Impala filled my thoughts and dreams much more these days. I'd sometimes think about it for hours. It couldn't be helped. The shit was worrying me so bad I was scared that I would eventually need medication to make it through the fucking day. I just couldn't escape it.

Chills ran down my spine and my heart plunged to my stomach every time I thought about the possibility of what may have happened to my family. Maybe it was *him*. Lord knows he deserved his revenge if it truly was him behind the dark tent of the Impala's tinted windows. I had done the foulest shit to him. I had committed the ultimate double cross. And on top of all that, I'd taken away nearly every one he loved. The shit scared the shit out of me every time I thought about it.

I wondered sometimes if I was losing my mind. Although my eyes had seen what I thought was his face that night as I exited the freeway, it was still difficult to truly believe it was him. But if it was, one question tortured me every morning I awoke in my tiny cell.

Had he killed my family?

My eyes were red and feeling as if they were going to well up with tears as I walked away from the pay phone for the millionth time. As usual, no one was answering. Lucky had even gotten a block placed on his phone. My heart was broken and I felt completely alone.

The place was taking a toll on me. I was always too damn worried and stressed to eat so I was losing weight. My hair was becoming nappy because I rarely combed it, instead, choosing to keep it in a ponytail. The jail was destroying my spirit.

It was also hell being this close to bitches all day long. I got no privacy or space from them. I'd never really trusted women, period. It was in their nature to be devious and sneaky so I definitely didn't trust these scraggly looking hoes up in here. Just being around them made my damn blood boil sometimes.

Stormy was just entering the dorm, returning from her latest visit when she saw me. She was always getting visits. Shit, she was getting them even on days when she wasn't supposed to. She definitely had pull.

"Still no answer?" she asked approaching me.

I shook my head.

Seeing the hurt in my eyes, she said, "Hold your head up, girl. You know you can't show weakness to these muthfuckas in here. They're like coyotes. If they smell weakness, they attack."

She was right but I could only manage a half-hearted nod in agreement. This place was breaking my ass down.

"I got some good news," she said.

"What's up?"

"I just spoke to my hook up."

"What hook up?" I had no clue who she was talking about and really didn't give a damn.

"The Foster Care hook up."

"Oh."

She looked at me with surprise. "Damn, nigga, you sure don't sound enthusiastic."

"My bad. I got a lot of shit on my mind."

"Well, you can't let that shit stop you from hustling. I'm looking at about ten years. Do you see me moping around?"

I shook my head. She was right. Stormy was still grinding and getting money. She had a hand in almost every hustle the County Jail could offer. From our dorm she had her prostitution hustle going strong. It was like a match-maker service where you get sex a la carte. Then there were the commissary hustles, in-mate protection services, and a whole lot more going on all over the jail. The bitch stayed getting money. She even had a few

85

C.O's in her pocket. I'd only been around her for a few days and already gotten V.I.P treatment from one C.O. just for delivering Stormy's homemade moonshine called Hooch to one of the inmates in protective custody.

She was wild, but just my speed. Over the past week I'd opened up to Stormy about my welfare hustle. Being the hustler that she was, she immediately wanted to fuck with it. She was always looking for new ways to make money.

"Now listen," Stormy said as she grabbed me by the shoulder and led me to a corner of the dorm, not wanting anyone to hear our conversation. "I got everything worked out for you. Once you get out, my girl is going to get you some foster kids ASAP."

My face twisted in disbelief. "How is she going to do that?"

"Don't worry about it. She got you. Once they're in your custody, the agency is going to pay you eight hundred dollars per child."

My eyes bucked open like I had cataracts. "Eight hundred dollars?"

She nodded. "Yup. All you've got to do is make sure you at least spend a hundred dollars a month on each of them. That's mandatory because them white folks ain't as stupid as they may look. They come around checking."

I nodded at each word, following her carefully. Money always kept my attention.

"Your house got to be presentable," she continued. "Clean the kids up a bit, too. Bathe them little muthafuckas because when they're in foster care, they pick up bad habits. Just like some of these bitches up in here, they don't like to wash their asses. They'll wear the same underwear over and over again. They'll even wear their socks until them shits start stinking through their shoes."

My look grew sour at her description.

"That's real talk," she stated. "They'll have roaches big as mice setting up shop in your house."

Just the thought of a damn roach made my stomach turn.

"That's the type of shit those white folks look for. So you got to make sure you keep them little fuckers clean."

I nodded.

"Also, every child should have their own room. But two girls can share one or two boys. No co-ed shit. Can you handle that?"

"Yeah."

My home had a basement that my mother had converted into a sitting room. There were two small rooms aligning it that I would be able to turn into bedrooms. Treasure, myself, Deniro, and Shane would take those rooms. The foster kids would take the other bedrooms. There were three bedrooms upstairs. That meant I could get at least three children, maybe even more. At eight hundred dollars a pop that would be twenty four hundred dollars. My pussy got wet at the thought.

"That's all I can tell you right now. When you get out, my homegirl, Drenna will put you up on all the details."

I was in the process of asking a few more questions when I felt a tap on my shoulder. I turned around and was surprised to see an old face from my past. It was my D.C. and Virginia connect, Tia. When I was out running my welfare scams, she was the key to it all.

"What's up?" I asked.

Her face twisted to an expression that was far more than just anger. "What the fuck you mean what's up?"

I quickly turned to glance back at Stormy, who watched Tia's every move. "Look, you need to fall back and check your tone," I warned.

"Fuck that!" Tia yelled, balling her hands into fists at her sides.

Card games stopped.

Dominoes fell.

Hair braiding ceased.

All eyes were looking at us.

"I'm in here because of your sloppy ass!" she belted.

87

"What the fuck are you talking about?"

"Bitch, don't play stupid! The police kicked my door in and got me behind your bullshit!"

"My bullshit?" I wasn't sure exactly what went down, since she was locked up in Maryland, but I wasn't about to discuss that shit in front of everybody. This was a side bar conversation.

"Well, that's the price of the game! Get yourself a lawyer and get over it!" I returned.

"You're foul, Keema. That's fucked up how you never paid off your debt to my friends. We kept our end of the deal and you didn't!"

The last thing I needed was for her to be giving me a bad rep in jail, especially in front of Stormy.

"I don't know what the fuck you're talking about. You must have me mixed up with some other petty chick that you deal with. I pay my dues!"

"Stop lying!"

Before I knew it, Tia caught me with a strong right cross that made my knees buckle. My eyes saw bright white lights.

"Oh shit!" someone yelled. "She just snuffed that bitch!"

I widened my eyes and tried to shake off the lights I kept seeing. As I tried, I felt her catch me with another punch to the jaw. The force of it dropped me to my knees.

The entire dorm erupted. Everyone began to crowd around us. I could hear them urging us on. I also heard Stormy warning bitches not to jump into it. She then started taking side bets.

My heart raced. My adrenaline pumped. Although dazed, I jumped up and pushed Tia backwards until she tripped over her feet and fell to the floor with me on top of her. My vision hadn't come back completely, but I could see just enough to take aim at her face and swing. My fist connected with her mouth.

"Ewwwwwww!" the surrounding inmates yelled.

I caught her with another one. But it wasn't hard enough to daze her. "Bitch, I opened up my home to you and your fucking daughter. You ratchet bitch!" Tia reached up and dug her thumbs into my eyes.

"Owwww!" I screamed. I was forced to let her go and grab her wrists as she wriggled underneath me.

"You scandalous bitch!" she screamed, trying her best to put my eyes out.

With a tight grip on her wrists, I was finally able to tear her thumbs loose from my eyes, but she somehow managed to catch me with a strong punch that knocked me to the floor. It hurt so bad that I had to grab my jaw. In pain, I looked up just in time to see her charging towards me. Just as she was about to dive on me, I raised both of my feet and kicked her in the stomach as hard as I could. She immediately hunched over. At that point, I quickly jumped to my feet and punched her in the side of the face forcefully, causing her to fall to the floor.

"Keema," Stormy said, stepping to me as everyone around us screamed for more. She pulled a shank from beneath her shirt, placed it in my hand and said, "Finish her ass off. I'll give you fifty percent of the money I'll make if you do it. Who thinks she got the guts?" she shouted to the inmates, urging them to place bets.

Taking the shank in my hand, I looked her directly in the eyes wondering what type of person she really was.

"Do it," she told me forcefully.

My skin cringed.

Behind her and over the shoulders of the cheering inmates I could see several guards rushing into the dorm.

"Kill that bitch!" one of the inmates yelled. Then they all began to chant, "Kill that bitch! Kill that bitch!"

"What you waiting on?" another asked. "Murk her ass!"

My eyes dropped to Tia laid out near my feet. She was holding her stomach and curled into a ball. A part of me wanted to kill her, but most of me wanted her alive. I wasn't a killer; simply a hustler; a woman on her grind. I looked at the shank in my hand.

"Hurry up!" Stormy yelled. "I held the guards up as long

as I could."

As soon as she said that, I looked up to see the guards finally beginning to force their way through the crowd of inmates. My eyes dropped back down to Tia.

"Kill her ass, Keema!" Stormy shouted angrily.

I squeezed the shank tightly in the palm of my hand. I wanted to do it so badly, but the thought of life in prison scared me. Shit, it terrified me. Although I was facing time in prison already, at least I would one day see sunlight again. But if I killed this bitch, this hell hole would become my reality forever. The realization made me drop the shank to the floor. I looked at Stormy to see obvious disappointment on her face. That was the last thing I saw before the guards rushed me to the floor and Stormy's eyes sent me a death sentence.

11

When I finally get my ass out of jail, I'm gonna change my life, I thought to myself. That was real talk. I'm sure every jail house muthafucka said that, but my words were sincere. I never wanted to set foot in this spot again.

Being in jail was a nightmare, but being in the solitary confinement or the 'hole' as most called it was even worse. I'd spent day after day staring at four walls with nothing else to do but think. I even tried sleeping my time away, but a human being can only sleep for so long. The rest of the time was spent crying my damn eyes out. In between it all, I ate the soggy ass bologna sandwiches they gave me and drank out-dated cartons of milk. A bitch was hungry so I had no choice. On top of it all, I was cold all the time because they never turned off the air conditioning. At times, my cell felt like a refrigerator. My sheets were too thin to ward off the cold.

Countless thoughts ran through my mind every day and night. I would lie in my bunk and stare at the ceiling while think-ing about my life and all the decisions I had made, especially the ones that led me here. Those thoughts often made me wonder if it was karma that had been beating me over the head lately with bad luck. I'd crossed a lot of people and done a whole lot of lying. Maybe the shit was finally coming back to haunt me. It had finally caught up.

The faces of my mother and my dead son Cash came back to me several times. I missed them like crazy. Despite my mother crossing me, I still loved her and wished she was here. As far as Cash, he was my heart, my youngest baby. I could still remember how he used to mispronounce McDonald's because he didn't quite know how to say his words so good. The last moment I saw the two of them constantly filled my nightmares as I sat on the cell's uncomfortable bunk. I could still remember Cash's smile before he died that day. It broke my heart to remember it. He was my child. I was supposed to protect him. I was supposed to have never left him on my mother's doorstep that day.

If I'd been the mother I was supposed to have been, he'd still be here. The shit had me sitting on my bunk with my knees pulled to my chest crying like a crazy woman. Guilt was all my heart and soul could feel. Everything was my fault. I vowed to do better as a mother if the good Lord ever let me out.

Obviously, I was already stressed the fuck out before they threw my ass in the hole. Now, the stress had doubled. It was sheer torture to have to sit in a small room like a wild animal. The shit was inhumane. I'd always heard of muthafuckas who went in and out of the hole on a regular basis. I'd heard some of the bitches back at the dorm who'd done time in prison say that they preferred the hole because it allowed them to get away from the bullshit they were surrounded by. However, me myself, and I couldn't see how they managed. I was surprised that I still had my sanity. Every day I awoke, I wondered if that would be the day my mind would finally snap.

I had spent nearly two weeks in solitary when the door finally opened and a tall dark skinned, male C.O. told me to come on out. As I stood from the bunk and exited the tiny cell, I looked a hot mess. My eyes were red and tears were rolling down my cheeks. My hair was nappy and thickly matted and my jumpsuit was beyond wrinkled. I'd taken a few birdbaths in the cell's sink, but the urge to keep myself up was leaving me. I no longer cared how I looked.

I was dying in here.

Wiping the tears from my eyes, I stepped out into the hallway. "Am I finally getting out?"

"Yes," he said, closing the cell door. "Good timing, too."

"Why?"

"You've got a visit."

"Huh?" I didn't think I'd heard him correctly. The news caught me completely by surprise.

He nodded as we began to make our way down the hall. "Who is it?"

"Don't know. You'll find out when you get there."

Immediately, I wondered if it was my public defender. He was supposed to show up last week, but I hadn't heard a word from him. Since I was in the hole, I couldn't even call him.

"You want to take a quick shower?" the guard asked.

Realizing I looked and smelled horrible, I nodded yes. Moments later, I was standing underneath the shower's cascading warm water. Every drop felt good as it rained down on my skin.

As I washed my body quickly, I hoped the public defender had some good news. I hoped he would tell me I would be going home soon. That would be the best news in the fucking world right now.

I stepped out of the shower and got dressed within minutes. Minutes later, I was being escorted to the visiting area. It was a long hallway with narrow cubicle like booths lining its entire left hand side. Each of the booths had a steel chair, a phone, and a window of bullet proof glass. It immediately reminded me of that scene in the movie *Menace to Society* where Caine went to see Pernell.

The guard stopped me at booth number ten and told me to have a seat. As I sat down, he walked off. I looked at the bullet proof glass, but there was no one sitting on the other side. After several minutes, I heard a door open and shut. I then heard footsteps. Seconds later, my eyes brightened. I couldn't believe who'd taken a seat across from me. The entire blanket of darkness that I'd been covered with for the past several weeks lifted.

It was Treasure.

She looked so grown. Her hair was neatly done and hanging to her shoulders. Her nails were also freshly manicured, and her lips were glossed and shiny. Both her ears had diamond studs in them and she was dressed in a cute pink fringed tank top and some leggings.

"Oh my God! Treasure!"

I wanted to hug her, but the glass between us wouldn't allow me to. Quickly, I grabbed the phone and placed it to my ear. "Baby," I said with tons of excitement and a huge smile. "I can't believe it's you."

Treasure placed the phone to her ear, leaned back into her chair, and dropped her eyes to the floor. There was no excitement in her demeanor or expression. I didn't care though. I was just happy to see my child, to know my baby was alive. Seeing her made my day.

"How did you get in here?" I asked, knowing a person had to be at least eighteen to visit by themselves.

Treasure reached into her bra and pulled out a wad. "Money can get you whatever you need in life. I knew the right guard to approach," she told me bluntly.

It took me several seconds to digest what she'd just said then I thought about the fat stack of bills.

"Girl, where did you get that kinda money?"

"The streets," she said curtly and stuffed the money back into her small breasts. Still, there was no excitement in her.

"Sweetheart, aren't you happy to see me?"

She nodded, but refused to give me eye contact.

"How is everything? How is everybody? Are you guys okay?" I prodded.

"We're alright."

"Where's Shane and Deniro?"

"At home."

"At home? Why didn't you bring them?"

She simply shrugged her shoulders. "Didn't really think about it."

Her nonchalant attitude was beginning to turn me all the way off. "Treasure, you knew I would want to see them. What do you mean you didn't really think about it?"

"I just didn't," she said with another shrug. "Besides, school started this week. I came straight here after lunch."

I wanted to ask her why she didn't finish out the day then realized my words didn't matter to Treasure. She was doing shit her way now, obviously.

"Wow, school huh? Well I'm glad you're enrolled and going. I've been worried sick about you guys. I thought something happened to you. I haven't been able to eat or sleep. You guys are on my mind every moment of the day."

She sucked her teeth slightly as if she didn't believe me while still choosing to look at the floor.

"I've been calling the house. Why hasn't anyone been answering the phone?"

"You know how high these phone bills can get."

I gave her a strange look. "Treasure, I'm your damn mother. When I call, you're supposed to answer."

"We've got enough bills. We don't need any more."

I couldn't believe what I was hearing. Was she fucking serious? Was she *really* fucking serious?

"What happened to your cell phone?" I asked. "I've been calling it and it's been turned off."

"I had it disconnected."

"Why?"

She finally raised her head and looked at me. There was annoyance in her eyes like I was getting on her nerves or something. "I just told you," she said. "We got enough bills. The last thing we need is to stretch our finances further than they already are. You're not around to take care of us, so I had to do what I had to do."

"Where's Shy?" My eyes quickly looked behind her.

Treasure's eyes dropped to the floor again and she folded

her arms. "I don't know," she said with a shrug.

"Treasure, what do you mean you don't know? I left her in charge. She's supposed to be holding shit down. She was supposed to…"

"Look, she comes and she goes," Treasure said interrupting me. "I see her every now and then. What she does is her business, not mine. I've gotta look out for my brothers."

This shit was like a bad dream. I couldn't believe what the fuck I was hearing. *Damn it, wait until I get my hands on Shy*, I thought to myself angrily. When I finally got my hands on that bitch, there was going to be some serious furniture moving going on. I was going to warm her black ass up like a hot bowl of grits.

"She's supposed to be getting me out of here," I told Treasure. "She knows that. That was last thing I told her when they were arresting me."

"Then that's between you and her. I'm focused on keeping a roof over me and my brother's heads."

She seemed so cold and uncaring. The shit made no sense to me. It was as if she hadn't missed me at all.

"Treasure, do you know what I've been going through in here?" My voice began to rise. "This place is fucked up. I'm going crazy up in here."

She simply crossed her legs and stared at the floor again as if my words were boring her.

"Who's running my business out there? Who's handling everything?"

"Me, who else?"

"And it never dawned on you to find someone to get me outta here? It never dawned on you to even put some damn money on my books? I've been struggling up in here."

Once again the little bitch sucked her teeth like I was getting on her nerves. I wanted to snatch her little ass through the glass.

She looked nonchalantly at her manicure.

I was fed up. Slamming the palm of my free hand down

flat on the table, I said, "Look, damn it! You need to get me out of here and you get me out of here *today*, Treasure! I'm not fucking playing!"

She raised her eyes to me.

"My bail is five thousand dollars. Hit my stash. I should have about a few stacks in it. Also, get your ass out there and round up my money from the cards. That should cover it. If it doesn't, call Lucky. Tell him what's up and that you need some money to bail me out. Tell him I'll pay him back in less than a week." Being that someone could've potentially been listening to our conversation, I hoped Treasure knew that I meant gift cards.

I knew Lucky couldn't tell Treasure no. Shit, she could probably get the entire five thousand from him.

"You got me?" I asked.

She nodded and dropped her head again.

Fuck a damn nod. I needed verbal confirmation and eye contact. "Treasure!"

"What?" she said, raising her head.

"I said, do you got me?"

"Yeah, I got you."

"Has Drake called?"

"Yeah."

"Is he out?"

"Yeah."

Thinking about the money he had stashed, I continued with my questions. "Well, have you seen him?"

"Yeah, he's been by a few times."

"A few times?"

Treasure nodded.

"Well, doesn't he know I'm in here? Didn't you tell him?"

"Of course, I told him."

"And he never mentioned anything about coming to get me out?"

Treasure shook her head as if there was nothing wrong

97

with what she was saying.

I leaned back into my chair and stared at her. Obviously, there was a lot not being said. There were some things she wasn't telling me. Everything seemed highly suspicious. But I wouldn't be able to find out anything while locked up in here. Soon as that bond was paid though, I'd find out every mutha-fuckin' thing.

"So, how much have you made off the cards so far?" I asked firmly.

The little winch shrugged her shoulders again.

Just as I was about to go in on her ass a guard showed up behind her. "Time's up," he told her.

"I gotta go," she said quickly as if the guard had just saved her life. "Oh, I forgot to tell you, some social worker and other strange people keep coming by the house. They probably wanna take us away like they did before, so we keep the doors locked at all times. Don't worry though. I got this."

I sat back with frustration, mouth wide open and watched my child walk away. *What the fuck have I created*!

12

My eyes ran across the name, address and phone number written on the small piece of paper in my hand. It was the info to the foster care connect Stormy had hooked me up with. After refusing to stab Tia, I honestly thought she wasn't going to fuck with me anymore, but when I got back to the dorm, she was good with it. She said not every bitch was meant to be a killer. Not all of us had it in us. Besides, business was business. She knew that I could make her money on the outside which meant more to her than killing someone she had no beef with. And thank God I didn't kill that bitch. If I had, I wouldn't be walking out of the County Jail's front doors at this very moment.

It was just after dawn when I stepped out into the night. Pausing at the top of the stairs, I took everything in while searching for my ride. It all seemed surreal. I watched the cars pass by. I smelled the air. It was all more beautiful than I had ever remembered. For a moment, I just closed my eyes and let my ears listen to my surroundings.

There was nothing at all in the entire world like being free. I mean absolutely nothing. I missed the smallest things like just being able to go to my refrigerator and make myself a sandwich. But now that I knew what it was like on both sides of the fence, I wouldn't take shit for granted anymore.

I had also decided I would never go back to jail. No matter what verdict the judge handed down on my trial date, I'd already told myself I'd die trying to escape if things seemed to not lean in my favor. Whatever it took…I would stay free. I didn't give a fuck. And hustling harder than before, stacking money, was now my mission. I didn't quite know how my case was going to turn out. However, I did know that if the police ever wanted to get their hands on my ass again, they would definitely have to do their job. They were going to have to *catch* me.

"God, thank you," I whispered taking a few more steps toward the street.

A part of me was ashamed. When I was on the inside, I'd promised God I would change my ways once I got out. I really did mean it. I really did want to. But I was going to have to get some things in order first, mainly my money and business affairs. That was going to cause me to have to go back to the old me for a moment. One thing was for sure, being a better mother was at the top of my list.

My eyes opened and I began to speedily ramble through my purse to check and make sure all my belongings were inside. It wasn't much, but it was still mine so I hoped those cocksuckers didn't steal my shit. Seeing that my cell phone and everything else was there, I pulled the envelope of money from inside and opened it. After counting out the two hundred dollars it was stuffed with, I was satisfied to know the police hadn't ripped me off. Quickly, I turned on my phone and was happy that I had a small amount of battery left before my phone went dead.

My eyes rose from the purse to the street. They began to search for a familiar face. I'd assumed Treasure paid my bond, but wasn't positive. Maybe it was Lucky or even possibly Drake. I didn't quite care who just as long as it was paid.

I took the last two steps to the street and let my head swivel to both ends. *Was anyone going to pick me up*, I wondered? *Was anyone going to meet me*? If so, where the hell were they? With my hands on my hips, I stood on the sidewalk. After several moments I decided to walk up the block to see if maybe they'd gone to the store for some cigarettes or something. As I neared the end of the street, my phone rang. The sound was something else I'd missed while I was locked up. The name and number on the screen was Raven's.

"What the fuck?" I whispered to myself.

The call threw me for a loop. She was the last person on the entire planet I expected to be hearing from. What was she calling for? Had she been the one who bailed me out? She had to be, I realized. Why else would she be calling at this particular moment? Evidently she realized that crossing me was foul as shit and she felt the best way to make up for it was getting me out of jail.

I was still pissed at her for stealing from me, but sitting in jail had made the anger subside somewhat. I hadn't totally forgiven her, but she was family. For that, I was more than willing to go ahead and let bygones be bygones. I'd accept her apology. We could possibly even go back into business together. After all, she was the nigga who taught me about the gift card hustle.

"Hello?"

"You think you're cute, huh, bitch?" Raven said angrily.

I truly wasn't in the mood for this shit. "What are you talking about?"

"Bitch, you know what the fuck I'm talking about. Don't get cute. That's some dirty shit you did. How could you be so ratchet?"

"Raven, look, I ain't trying to argue with you right now about…"

"Fuck that, you back stabbing hoe! First you accuse me of stealing from you! Then you fuck my man!"

Damn, I'd forgotten about sucking Dollar's dick.

"Raven, I…"

"When you accused me of stealing from you, I was going to let that shit go! We're family, so I was willing to forget it! But when you slept with my nigga, that was some low down shit! That was grimy!"

She'd pissed me off. "Raven, I didn't force that sorry ass

nigga to pull his dick out!" I screamed back. "Shit, if you would've been sucking his dick right, he wouldn't have been stalking me! Don't get mad at me because you don't know how to please a nigga!"

"You low down slut!"

"You can have the nigga back anyway! I didn't want him. He served his purpose and I sent him back to you!"

"You're a devious, miserable muthafucka!"

"Whatever, Raven. Your sex game is bummy! Everything about your damn jealous ass is bummy! Get on my level then maybe you won't have to steal money from me! Maybe then your niggas won't be out here creeping on your dumb ass!"

"I can't believe you. I brought you into this game! I taught you how to get money off those gift cards! It was me! And this is how you repay me?"

"You stole from me, Raven…remember! You stole from me! It's you who made shit this way! Don't try to flip it around! You cross, you *get* crossed!"

"I didn't steal shit from you! I didn't steal a dime!"

"Well, bitch, my shit didn't just get up and walk off by it-self!"

"It wasn't me! It was one of them muthafuckas around you!"

"Whatever!"

"You know what? Fuck you, Keema!"

I rolled my eyes.

"You're about to wish you'd never crossed me, ho! From this point forward, it's T.O.S! Terminate On Sight, bitch! When I see you, you're dead! You're fucking dead!"

"Blah, blah, blah, whatever," I said then hung up.

When I reached the end of the street and looked around, there was still no sight of Treasure or anyone.

"Where the fuck are they?" I'd grown impatient. Raven had pissed me the fuck off with her nonsense so the last thing I felt like doing right now was waiting. I wanted to go home, hop in the shower, and climb in my own bed.

I shook my head at the conversation I'd just had with Raven. She had a damn nerve. The bitch had stolen from me then had the audacity to get mad because I got some get back on her lame ass. Fuck her! She deserved what she got. And I wasn't sweating her threats. If she wanted it with me, let her come.

Heading back down the street, I watched every passing car, hoping to see someone I knew. What the fuck was going on, I wondered for the millionth time. Why wasn't anyone out here to pick me up? It was obvious that when I got home, shit was going to have to be tightened. First, muthafuckas left me in jail for damn near a month. Then when I get out, they're not here to pick me up. This shit wasn't going to go unpunished. I was going to be a real cold hearted ass bitch from this moment on. Mutha-fuckas were going to respect my gangsta. That was for damn sure.

As I walked, I heard the brakes of a car squeaking as it slowed beside me. Just before looking at it, I automatically fig-ured it was Lucky, Shy, Drake or someone I knew. Finally, damn it! My head turned toward the car. The sight made me gasp in fear. My feet stopped moving. I completely froze up.

It was the black Impala!

My bottom lip dropped. My eyes widened. My heart began to pound like a bass drum. My adrenaline raced through my veins.

At that moment, the passenger side window of the Impala rolled down. As soon as I was able to see inside of it, the fear I'd just felt a second before was nothing. The sight of the car had paled compared to the face I was now staring into.

It was him! It was really him!

It was Frenchie!

Immediately, I remembered the night me and Imani had killed him. The sound of the gunshot was still fresh and ringing in my ears. I could still see the flame blazing from the nozzle as the bullet exited the gun and ripped into his chest. How the fuck did he survive?

I had to be staring at a ghost. I had to be. Both me and

Imani watched him die. We'd watched him take his last breath. This moment just couldn't be.

Frenchie stared at me with the coldest eyes I'd ever seen. They never blinked even once. His jawbone was clenched tightly. Something much more than just anger was written in his expression. It was far beyond.

My body couldn't move as it stood there on the sidewalk shaking. My eyes were locked on his. I had no idea what to do.

Suddenly Frenchie threw the car in park, reached for the handle of his door, and opened it. Before he could get a foot out of the door, I took off as fast as my feet could carry me. Behind me, I heard Frenchie's door slam shut.

Immediately afterward, I heard the Impala's engine roar and its tires rip loudly into the pavement as he smashed down on the gas pedal. Horns blew, causing me to turn around for a brief second to see him making a U-turn in the middle of the street and coming after me. Knowing I couldn't out run the car, I ran back toward the County Jail, dashed up its stairs and back into the building. I was breathing hard and heavy as I turned to look out the window. The car screeched to a stop across the street. Frenchie stared at me.

"May I help you, Miss?" a cop asked from behind the desk.

Ignoring him, my eyes and attention remained on Frenchie. What could I tell the officer anyway? Hey, the man I killed in cold blood is chasing me?

I had no idea what to do.

"Miss, are you okay? Can I help you?"

Suddenly Frenchie sped away from the curb. My eyes followed until he was completely gone. Once the car disappeared, the terror inside me remained. I couldn't stop shaking. My heart wouldn't stop pounding. I was super terrified of stepping out of the door. What if he hadn't gone anywhere? What if he was waiting around the corner? What if he was waiting for me to step outside so he could do a drive by and spray me on the front steps?

Suddenly another question dawned on me, one much scarier than the others. What if he was headed back to my house?

"Oh God," I whispered in horror as I thought about my kids. What if he was headed back to kill them?

"Miss, can I help you?" the officer asked again.

Ignoring him, I fell to the floor in a pool of sweat.

13

As the bus slowed and pulled to the curb, the wait for it to come to a complete stop and open the doors racked my nerves. The only thing that matched it was the forty-five minute ride itself. It was a fucking wonder I hadn't pulled all my damn hair out while spending the entire ride worrying, looking out the window for Frenchie and biting my nails, which were already down to the nubs.

As I sat in my seat, my body couldn't remain still. It trembled and felt as though it needed to get up and move around while my foot patted the floor nervously. Now, as the bus finally stopped and the doors began to part, my hands and body slid impatiently through them before they could open completely. With no hesitation, my hand clutched the strap of my purse and my flip flops headed quickly down the busy street and bent a corner. My street was several blocks deeper into the neighborhood.

While jogging, my head rotated constantly. My eyes surveyed everything around me. My ears listened carefully to every sound. Frenchie was on my mind heavily. Seeing him back at the jail filled me with a terror unlike any other thing I could imagine. Now, as my feet carried me quickly through the night's darkness, I was terrified that his Impala would come down the street at any time or pull out of nowhere and meet me at one of the approaching corners. Every car that passed by me, especially the black ones made my eyes lock on them, preparing myself to dash up into a backyard if needed. From a distance they all looked alike. They all made me nervous. But each time they reached and passed me, relief spread over my body as I realized it wasn't Frenchie.

As the jog from the bus stop to my block took forever and longer than I imagined, my mind ran through countless scenarios, each violent. Visions filled my head of my children's dead bodies. My thoughts forced me to picture them with nickel sized bullet holes in the center of their foreheads while they laid on their backs staring lifelessly up at the ceiling. I could see and smell blood pooling around them. The shit was pure torment. Losing a child is definitely the most horrible experience for a parent. No one knew it more than me. I'd already lost one. I seriously doubted that there would be enough strength left inside me to take losing another.

Finally, I reached my street. As I approached the corner, with a mind of their own, my feet stopped running. My eyes squinted underneath the golden glow of the overhead street light into the far off darkness. Cars lined the curbs on both sides of the street but it was too dark and my house too far down at the opposite end of the street for me to tell if Frenchie was around. There was no way to tell if he was possibly somewhere on this dark street waiting for me. My heart rate stepped up its speed as I realized there was only one way to find out. I headed down the block. This time, though, my feet walked instead of jogged. With each step the street seemed to grow longer and longer, but I refused to stop or slow my pace. After what seemed like an hour of walking while cautiously watching every door, car and driveway, I finally reached my house.

The winds blew strongly for a September night, but it felt good. On the sidewalk beneath my lawn I stopped and looked up at my home. All of its lights were out and I couldn't see any movement inside. All of the windows were totally dark and my Camaro wasn't in the driveway. It looked like no one was home.

Once again, I couldn't help wondering who'd bailed me out of jail and why hadn't they come to get me. Those questions were immediately set aside as I remembered what I had bailed so quickly to the house for.

FRENCHIE!

Quickly, I ran up the lawn and reached the porch. In three seconds flat, I was up the steps and searching my purse for my keys.

"Fuck!" I yelled angrily after realizing I'd given Shy my keys the day I was arrested.

Immediately, my fists began banging on the door while I turned to look around behind me, expecting the Impala or Frenchie himself to appear out of nowhere. When no one answered, I made my way back and forth across the porch peeking through the windows, hoping to see my kids, hoping they were maybe asleep. But it didn't take more than a few brief moments to realize neither was the case. No matter how many windows I looked into, they were nowhere in sight. And no matter how hard my fists banged on the door, no one answered.

"Treasure!" I shouted but received no answer.

"Shane!" I called but still received no answer.

After calling my children's names several more times and making my way around the entire house, looking through more windows, something far worse came over me. Had Frenchie taken my kids, I wondered? Had he killed them? Were they maybe somewhere in the house dead? Or maybe they were somewhere with him at that very moment being tortured?

"Oh God," I whispered. Could Frenchie be that heartless? Could he be so thirst filled for revenge that he would hurt or even murder innocent children?

My hands grabbed both sides of my skull stressfully as my mind pictured my babies in a dark basement somewhere screaming for me as Frenchie did only God knows what to them. The thoughts made me begin to pace the porch nervously. Suddenly, I thought about Shy. She lived several houses down. Maybe she had the kids. With no more thought, I ran down the stairs. As I reached the bottom of them, I heard a door open across the street and looked to my neighbor coming out of his house and headed to his old, beat up Volvo in the driveway.

I never liked him. He always seemed like an old pervert to me. I'd notice him at times peeping out of his front window at me. There were also times when I could've sworn I saw him peeping out at Treasure, too. But despite my dislike, I headed across the street towards him.

"Excuse me," I said sweetly. "Have you seen anything strange going on around my house?"

Just as I figured, his eyes dropped straight to my breasts. The old nigga wasn't even sly about the shit. He did it, not caring how much of a pervert it made him look.

The old man looked to be about sixty-five years old and had a tooth pic dangling from the corner of his mouth. His hairline had receded all the way back to nearly the center of his head, but he still had the nerve to be rocking it slicked back into a greasy ponytail. He wore played out gold horse shoe earrings, a pair of dingy jean shorts, black silk dress socks pulled up to his damn knee caps, and a pair of gators. The nigga looked a total mess, like the seventies had passed him by. He reminded me of Jerome on the old Martin episodes.

"Hello?" I said, snapping my fingers, trying to get his attention off of my breasts. "Up here."

He gave me a smile, exposing a gold tooth. The rest of his teeth were the ugliest shade of brown I'd ever seen in my life. They immediately turned my stomach.

"I'm sorry, Lil Mama. What'd you say?"

"I said have you seen anything strange going on across the street at my house lately."

"Lil Mama, I stick to my own. I don't get into nobody's business."

That was a fucking lie. My mother had always told me about him. She said he was as nosey as they came. Shit, it seemed like every time I pulled up to my house, he was sitting on his porch watching my every move. With no time for bullshit,

I exhaled annoyingly, reached into my pocket for some money and gave him a twenty dollar bill.

"Now, have you seen anything strange going on over at my house lately?" I asked again, this time with a hand on my hip and my body weight slung onto one foot.

He raised the bill over his head and looked at it carefully underneath the glow of the street lamp to make sure it was real.

He was pissing me all the way off. Now, both hands were on my hips as I exhaled again impatiently.

Satisfied that the bill was real, he folded it and held it in the palm of his hand. "Yeah, Lil Mama," he responded in a raspy sounding voice like he'd smoked entirely too many cigarettes. He even sounded like Jerome. "It's been a lot of action going on around your house lately."

"Like what?"

"Police have been over there. I saw a few social workers and government cars." The tooth pick in the corner of his mouth bobbed up and down as he spoke.

"What about my kids? Have you seen them?"

"Nah, not in a few days. Your house has been quiet for the past two days or so. Haven't seen anybody."

"Did the white folks take my kids with them?"

"Nah, not that I seen or know of."

I didn't quite know what to think. If the county had taken my kids, I was sure they would've notified me.

Seeing the wonder on my face, he continued. "Besides them social workers, there was a whole lot of fancy cars in and out your driveway."

That took me by surprise. "What do you mean?"

"Benzes, Jaguars, BMW's, a lot of nice ones."

I had no clue who the cars belonged to. Then Lucky crossed my mind. He was the only nigga I knew who was getting enough paper to ride like that. As far as I knew, he didn't keep an entourage or goon squad around him. But since he'd been doing business down here in grimy ass Baltimore, maybe he decided it was best to surround himself with a little protection. Shit, it

111

could've possibly even been Drake and his crew. He'd most likely gotten hold of his stash by now.

"What did the guys driving them look like?"

"Young boys. Slick looking niggas.They be over your friend's house all the time; the girl who lives down the street."

Not interested in hearing anything more, I took off for Shy's house, leaving the old man standing there. Within seconds I was in front of Shy's house. In her driveway was a brand new burgundy Honda Crosstour with paper plates.

Was it hers?

Well, whether it was hers or not, she had a whole lot of explaining to do on top of telling me where my babies were. I looked up at the house. It was just as dark and motionless as mine but it didn't stop me from stomping my way up the lawn and onto the porch. As soon as I reached the screen door, I snatched it open and began to bang on the door.

"Shy!" I yelled.

No answer came from inside the house.

"Shy!" I screamed again while glancing down the street to see that the old man was still watching me with his arms folded across his chest.

"Shy!" I yelled again, this time much louder as my fists pounded on the door harder. "Open the door! I know you're up in there! I see the fucking car out here! Where my kids at?"

Still no answer.

My worry soon shifted into pure anger for Shy. While I was locked up, she was out here buying new cars and fucking with niggas who get money. What the fuck? She'd left me in there for dead. I was so pissed that as my eyes glanced over at the Honda, I decided to put a brick through the window. I ran down the stairs to the side of the house, grabbed a brick and headed towards the car. As I neared it and began to raise the brick over my head, I noticed the headlights of a dark colored car slowly creeping down the street. My eyes narrowed into a squint in an attempt to get a better look at it from the distance.

"Shit," I said, realizing what kind of car it was.

It was the Impala.

Dropping the brick, I ducked back up into the driveway and planted my back to the side of Shy's house. Swallowing a lump in my throat, I could hear my heart rate pounding again. I didn't know if I should run. I wasn't sure if he'd seen me. Running into Shy's back yard wouldn't do me any good anyway. She had a brick wall that surrounded her entire backyard. There's no way I'd be able to climb it.

I was a sitting duck.

The moment seemed like eternity. I had no idea what to do and I was too scared to peak out from beside the house to see how close the car was. All I could do was stay pressed against the wall. Finally, I heard the car approaching. I reluctantly turned my head to see it, expecting the Impala to stop in front of the house, but surprisingly it kept going, allowing me to see with a relief that it wasn't an Impala at all.

It was a Mercedes CL coupe.

I exhaled, relieved as the Benz sitting on chrome rims passed by without stopping. Ducking my head out from behind the house, I looked down the street to see the car's tail lights. It was heading down the street, causing me to drop the brick and step out from my hiding spot.

Then I noticed it pull over to the curb where the old man was still standing. I stood and watched as the driver, whom I couldn't see from the distance, rolled down his window and said something to him. Both men began to have a conversation that I was too far away to hear. As they talked, the old man looked up the street directly at me. At that moment something inside me felt strange about him and the car. I couldn't describe what I felt, but something just didn't feel right. The old man looked back at the driver, said something else, and several seconds later the car pulled off.

After taking a quick look up and down the street to make sure I didn't see Frenchie, I headed back down the street towards my house. As I approached, the old man looked at me from across the street.

113

"There's been a lot of that!" he yelled.

"A lot of what?" I asked, having no idea what he was talking about.

"Strange cars riding slow up and down the street lately at this time of the night."

I was a few steps away from my house.

"I know that Benz, though. That's them Mexican boys who've been looking for you."

I stopped and turned. "What?"

"Them MS-13 boys."

My stomach dropped at the sound of their name. Quickly, I headed back across the street. "What do you mean MS-13?"

"MS-13," he said. "I'm too old to keep up on all these young gangs y'all young cats got out here nowadays, but I know about *them* though. They're the type who'll cut momma up right in front of you."

"What do you mean they were looking for me?"

"They've been riding through here almost every night over the past couple of weeks asking about you. They just asked about you again."

"What did you tell them?"

He smiled again, showing off that tacky ass gold tooth. "I told you before, Lil Mama, getting into people's business ain't my thang."

This nigga wanted more money.

I'd lost all patience with his ass. There was no time for bullshit. I pressed up on him. "Muthafucka, don't play with me!" I screamed. "My kid's lives are at stake! This ain't no fucking game! What did you tell them?"

He stepped back and put his hands up in defense. "Damn, pump your breaks, girl. I ain't tell 'em nothin'."

"You sure?"

He nodded.

My kids' faces and smiles appeared in my mind. "Nigga, if you're lying to me, I swear...I'll come back and kill you and your whole family."

He took a couple more steps back.

Quickly, I turned on my heels and charged across the street to my house. I darted up into the backyard, grabbed a brick, and tossed it as hard as I could through the window of the backdoor. Glass flew everywhere. Within a few quick seconds, I'd reached in, unlocked the door and rushed inside.

"Treasure, Deniro, Shane!" I called as I made my way through the dark house. I didn't get any answer, but continued to call and search for them anyway. It turned out to be all for nothing. No one was in the house.

For a moment I thought about staying in the house and waiting to see if anyone would come home. But after what the old man had just told me, I realized that would be a bad mistake. I had no idea what he'd told those Mexicans. Shit, he was probably on the phone with them right now.

With no hesitation, I hit my bedroom and headed for my stash, but my money was gone. There wasn't a single penny of it left.

"Damn it!" I shouted.

I wanted to flip out, but realized there was no time. Like a mad woman, I snatched up a gym bag from the closet, hit my dresser drawers and began tossing clothes into it. I then snatched my cell phone charger from the nightstand, knowing it was going to be important to keep my phone charged so I could keep calling Drake, Lucky, and Shy as much as possible. I had to know if they knew where my kids were.

After packing and tossing the strap of the bag over my shoulder, I darted across the room to my bed, lifted back the pillow and grabbed my .380 pistol. Moments later, I headed for the front door. Approaching the living room, I glanced into Treasure's room and saw that her bed was covered with Gucci boxes and bags. There were also shopping bags on the floor from Neimans and Saks.

"What the hell?" I said to myself. Had the little bitch been spending *my* money on this shit, I wondered. Had she been out here partying and tricking off my hard earned money?

My mind split in several different directions. It was filled with anger, fear, shock, disappointment, and so much more. I had questions, but no one to answer them. So many things weren't right, but there was nothing I could do about it.

Quickly, I began to go through her drawers, searching for money and gift cards. I found nothing except more new clothes. The majority of them still had the price tags on them.

I fumed, but realized I had to go. Tossing the bag onto my shoulder and snatching up my purse, I headed for the front door, not quite sure where I would go for the night. I grabbed the door knob and turned. As I began to open the door, I could hear the sound of a car's brakes coming to a stop outside. Quickly, I shot to the front window and peeked out. My eyes widened at what I saw.

It was the Benz.

I locked the door, charged through the living room to the back of the house and ran out the back door into the night.

The backyard was so dark I could barely see too far in front of me but my feet kept moving as fast as they could any-way. They stumbled a few times, but out of fear for my life, I managed to keep from hitting the ground. Within seconds I was at the fence. I tossed the suitcase over and then climbed over it myself. As soon as I was on the other side, I hit the ground, snatched up the suitcase and took off, looking behind me occa-sionally for the Mexicans.

Not seeing anyone, I dashed through the backyard and along the side of the house towards the street. Once again, I looked behind me. Without a soul in sight, I faced the street again. However, I was immediately startled at what was ahead of me. The image made me freeze in one spot and gasp in terror. From head to toe, I shook uncontrollably. My eyes were wide. My heart felt like it would burst.

In front of me leaning against the black Impala was Frenchie.

Not knowing what to say or do, I realized I was trapped. His face was like something out of a horror film; cuts, bruises, scabs, stab wounds. I realized there was nowhere to run. I could only stand there and wait for the death that I definitely deserved. Strangely, he leaned against the car staring at me while holding a .45 Smith & Wesson at his side.

For a moment we both stood in silence, with me barely able to breathe. Finally, I begged, "Frenchie, please don't kill me! I swear I'm sorry. I really am."

The words fell from my mouth in desperation and at a machine gun's pace.

"Your triflin' ass deserves to die right here and right now, bitch," he finally sneered. His voice was dominant and venomous, shaking me to my core.

I could only remain silent. I was too scared to say one word at that point.

"You deserve to be mutilated."

My knees were weak. It took everything in my power to remain on my feet.

"But I allowed you to live and even got you out of jail because you owe me," he informed.

At least I now knew who had gotten me out of jail, but now wasn't the time to thank him. My head quickly swiveled around for the Mexicans, but they weren't there. I faced Frenchie again.

"Anything, Frenchie. I'll give you whatever you..."

"Bitch, shut the fuck up and listen!"

I did as I was told, scared to death of pissing him off.

"The only reason you're alive is because I need you. Since my brothers were gunned down, my nephews are the beneficiary to my estate, and you're their guardian. So, you'll get the money."

It seemed obvious from his expression that he had no idea I was behind the death of Rick and Dupree. Thank God for that!

"I need that money," he continued. "And the only way I can get it is through you."

I didn't quite understand. "But you're alive. The estate is yours. Why can't you just collect it yourself?"

"Because certain people want me to stay dead. Besides, I'll collect way more this way. But that's some shit that doesn't concern you. All you need to focus on is gettin' with your attorney and gettin' this shit sped up and finalized."

"I've been trying."

"Well, try harder."

"What do I get out of this? What's my cut of the money?" I questioned.

"Bitch, your cut of the money is *zero*! What you get out of this is your damn *life*! Or I can just smoke you now for tryna kill my black ass!"

Frenchie's eyes narrowed and his face twisted into pure evil. He reminded me of Screwface in the movie *Marked for Death*.

"Do you know how hard it is right now for me to keep from blowin' your damn head off?" he asked, then held the gun up. "I want to put a bullet through your face more than anything in the world."

My body tensed from the horrific possibility that he might do it.

"But, I'm lettin' your ass live because I've gotta get that money."

I didn't say anything.

Frenchie began to make his way around the hood of the Impala to the driver's side. "Get that shit taken care of," he demanded. "And give me your fuckin' cell number. That shit better stay on at all times, too!"

Quickly, I rattled off the number.

"And don't try anything stupid. I'm watchin' everything your sneaky ass does. If I think you're tryin' to play me, I will body your ass; money or no money."

Frenchie opened the door of the car. From over the hood, he said, "And by the way, how's Shane?"

"He's good." I kept a straight face.

Looking me straight in the eyes, he said. "You sure about that?"

I nodded.

"That better be the truth. If I find out any different, what them Mexicans got planned for your ass won't be shit compared to what I got in store for you."

At that moment, he climbed into his car and pulled off, leaving me standing on the sidewalk alone and afraid.

Still GRINDIN' BY: KENDALL BANKS

120

14

This place had me going crazy. It was almost just as bad as the County Jail. I mean, wall to wall bitches, no privacy, muthafuckas scared to hop their funky asses in the shower, feet smelling like stale corn chips, and a whole lot more unkosher shit I definitely wasn't feeling. The only difference from jail was there weren't any bars or walls to keep you inside.

Every trick in this shelter had a story and had fallen on some kind of hard times. From homeless situations and drug addictions to fleeing super abusive niggas, these women and their children had gone through it. Their scarred and bruised faces showed it.

This was not my scene at all. These bitches were charity cases. I was a hustla; born that way. We were totally different and had nothing in common. That was why on my second day in this place, I had to get out and at least get some damn air. I couldn't take another second of being cooped up in here. Besides, I still needed to find out exactly what was happening on the home front. I was still in the dark on what had been going on with my business while I was sitting in The County.

"Keema, I don't know your entire story because you won't let me all the way in," Mrs. Kyle said as we headed from her tiny office, and down the narrow hallway of the women's shelter. She was one of the shelter's caseworkers.

I hadn't told her why exactly I'd come in the other night. The only information I was willing to volunteer was that I was out on the street and needed someplace to stay. That's it and that's all.

"But I do assure you," she continued, "that we have a whole lot of programs and resources here to benefit you."

It was taking everything in my power to keep from rolling my eyes. The bitch had just had me in her office for the past half hour trying to get up in my personal business, asking me question after question. She had me filling out paper work and wanted me to stick around for a house meeting that all the women had to attend every evening. To hell with that. I played it off like I really had some place I needed to be and would be back later that evening as soon as I could. The last thing I wanted to do was sit around and listen to a bunch of bitches whine about their damn problems.

"Keema, you're a very bright and beautiful young woman. I've seen a lot of them like you come through that door but they leave without taking advantage of what we have to offer. I'm truly hoping you won't be one of those women. I'm hoping you'll really be back this evening. Something in those streets brought you in here in the first place. I hope it won't pull you all the way under this time. "

"I'll be back this evening," I told her quickly, growing annoyed at the sound of her voice. Without missing a step, I finally reached the door and headed out without looking back. A bitch had no intentions of coming back. I'd only stayed because I had nowhere else to go the other night and needed to lay low for a moment.

The past two days had been stressful and painful. Problems were hitting me left and right. No one was still answering their phones. I'd called everyone and still couldn't reach any of them. The shit had me crazy with worry. Besides, after seeing Frenchie and realizing why he'd decided to let me live, I had to find Shane and Deniro ASAP. The thought of each issue had my head spinning. I quickly thought about those crazy MS-13 muthafuckas pulling up outside my spot the other night. I had no choice but to worry and stress out. These folks were stone cold killers and they were looking for me. I had no idea if they had done something to my kids to get back at me. The possibility made me so nauseous at times over the past couple of days that I'd thrown up a few times.

Within moments, I was on the bus headed back to my house. While taking the long ride, millions of thoughts raced through my mind. Who had my car? It wasn't in the driveway the other night. What if I couldn't find the kids before Frenchie wanted to meet up with me? Would he want to kill me knowing that without them he'd never get the money he wanted?

With that crazy thought, I picked up my phone and called Mr. Hyde who was in charge of the inheritance. He answered real smug-like as if he were super busy.

"Mr. Hyde, it's Keema. I keep calling you. What's up?"

"Ahhhh, Ms. Newell. I can't really talk right now."

"Well when? This bullshit is taking too long."

"I'm sure you're antsy but as I told you the other day, these things take time. And I definitely need more time to get you the documents you requested."

My antenna went up. What documents? I hadn't requested any documents. And what did he mean by, as he told me the other day?

"Look, I'm not sure what kinda games you playing but I need to come see you." There was loud chatter from behind.

"Ms. Newell, I gotta go. I'll call you tomorrow for sure."

I hung up wondering why he was giving me the run around. That money needed to come my way quick.

Within a half an hour I was off the bus and approaching my street cautiously, not sure what I was hoping to find or see. I was honestly expecting the worse. But no matter what, going back was the only way to find out.

I reached the corner of my street and took a deep breath as the small houses came into view. My hand dug into my purse

and grabbed the handle of my gun, keeping it hidden and ready
to pull out. My eyes were peeled for that Mercedes Benz the
Mexicans had been in. So far, the coast was clear. It was
midafternoon and the street was silent. The silence did little to
ease my worries though. Silence couldn't protect me from what
them niggas wanted to do to my ass. As I headed down the street
there was a UPS truck parked directly in front of Shy's house.
She was standing in the front yard with her back to me signing
for a package. Immediately, as the UPS man handed her the
package and walked away I darted up the lawn behind her. The
bitch had explaining to do and there was no way I would give
her a chance to run.

"What's up, Shy?" I shouted.

Shy turned around as soon as she heard my voice. The
bitch was spooked. It showed all over her face. She'd been
caught off guard. "Hey...hey...hey, Keema," she stuttered and
attempted to give me a fake smile like everything was all good,
like she hadn't left me in jail to fend for my damn self. I wanted
to haul off and smack the shit out of her.

Unable to totally hold back, I had to let her know I wasn't
in the mood for games. My hand popped out with the gun. I
pointed it directly at her stomach.

"Keema, what are you doing?" Shy asked with a heavy
gasp and wide eyes, terrified at the sight of the pistol. It looked
like she was getting ready to piss on herself.

"Bitch, don't fucking play games with me," I said angrily.
"Why haven't you been answering my damn calls?"

"I...I...I..." was all she could manage.

"Why didn't you come get me out of jail, bitch? I specifi-
cally told you to come get me."

"Keema, I...I...I."

"Fuck that damn 'I-I-I' shit! You played me!"

She raised her hands defensively. "I was gonna come and
get you, Keema. I swear to God I was." The bitch was petrified.

"I put you in charge of my shit and you fuck me over?"

She was practically ready to cry. "No, Keema, I didn't

fuck you over."

"Yes, you did!"

I noticed the Honda Crosstour again parked in the driveway. The muthafucka shined like she'd just gotten it detailed. There wasn't a spot on it. The sight of it had me hot enough to pull the trigger.

"Look at that shit, bitch!" I said, pointing at the car. "While I was locked down, your ass was out here copping new whips and shit! You rocking new clothes and your muthafuckin' hair and nails are fresh!"

Shy was at a total loss for words. She could only stand in place, nervously. She knew she deserved to get dealt with.

It took everything in my power to keep from blowing a hole in her ass. She had me pissed all the way off, but although my finger clutched the trigger, anxious to squeeze, something inside me held back.

"Where are my kids?"

"They...they...they..."

I jabbed the gun directly into her belly button. "Where are my damn kids, Shy? Fuck all that damn stuttering! Start talking or I swear on everything I love I'm gonna blow your guts through your back! I left them with you! Where are my kids?"

Tears began to roll down her cheeks. "They're with Drake," she finally said.

The shit surprised me.

"They're up in a spot out in Fell's Point."

"And when the fuck were you planning on telling me this, Shy? I left *you* in charge of them!"

Her eyes could only drop to the ground shamefully. She'd betrayed me.

"Your ass didn't even ask me if it was okay."

Her eyes rose to mine. "Keema, I know I should've told you but giving them to Drake was the only way to keep them safe."

"What the fuck does that mean?"

A look even more fearful than the one she had of the gun

125

came across her face. Tears welled up in her eyes.

"Well?" I asked, impatiently.

"They keep coming back looking for you," she said.

Immediately I thought about Frenchie. "The guy in the Impala?" I asked.

She shook her head. "Nah, I haven't seen that car since the day you went to jail."

"Then who are you talking about?"

"Keema, I really don't want to be in the middle of this." Her words sounded as if she were pleading with me.

"Bitch, who the fuck are you talking about?"

I could've sworn I saw her body tremble with chills. Just the mere thought of what she was about to say had her terrified. "Keema, those MS-13 Mexicans keep coming around here. They're asking all kinds of questions about you and that Mexican you guys killed. As a matter of fact, they were here about fifteen minutes ago."

Knowing that I'd just missed them made me more scared than I was the night I saw them. If I woulda showed up several moments earlier, I woulda ran right into them.

"Keema, they killed Dollar!"

"Really? Ohhhh Shit!" I dropped the gun to my side and began to run my hand over my head nervously. I'd gotten myself in some real deep shit and had no idea how I would get out.

Fearfully she said, "The first day they came to ask about you they rode up on me and showed me Dollar's head. They had it stuffed in a bowling ball bag. It was so sickening seeing his dreads and everything," she whined. "There were maggots crawling out of it and everything. I'd never seen anything like that before in my life. I mean, what type of lunatics ride around with a nigga's head in their car?"

My face flushed at what she'd just said. Those muthafuckas were more than heartless.

"They told me my head would be next if they found out I was hiding any information about you from them."

For a brief moment the visual of her head stuffed in a bag

filled my mind. The shit was horrifying. Those Mexicans were monsters.

"Keema, that shit scared me to death. I had to let Drake take the kids. It's the only way I could keep them safe. Besides, I don't want no beef with them fools. They're crazy. They take death and murder to a whole new level."

Words wouldn't leave my mouth. What they'd done to Dollar was fucking with me. If they cut off his head, what were they going to do with me?

Shy reached into the pocket of her jeans, pulled out a small piece of paper, and handed it to me with a trembling hand. There was a name and number written on it.

"What's this?" I asked.

"One of their names is Rios. He's covered from head to damn toe in tattoos. I mean, he even has them all over his face. That's his number. He said to give it to you. He said you guys need to talk and asked me what you look like."

I stared at the number. "Did he say what he wants to talk about?"

"No, but if I were you, I wouldn't call him."

"Did you tell him what I look like?"

"No, girl. I just said a little like me. But definitely don't go near him. Those muthafuckas are scary. They'll make sure you come up missing."

I glared at the number again. What did they want to talk to me about, I wondered? If niggas want to kill you, they don't give out a number and ask you to call them.

She reached into her pocket again and pulled out another small piece of paper. "This is the address to where the kids are," she said, handing it to me.

Accepting it, my mind was still dejected. It was still caught up in wonder about what Rios wanted me to call him for.

Shy pleaded with her eyes. "Keema, I really didn't play you. I was scared and didn't know what to do."

She wasn't getting off that easy. "Bitch, you couldn't have been too damn scared. You bought a brand new car. You've

127

been getting money."

An uneasy look came across her face. "About that; there's something else you need to know."

I was about fed up with surprises.

"Keema, It wasn't Raven who stole your gift cards that day," she revealed, looking more and more uneasy with each word, as if scared to tell me.

"Then who did?"

The upcoming words pained her to say. "It was Treasure."

I looked at her like she had lost her mind. "What do you mean it was Treasure? Don't lie on my seed."

"I found out a little bit after you went to jail. I overheard her telling someone about it on the phone."

My face was twisted in disbelief. "Are you sure?"

She nodded. "Keema, you underestimate Treasure. I know she's twelve but she operates with the mind of a thirty year old." She paused to clasp her face in between her hands. She was clearly frustrated. "Not only that, she's running with Raven now, too."

"Raven? What do you mean?"

"They've got a couple hustles going on. They even got some credit card fraud scheme going on. They're gettin' big money from it. Raven pays me five hundred dollars a week to help out. That's how I got the car."

The talk about Shy's car made me think of my own. "Where the fuck is my car, Shy?"

She hunched her shoulders.

My blood boiled over. There was no time to figure out if the state had my car, the police, or if it had been stolen. I could only think about Treasure, my own child, who'd stolen from me. And now on top of that, she was running with my enemy? She'd made me look like a damn fool. I wanted to snatch a knot out of her little skinny ass. Taking a quick glimpse at the address on the paper, I fumed, headed up the sidewalk, leaving Shy standing on the lawn behind me apologizing.

15

The woman whose name I'd forgotten was trying to make small talk as she drove me through Fell's Point. I knew it was impolite to not return it as I sat in the passenger seat of her Lexus but I couldn't help it. I was not in the mood for conversation or making any new friends. My mind was on a million other things anyway. After getting to Fell's Point I couldn't find the address Shy had given me. Shit, I couldn't even find the street after walking down more of them than I could count. The neighborhood was like a maze. I had to stop at a gas station and ask the lady I was now riding with as I saw her pumping gas. After giving me directions and realizing I was walking, she offered me a ride. There was no way in hell I was going to turn down that opportunity.

Fell's Point, a quiet and historic neighborhood filled with shops, cafes, parks, museums, and old fashioned homes had a good feel to it. Crime was nearly nonexistent there. People strolled up and down the streets and through its parks with their dogs on leashes while others jogged or sat on their porches in conversation. It was a beautiful neighborhood but admiring it or enjoying the sites was impossible. I was too angry, nervous, worried and so much more to give any thought to the beauty passing by my window over and over again.

What the fuck was up with Treasure, I wondered as cool

AC blew from the dashboard vent into my face. What was going on with her? How could she steal from her own mother? How could she start rolling with Raven, my enemy? Why had it taken her so long to come visit me? And if she was truly out here getting money with Raven, why hadn't she gotten me out of jail? Shit, the little trick hadn't even called me since I'd been home. Did she even care if I was out or not? Did she give a damn? What the fuck? It was as if she'd wanted me to stay in jail.

I couldn't help going back to the day in Arizona when I laid on my back with blood gushing out of my shoulder and pooling around me as she stood over me with guns pointed in my face. Before that, I'd never imagined she would have the heart to do something like that but she did. It was at that moment that she truly became something or someone I didn't recognize. It was at that moment that I realized exactly how angry she was at me for what had happened to Cash and her grandmother. I sympathized with her broken heart that day and thought we had moved past it.

Stealing from me though was completely different. I couldn't sympathize with her on it. I hated a thief. Especially one I took care of, fed and whose head I kept a damn roof over. That was just straight up ungrateful. She had me pissed off.

Drake also had me angry. The sorry son of a bitch was out of jail, had my kids, and didn't feel it was important to come and get me out, or at least come visit me? The muthafucka couldn't even put a few dollars on my commissary. What kind of bullshit was that? I shook my head angrily as I stared out the window. Both of them had me steaming. There was no excuse for what they'd done. I couldn't understand why they seemed to have left my ass for dead. Whatever the reason, though, I was going to find the fuck out. Both of them were getting ready to get cursed out and Treasure's little sneaky ass was going to get her little narrow ass two-pieced.

"It's only about three more blocks from here," the lady in the driver's seat said.

I abruptly came up out of my thoughts at the sound of those words. "Can you drop me off right here?" I asked.

130

"Are you sure? I can take you directly to the house. It's not a problem."

"I'm good right here."

"Okay," she said and pulled over to the curb.

"Thanks." I smiled, hopped out and closed the door.

"No problem."

The Lexus pulled away from the curb and headed up the street.

I looked around to make sure I hadn't been followed. Besides Treasure and Drake, of course I couldn't get Rios off of my mind.

"Damn it," I said to myself. "How the fuck do you get yourself into these messes, Keema? How do you do it?"

As I stood on the side of the road, I thought about my life and how it had become overwhelmed with death. I thought about the friends and family I'd lost, each victims of shit I had done. Each had lost their lives because of *me*. In all honesty, I deserved to be dead, not them. Damn, the guilt made me put my hands on my hips and drop my head shamefully.

Memories of those lonely nights I spent sitting in my jail cell crying and missing my kids filled my head and heart. I'd promised God that if he let me out, I would change. I'd promised Him I would be a good mother and leave the schemes and games alone. I really meant it, but the moment I was back out, the itch to hustle had consumed me once again. I couldn't let it go. What the fuck's wrong with me?

FUCK!

I'd thought about the ladies back at the shelter and the circumstances that had gotten them there. I realized just by them deciding to stay there instead of going back to the Hell's that had led them there, they had grown strong enough to leave the past behind and accept the help Mrs. Kyle was offering. Could I be one of those women, I wondered? Could I have the heart to walk away from this shit, get into one of the shelter's programs and get my life back on track; this time the right way?

My luck had been terrible. I'd gambled, putting it all on

the line and lost tremendously. My youngest baby was gone. My mother was gone. My best friend was gone. My daughter hated me. I'd even pushed away a good man; Lucky. I had nothing left to gamble with. My life was a mess. Tears began to roll down my cheeks. I needed change, a whole new start but I wasn't quite sure where to begin. It was time for a new life.

I raised my head and through the blurred vision my tears were creating, I grabbed my phone from my purse. Change was going to come, I promised, but before it could happen, I had to straighten a few things out. My finger pressed the digits of Rios' number into my phone. As the phone began to ring, my ear listened to each ring. My heart beat hard and powerfully.

"Hello?" a man answered.

The sound of his voice made all my bodily functions go haywire. Then my stomach dropped. "Hello?" I said fretfully.

There was also some kind of Mexican hip hop playing in the background. I couldn't understand its words but it was loud.

"Whut's up?" he asked in a thickly coated Mexican accent. "Who's this?"

I paused for a moment. I was scared to death to go on. Just the sound of his voice had me shook. I could picture Dollar's head in that bowling ball bag Shy was talking about. The thought almost made my knees give out.

"Yo, who is this?"

I swallowed the developing lump in my throat. "Can…can I speak to Rios?"

"This him. Who's this?"

"It's Keema." I closed my eyes.

He immediately said something in Mexican, Spanish, Dominican; or whatever language he'd chosen to blast off in. He said a few more words to someone around him and the music went silent. I was terrified.

"You've got a lot of people around here pissed off and looking for you."

I didn't say anything.

"You touched one of ours, puta. Not only was he one of

ours, he was my blood. He was my uncle."

"Oh God," I whispered with my eyes still closed.

"Punishment for that shit is death. We can't let you walk around breathing in all this good air after you kill one of ours."

"But…"

"There are no *buts*!" he spewed loudly. "You kill one of ours, you die, bitch! There are no in-betweens!"

"Rios," I pleaded. "I'm sorry about your uncle. I swear I am. But I had nothing to do with it."

"What the fuck do you mean you had nothing to do with it? Don't insult my muthafucking intelligence!"

"I'm not, Rios. I wouldn't do that to you. Someone set your uncle up and I know exactly who it was."

"Who?"

"I can't tell you right now."

"Don't play games with me!"

"I'm not playing, Rios. I'm really not. I can't tell you right now who it was but I'm willing to meet up with you tomorrow and tell you then."

"Where do you want to meet?"

"I'll call you first thing in the morning. I promise."

"Fuck a damn promise! Call me tomorrow morning for our meeting or I promise there will be no place on this earth for you to hide. What I did to your friend Dollar is *nothing* compared to what I'm going to do to you if I find out you're bullshitting."

"It's not a game, Rios. It's the truth. I'm going to call you first thing tomorrow morning."

"Make sure."

CLICK!

The line went dead.

My hand trembled as I took the phone from my ear and stuffed it back into my purse. My knees felt rubbery. Fear had me dizzy. I raised my head and let out a deep breath to compose myself. Exhaling hadn't taken the fear away completely but it gave me a little relief. I had a plan to get Rios off of my ass and wasn't quite sure if it would work. Unfortunately, it was the only chance I had to save the lives of myself and my babies.

I headed down the street. After three blocks I turned down a side street, pulled the small sheet of paper from my pocket and began to look at the addresses of each house. The area seemed so peaceful, making me feel privileged to even walk the streets of their neighborhood. As I walked, a pearl white Aston Martin came darting down the street ahead of me and pulled to the curb several houses ahead and across the street. I watched it. Seconds later, I couldn't believe my eyes when I saw who climbed out of the driver's seat.

It was Drake.

Dressed in expensive looking gear, he had a cell phone to his ear as he made his way around the car's hood and stepped up onto the curb. Diamonds dripped from his neck and wrists.

"Son of a bitch," I whispered as Drake walked up the staircase to a midsized gorgeous home, turned the knob to the front door and walked inside.

I remembered Shy saying that Raven was now getting major cheese. From the looks of it, all these muthafuckas was getting major cheese. Drake had obviously gotten that money he'd stashed and was living well off of it. I was more pissed than before. After all that shit he had talked in prison about wanting us to be together, the sorry ass nigga was up here living high on the hog and had forgotten all about me, the mother of his damn child. I stomped across the street looking dead at the front of the house. I couldn't wait to get inside and snap on that sorry ass nigga. As I approached, something in the driveway caught my eye.

"What the fuck?" I whispered in both anger and disbelief.

In the driveway was my Camaro. But it wasn't just the site of it that had me frozen in my tracks. What had a bitch fucked up was what was written on the license plates. They read...TREASURE.

My jaw dropped. I had no idea what was going on.

16

After my thirty second breakdown, I finally picked myself up off the ground. I had to sit down after seeing my ride with personalized tags that I never approved. With no more hesitation I crossed the street, stomped up the stairs to Drake's spot and rang the doorbell. As I waited for someone to answer, a rage burned inside of me and my chest heaved back and forth. Finally, after what seemed like forever, the door finally opened. Dressed in a pair of J Brand skinny jeans, a long sleeve color-block t-shirt, and studded Gucci ballerina flats, Treasure laughed wildly into an I-phone. Her ass was so deep into the conversation that she didn't have time to duck out of the way. My backhand caught the side of her face so hard its force immediately knocked the phone out of her hand and dropped her frail body to the floor. It had been a long time coming, but it was time I let her know who the head bitch in charge was.

My eyes burned through Treasure as she sat on the floor looking up at me and holding the side of her face. I'd slapped her ass so hard my hand stung from the contact it made with her skin.

"Treasure, you okay?" Drake called out from somewhere in the house.

She didn't respond. It was that soldier shit running

through her blood that made her deny his help. Neither of us spoke for a moment. Our eyes did all the talking. We both knew the amount of animosity between us.

While staring down at Treasure, my eyes scoured her clothes and swag. She'd been fly before I went to jail, but now her swagger was off the fucking meter. Before I went to jail she still rocked high buns and braids. Now, the bitch had a fourteen inch weave. And I'm not talking store brand hair either. Her high dollar shit was straight from India. Her diamond bracelet and earrings glistened loudly. Before I went to jail she wasn't rocking jewelry at all. She even had green contacts now that gave her eyes an exotic look. The bitch had definitely stepped up her game.

Once again, I thought about what Shy had told me. On the way over, I wanted to believe what she'd said about my baby wasn't true. My hope was that she hadn't betrayed me and that there was a perfectly good explanation for everything. Still, a huge part of me knew the only explanation was pure betrayal, especially when I spotted my Camaro parked in the driveway with Treasure's name written on the plates. Obviously, the identity thief wanted to *be* me the entire time. She obviously wanted everything I had.

How could she have been filled with so much envy for her own mother? Everything that was mine was hers. She was my baby, my flesh and blood. How could a daughter envy her own mother? How?

Immediately, I began to wonder about Shane and Deniro. I raised my eyes from her and quickly surveyed the fully furnished living room for them. "Where the fuck is Shane and Deniro?" I asked her.

Treasure didn't answer. She stood up still holding the side of her face, while staring at me. If I didn't know any better it looked like she wanted to try me.

"Where are my damn kids?" I screamed, ready to lay her skinny ass out again if she got froggish enough to leap.

Suddenly, Drake raced out of the kitchen. "What the fuck

is this?" he asked in surprise when he saw me.

I shoved Treasure out of the way and marched across the room to him. "Where the hell are my damn kids, nigga?"

"Keema, I thought you were locked up," he said, still in surprise.

"Fuck all that! Where are my kids?"

"They're not here," Treasure said behind me.

I turned to her. She had a cold and bitter look on her face. "What do you mean they ain't here?"

"Exactly what I just said," she told me, working her little scrawny neck with attitude.

"So, where the fuck are they?" I questioned.

"Shane ran away."

I looked at Treasure like she had five heads. I couldn't believe how nonchalantly the words had come from her mouth. It was as if she didn't care. It was as if there was nothing wrong with an autistic, seventeen year old boy who didn't know how to take care of himself roaming the streets alone. Immediately, thoughts of Frenchie killing me in broad daylight entered my mind. Without being Shane and Deniro's guardian, I wouldn't be able to get the money from Frenchie's estate.

Worry filled my face. "Bitch, what do you mean he ran away?"

Treasure worked her neck again as she said, "Did I stutter? He ran away. He put one foot in front of the other and went on about his business."

Drake quickly stepped in between us. He knew she was about to get her head bashed in. It was fucking child abuse time.

"When, damn it, when!" I screamed.

"A couple of days ago," she answered.

"What? Are you serious?"

She rolled her eyes.

My mind, body and soul became bombarded with worry. I could picture Shane sitting somewhere at this very moment terrified and wondering why I'd left him. The thought had me scared for him.

Deniro appeared in my mind. I turned to Drake. "Where's Deniro?"

He didn't say anything. An uneasy look came across his face. I didn't like it at all. I knew it held bad news.

"Nigga, where is he?"

"CPS has him," he finally replied.

"What? Aweeeeeee, nah! What the fuck!" I wailed.

Drake took a step back, knowing I was ready to snap on him.

"What the fuck is my baby doing with CPS?"

"I had no other choice, Keema. You were locked up and I had nobody else to leave him with. I can't be babysittin' some other nigga's kids."

"Yeah," Treasure chimed in, agreeing with Drake.

I took two steps toward her.

"We're running businesses," she stated proudly. "We're getting money. We ain't got time for dead weight. Shane and Deniro wouldn't have done anything but slow us down. We're better off without them."

My body shook with anger. "You narrow bitch! How can you even fix your lips to say some shit like that? Those are your brothers! They're your family!"

"Just because you're born family doesn't mean you stay family."

My eyes narrowed at her. "You little bitch," I growled, taking step towards her with my fists clinched at my sides. "You miserable little bitch."

I hated her. I hated my child.

"I didn't want to believe Shy," I said, while shaking my head. "I didn't want to believe her, but it was true. You really did steal from me and you really are running with Raven, aren't you?"

Treasure folded her arms across her chest as if to say, "So what."

"How could you, Treasure?" My voice cracked a little. My heart surprisingly had become weak.

138

"The game ain't fair," she said nonchalantly. "I saw a chance to get money so I took it. That's what you taught me, right?"

I stared at her. "How could you make me think Raven took the gift cards? How could you turn us against each other like that? You knew she was the only family I had."

She shrugged her shoulders.

"And how in the fuck did you change my tags without my permission?"

"I didn't need your permission," she shot back. "I sent off the car note payment so Shy took me to the Motor Vehicle place to fill out the form for personalized plates. We didn't need you for that. We just needed the registration info."

Her eyes were cold.

Harsh.

"Treasure, what's wrong with you? What happened to you?" I asked.

"Look, I'm not in the business of explaining myself to anybody. The game of making money is cold and heartless. Only the strong survive. That's all to it. Grindin' 101, right?"

That was it. I couldn't take anymore. In a fraction of a second I was on her ass. My hands wrapped around her neck so fast she hit the floor with me on top of her. I squeezed for dear life seeing Drake headed for us.

"You triflin' bitch!" I yelled in her face as she clawed at my hands, trying to get them to turn her lose. Her eyes began to bulge and a thick swollen vein bulged in the center of her forehead.

"You muthafuckin' no good bitch!"

The goal was to suck all life from her foul little body.

"Keema, stop!" Drake shouted as he ran up behind me. "Get off of her!"

"I'm gonna kill you!" I threatened Treasure, really meaning it. She'd taken me there.

"Get off of her, Keema!" Drake demanded as he tugged at my body and pulled me off of her.

"Get the fuck off of me, Drake!" I fought to break free and get my hands back on Treasure.

She coughed and breathed hard as she got back to her feet.

Drake slung me to the side and stood between me and Treasure. Over his shoulder I could see her smiling deviously as if making me snap on her was what she'd wanted. Who the fuck was this bitch? Where did my little girl go? The girl I was looking at was not the child I'd labored for nearly nine hours with.

Suddenly, I remembered what Lucky had said the last time I saw him. I realized he was right. I'd allowed Treasure to see far too much. I'd involved her in things she shouldn't have been a part of. It was me who caused her to grow up the wrong way. The realization made my shoulders drop with defeat. The only person I could truly be mad at was myself.

"Lucky was right," I told Treasure over Drake's shoulder. "Damn, I made you grow up too fast."

She rolled her eyes.

"I heard about that nigga," Drake said. "I don't like him and I better not ever catch him around my daughter again."

I looked at him like he'd blown a damn fuse. "Nigga, who the fuck do you think you are? He drove your daughter to see you in jail. Did she tell you that?"

Drake gave Treasure the evil eye before looking back my way. "Keema, look…"

"No, fuck that! Nigga, *you* look! Where the fuck do you get off trying to tell me who can be around my daughter? You've never been a father to her! You've never spent time with her until now! You've always been too damn busy running the streets and going to jail!"

"Well, that's changed now because I'm doin' lovely. Lots of time and money."

His voice annoyed and aggravated me to the core. I couldn't take it. "You know what? Fuck you, Drake!"

I made my way around him. "Treasure, let's go!"

"I'm not going nowhere with you," she said, poking her

little chest out. "I'm staying with my daddy."

"Don't get it twisted, Treasure. You're still my child. You still do what I say do."

She folded her arms again.

"She ain't going nowhere," Drake said, moving between us again. "She's stayin' right here. But you, on the other hand, got to go."

"Drake, move out of my way. My daughter is coming with me!"

"No, she's not," he countered.

"Keema, I don't want to put my hands on you. But I will if that's what it's goin' to take to get you out of here."

I was ready to fight him physically for my daughter. I had to take her somewhere, retrain her mind. I stepped towards him, but out of nowhere heard a snicker come from behind me. I turned around. My jaw nearly dropped. My eyes couldn't believe what they were seeing.

It was Raven.

Raven was standing at the bottom of the stairs with her arms folded. She was dressed in a robe that was open enough to reveal black lingerie. She had a sick and twisted smile on her face as she stared at me.

"What the fuck?" I mumbled, unable to think of anything else to say. I was completely caught off guard.

I turned back to Drake. "What is she doing here?"

"That's a silly question to ask," Raven responded.

I turned back to her.

"Why wouldn't I be here? Shit, I live here," Raven said.

My head darted back and forth from Drake to Raven. What the fuck was going on?

"What does she mean she lives here?" I asked Drake. "Just a month ago, you said you loved me…wanted to marry me."

"Keema, I'm the woman of the house," Raven inter-jected. "Don't ask my fiancé questions you should be asking me."

141

Fiancé, I thought to myself in surprise. The word hit me like a sledgehammer. I turned to her.

Smiling even bigger than before, Raven held out her hand. "We just got engaged a few days ago," she stated proudly. "You like the ring my baby bought me?"

On her ring finger was a huge emerald cut diamond; at least five carats.

The room spun. The moment was worse than death. The bitch had my daughter *and* my baby daddy. She'd turned them both against me. She'd gotten the ultimate revenge.

"It's time for you to go," Drake said as he opened the door and stood beside it.

"Yeah, Keema," Raven agreed. "It's time for you to go so me and my *family* can spend some quiet time together."

The bitch knew placing emphasis on the word *family* was enough to cut through me like a knife.

"Besides," she continued. "Me and my boo are still enjoying the honeymoon stage of our engagement."

"Whatever, bitch. Treasure, let's go," I said.

"I'm not going anywhere with you," she shot back.

"That's right. She's not. She lives here with me," Raven added.

I frowned. "Raven, you're not taking my child."

"Keema, you've already lost your child. You did that shit on your own. Treasure was never feeling you. She…"

"Shut up, Raven," I interrupted and looked back at Treasure. "Let's go," I told her.

"Keema, just think," Raven continued badgering me, "Treasure is the one who called the cops on you that day at your house. Stupid bitch, your own daughter had you locked up and gave the state info about your welfare scams!"

I exploded, then instantly charged at Raven. "You bitch!"

Drake grabbed me from behind before I could get to her. "Let go of me, nigga!" I demanded as I kicked, clawed, and scratched to get to Raven. "Let me at her ass!"

Raven never moved or budged from the wall. Her arms

remained folded across her chest and a smile remained across her face. She'd won. She'd beaten me.

"Let me go! Get the fuck off of me!" I belted.

Drake continued to drag me to the door while I continued to fight. I needed get back. I needed retribution. I needed to get my hands on that bitch. I needed it all like air and food. Then I saw something that took the fight out of me. I saw something that killed my heart. As Drake pulled me to the threshold, I was forced to watch as my baby, Treasure, sauntered over to Raven and innocently laid the side of her face against her chest. Raven then took Treasure in her arms as if she were her mother and rested her chin on the top of her head. She consolingly rubbed her back as the two of them watched me. That sick twisted smile never left her face.

She had my daughter.

Tears began to pour from my eyes as Drake slammed the door in my face. I couldn't hold them back as I realized I was all alone. My heart was broken. What would I do? Where would I go?

Suddenly, the sound of the door opening back up startled me.

"Here," Treasure said, tossing me some money and my car keys like I was a bum on the street. "Take this two hundred dollars and my new phone number. I hope you get yourself together."

With those words said, the door slammed in my face again. I couldn't move. I couldn't speak. All I could do was crumple to my knees and cry.

17

The tears were endless. The sobs were heavy and deep. The pain seemed like it would never fade and I seriously doubted that it ever would. My heart would be broken forever. My entire world had turned pitch black and meaningless. I'd never felt a pain as bad as this one, not even the day I got shot back in Arizona. It was torment beyond torment.

I sat in Mrs. Kyle's office balling my eyes out like a newborn baby. I had nowhere else to go, no one else to talk to. I was now all alone in this world. For the past hour, between falling tears, I told Mrs. Kyle my life story. I told her almost everything that had led up to this point, only choosing to keep the part I played in actual murders to myself. Everything else, I spilled, refusing to hold any of it back. I had to. I needed to vent. I needed to explain myself and why I'd done the things I had done. It was like therapy.

Mrs. Kyle was an excellent listener. She was supposed to have gone home hours ago after her eight hour shift, but had chosen to stay and listen to me spill my heart out. If she only knew how grateful I was for her shoulder. I now, at this moment, saw her differently than I had when I left the shelter earlier in the day.

Mrs. Kyle was a pleasant and elegant woman. Her words and the tone she spoke them in were always soft and peaceful, never threatening. Her vocabulary didn't seem to contain a single curse word and her heart didn't seem to contain any anger or hatred. She didn't have that bitter and nasty sort of demeanor that so many people I'd come across. She was the total opposite. She seemed so genuine and honest. She'd come off like that the very first moment I met her, but after dealing with as many cut throats as I have in life, I guess I wasn't too eager to let my guards down before. Now was different, though.

Dressed in a black skirt that dropped below her knees, a white blouse that was buttoned nearly to her neck, and black heals that didn't expose her feet, Mrs. Kyle seemed to be somewhere in her early fifties, but she wore it more than well. Her hair was long without a single strand of grey. Her skin was the color of caramel and had no blemishes. Her lips were thick and her body was curvaceous, but she didn't rock her beauty like most black women I knew. She wasn't nasty with it. She carried herself respectfully and in good taste. Damn, how I admired her.

"I've been a horrible mother," I admitted through my tears. "I don't even deserve my kids back. I don't deserve to even see them."

The words were honest. I really believed them. After all I'd done, what right did I have to be a mother again? What right did I have to regain custody of them again?

"No," she disagreed, holding me in her arms and rubbing my head softly. "Don't say that. Yes, you made mistakes. But you're human. None of us are perfect, child. We all stumble at times."

"You don't understand, Mrs. Kyle," I told her, raising my head from her chest and looking her in her eyes. "My daughter hates me. She'll never forgive me 'cause I've taught her how to be some sort of monster." I paused to shed more tears. "And my stepson is somewhere out here probably hurt and wondering why I left him on his own. Then my other son, Deniro is with CPS probably thinking I bailed out on him. Mrs. Kyle, they all hate me."

With each word I spoke, more and more tears fell. The

shit was killing me.

"Baby, they don't hate you," she assured me.

"How do you know?" I asked.

She leaned back and pulled up the sleeve of her blouse to reveal needle tracks on her arm. I couldn't believe they were there. They weren't fresh, but nevertheless I would have never expected that from her. She just didn't seem like the type. My eyes went from the tracks to her face in wonder.

Seeing my wonder, she nodded and said, "Yeah, Keema, I was out here. I was out here real bad."

I was speechless.

"For thirty years of my life I was a heroin addict, a crack head, and a prostitute."

"Geez," I whispered, covering my mouth with my right hand. I felt so terrible for her. She seemed like God's most perfect angel. How could he do those things to her?

"I have two children. The streets had me so gone that I left my kids on their own for most of their childhood."

My ears and attention hung on her every single word. I wanted to hear each and everything she had to say.

"Baby, at times, just like you're feeling right now, I felt like my kids hated me. I felt like they would never forgive me for putting the drugs and the streets before them. I felt I didn't deserve their love."

Hearing those words made me drop my head in shame but Mrs. Kyle placed a hand underneath my chin and softly raised my head up to face her. "You know what I found out, though?"

"What?" I asked softly, curious to know.

"Baby, I found out that they *didn't* hate me. They *never* hated me. They hated the things I did, but not me. All they wanted was for me to be the mother they knew I could be. That was what they wanted more than anything else in the world."

I couldn't say anything.

"After all I'd taken them through; they still had more faith in my mothering skills than I did. They were just waiting

147

for me to come home and prove it to myself."

The words made me think. Did Treasure, Shane, and Deniro feel that way about me? Did they love me enough to give me a second chance? Did they still care? I was filled with so much doubt.

Mrs. Kyle got up, grabbed a box of tissues from her desk and handed them to me. I took one and wiped my tears. They hadn't stopped completely, but her words had slowed them.

Sitting back down beside me, she said, "Keema, I had to work hard to get myself off the streets and off those drugs. I had to realize my kids were the most important thing in the world to me."

I shook my head, unsure of whether or not I had what it took to turn my life around and be the mother to my babies they deserved. I mean, damn, I didn't even know where to start.

"Do you want your children, Keema?" she asked.

"Yes, I do." My words were so soft spoken.

"Then fight for them, baby. Nothing can stop you but you."

I looked just as deeply into her eyes as she looked into mine. Before this moment I'd never been too big on eye contact. Something about it always made me feel weird. I'd always turn away after a few seconds of glaring. But now, I couldn't let my eyes leave hers. I didn't want them to. Something about them seemed to welcome me in and promise me they wouldn't betray me.

"The first thing you've got to do," Mrs. Kyle said as she stood from the couch and headed to her desk, "is get off of Public Assistance. It's been your crutch for too long. It has tricked you into believing that it's all you deserve. In order to get your son back, you have to have a job. You have to show the state that you're willing to work. That's the very first step."

She picked up her telephone, dialed a number and placed the receiver to her ear. After several seconds, someone answered. A moment later, Mrs. Kyle had arranged a job interview for me. I couldn't believe it. As she and the person on the other line spoke, my cell phone rang. I dug it out of my purse and saw Lucky's number on the screen. Anxious to hear his voice, my hands damn near dropped the phone on the floor as I jumped up, turned to walk to a nearby corner and pressed the accept button.

"Lucky?" I said immediately, happy he was calling.

"What's up?"

"Oh my God! I'm so glad you called." My mouth began to run a mile a minute as I told him everything that happened since the day I'd put him out of my house. Everything just spilled out uncontrollably.

"Lucky, I'm so sorry for how I treated you. I'm so sorry for accusing you of doing anything with Treasure."

"Keema, that shit hurt me."

"I know, Lucky. I don't know what the hell I was thinking."

"What would ever make you think I wanted Treasure sexually? You know how I feel about her. She's like a daughter to me. How could you think I would ever cross a line or hurt her? How could you ever think something like that?"

I grabbed my head and shook it stressfully from side to side. "I don't know, Lucky. My life has just been moving so fast that I haven't been thinking clearly."

He didn't say anything.

I felt horrible for accusing him of something so foul. "Look, I'm so sorry. I swear I am."

"Don't worry about it," he finally said. "It's all good. How's Treasure doing anyway?"

"She's gone crazy," I spat quickly. "She had me locked up, stole my car, took her brother to CPS and…"

Of course I went on and on. I told him about the Drake and Raven situation. I also told him about Shane.

"Damn," Lucky said worriedly. "What are you going to do now?"

"I don't know. I'm staying at a shelter right now. I realize that I definitely have to get my life right. I've got to get myself together. Me and my kids can't keep living like this."

"That's good to hear, Keema."

I paused before saying another word. Something was on my mind. I needed to ask him something, but wasn't sure if I should. Finally, I couldn't hold it in any longer. "Lucky, could you ever have feelings for me again?"

He didn't answer.

"Baby, I know what I did to you was so wrong. I know I betrayed you, but I also know I never stopped loving you."

"Keema..." he stopped me.

"Baby, I was so wrong to do the things I did to you. I know it. I swear I'll make it all up to you if you give me a second chance."

Suddenly, I could've sworn I heard a female voice in his background. I couldn't make out what she said.

"Keema, I gotta go."

"But, Lucky..."

"Keep me posted on how things turn out with the kids. And if you or them need anything, call me."

"Lucky, I love..."

He hung up before I could finish my sentence, causing me to close my eyes with regret for everything I'd done to him. My heart sunk to my stomach when I heard the woman's voice in the background just before he hung up. Some other woman was now getting the love I should've been getting.

After a brief conversation with Mrs. Kyle, I headed back to my room. My roommate was asleep. Without taking off my clothes, I laid flat on my back in my bed and stared at the ceiling. My world felt so empty. Everything had been taken away from me. All my deceit and selfishness had gotten me nowhere but alone. Tears began to fall again. They rolled down the side of my face and dissolved in my pillow.

I pulled my cell phone out and went through the photo gallery. For close to an hour I looked at picture after picture of my babies, including Cash. God, their smiles shattered my heart. Being without them was killing me. Before I knew it, something beyond rage built up inside of me. I hated myself for what I'd done to my family. I had to get them back. I had to put all the drama behind me. Hopping out of my bed, I stormed out of the room and headed down the hallway dialing Rios' number as I walked. When I reached the bathroom, I walked inside and closed the door. My feet began to pace the room back and forth as I waited for him to answer.

"Bitch, you better have something good to tell me," he answered, evidently recognizing my number.

"Yeah, I got something to tell your wetback banana boat riding ass!" I screamed into the phone as I held it pressed closely to my ear. "I'm tired of running from you! I'm sick of this shit!"

"You nappy headed monkey! Who the fuck do you think you're talking to? Do you know what I will do to your ass? Do you know who I am?"

"Fuck you! Yeah, I killed Peppi. Hell yeah, I pulled his fucking plug!"

"You're dead, bitch! Do you hear me? You're dead!"

"Don't worry, muthafucka! You'll get your chance tomorrow night!"

I told him where to meet me. "Be there tomorrow at eight o'clock, nigga! I'm prepared for whatever!"

Before he could say another word, I hung up.

18

Damn, I felt weird and strange. It was the next morning when I strolled into the media room of the shelter dressed in a not so sexy, blue pant suit that someone had donated to the shelter and a pair of ugly patent leather heels. The suit was generic but clean and not too long out of style. Of course I wanted to wear something out of my suitcase, but after showing off two of my outfits to Mrs. Kyle, she said that they weren't appropriate for a job interview. She actually said they were down right hookerish. I had to admit, she was right. They were definitely a little too tight and showed off a little too much.

I couldn't help feeling ashamed and like a charity case. For as long as I could remember, I'd never worn anyone else's clothes, not even as a kid. Although my mom was in the streets a lot when I was young, even she made sure to keep me dressed in nice shit. My cousins couldn't wait for me to outgrow outfits so they could get my hand-me-downs. Now here I was wearing someone else's clothes. Damn, what a downfall. I felt like I'd been booted out of Heaven or something. I really wasn't used to feeling this way and was wondering if I could really go through with taking the first step of changing my life.

"You look beautiful," Mrs. Kyle said proudly as I walked into the room. She surveyed me from head to toe.

"Are you sure?" I couldn't help feeling like the interviewer would know the clothes I had on were used. He'd probably look at me funny.

Mrs. Kyle walked across the room to me and straightened my collar. "Baby, you look wonderful. It fits you perfectly."

"Mrs. Kyle, what if she doesn't like me?"

That possibility ran through my mind the entire night. I'd never been on a job interview, so I had no idea what to expect or what the interviewer would think of me.

"Keema, why wouldn't she like you?" Mrs. Kyle asked, looking at me strangely.

"I don't know. There are plenty of reasons not to like people. What if she doesn't like my eyes? What if she doesn't like the outfit?"

Without even thinking, I'd started chewing on my fingernails. They were already down to the nubs because my teeth had been nervously working on them most of last night.

"Sweetheart, don't worry about anything," she told me reassuringly while taking my hand from my mouth and placing it at my side. "They're going to love you. I guarantee it. Just be yourself."

"What if after being myself, she still doesn't like me?"

She took both of my hands into her own and stared into my face. "Keema, what did I tell you last night? Who is the only person who can stand in your way?"

I exhaled nervously, remembering what she had told me. "Myself," I answered.

"Right, sweetheart. Only you can stand in between getting your children back. All you have to do is believe in yourself and everything will turn out great."

I still wasn't convinced. Shit, I wished she could come with me. Surely, those feelings showed on my face.

She placed the palms of her hands gently against the sides of my face. "Say 'I believe in myself.'"

"I believe in myself." There was no fire or sincerity in my words at all.

Seeing that my words were filled with self-doubt, she said, "Keema, think about your babies. Get a clear picture of them in your head."

I did what she said. In my mind I saw their smiles. In my ears I heard their laughter. Around my body I felt their arms.

"Do you see them?" she asked, still holding my face in her hands as if she was my mother and I was her child.

"Yes."

"Keep that picture. Hold on to it, Keema. No one can take that away from you. When you walk into the interview, take it in there with you. If you get nervous, look at it. Trust me, sweetheart. It will give you the strength to move mountains."

I truly believed her. I really did. Throughout my entire life, no one had ever come at me like that. No one had ever spoken to me like that. She really made me feel special.

"Do you understand?"

I nodded.

"Now, straighten your shoulders and hold your head up. You're a black woman. We've been holding down families and giving birth to civilizations since the beginning of time. We've birthed kings and we've ended wars. We've been enslaved and raped, but still remain beautiful. Nothing breaks us. If we can do all of those things, a simple job interview is nothing. We can do that with our eyes closed."

Wow, I thought to myself. She was so deep. For a moment, I realized how blessed her children were to have a mother like her. I even wished she could be my mother.

Not wanting to disappoint her, I mustered the strength to get a hold of myself and raised both my head and my shoulders. The last thing I wanted to do was disappoint her. She seemed to really care about me. She seemed to really want to see me succeed. I'd betrayed Lucky when he cared enough to look out for me. I'd hurt him. But now I learned my lesson. I'd be damned if I would do the same to Mrs. Kyle. Letting her down wasn't an option.

She smiled. "There you go, child," she said. "I told you

155

that you had what it took."

Grabbing me by the hand, she took me back to her office. When we got there, she went into her purse, and handed me a hundred dollar bill. In shock, my hands wouldn't allow me to grasp the bill.

"Take it," she urged.

"Mrs. Kyle, I can't take that from you. I know you don't make a lot of money."

"Yeah, but you need gas in your car and you need to eat healthy. It costs to eat healthy." She grinned.

I was still filled with disbelief. She had to be the nicest person I had ever met in my entire life.

"Mrs. Kyle, are you sure?"

"Baby, I wouldn't be offering it, if I wasn't sure."

Finally, I accepted. I'd been using my remaining cash to survive, plus pulling money from the ATM out of the last three thousand from my mother's money. That was it; all I had to my name.

Looking at me, she said, "I've never done that before. I don't just give my hard earned money to just anyone. Something about you is special though. I see something special in you. And I'm a great judge of character. I'm never wrong about people."

Where had this woman been all my life? Why couldn't I have met her a long time ago? Maybe, if I had, so many lives wouldn't have been lost. If I'd had her advice and influence, maybe my past would have turned out so much better.

Mrs. Kyle wished me good luck. Seconds later, I was sitting in the driver's seat of my ride, still with tags that read, TREASURE, driving to my interview. A lot of things were floating around in my head. I thought about my past, my present and my future. I sincerely wanted to change it all. Finally, I felt like I was ready. Finally, I would leave the bullshit behind and do things the right way.

My stomach dropped though as I realized I wasn't completely out of the woods yet. I was leaving the game behind, but a few loose ends still had to be attended to. I couldn't be free until they were. The meeting with Rios couldn't be avoided. It was one of those loose ends.

Grabbing my cell phone from my purse, my fingers punched Treasure's phone number into the keypad. After three rings, she answered. I paused before speaking. "Hey, baby," I finally said.

She gave off a heavy sigh like hearing my voice had gotten underneath her skin.

"Treasure, I didn't call to annoy you. I just wanted to know if you have any idea whatsoever where Shane might be. I'm worried sick about him."

His whereabouts had been on my mind a whole lot. I'd called the police just the day before. They said I could only report a person missing after forty-eight hours.

"No, I don't," she spewed.

"Are you sure, because if you..."

"Keema, I said I don't know."

Wow. She was calling me Keema now.

I sighed in defeat. It was clear even if she did, she wouldn't tell me. Damn, I hated what I'd done to us. I hated what I'd turned her into. It broke my heart to see us at odds. But despite where we were now, I was dead set on making my daughter proud of me.

"Is Raven around?" I asked.

"Yeah, why?"

"Can I talk to her? I really want to apologize."

She paused for a second and then said, "Alright, hold on."

"Treasure!" I called out immediately.

"What?"

"I love you, baby."

Everything inside me wanted desperately for her to say those words back to me, still she didn't. Instead, she said, "Whatever, hold on."

The phone went silent. Several seconds later Raven said, "Hello?"

At the sound of her voice, I went into gear. "Raven," I pleaded. "I know we're not on the best of terms. I know we're not, but I really need you right now."

My words were quick and desperate.

"I understand that being with you is the best place for Treasure. You're the only person I trust to take care of her. You have my blessing."

Purposely, I breathed loudly into the phone to make it sound like I was possibly being chased or something.

"Keema, your blessing doesn't really mean anything to me. I don't need it. What are you telling me all this for?"

"Because people are looking for me. They want to kill me, so I'm leaving town tonight. The money from Frenchie's will finally came through and I want to make sure Treasure is taken care of," I informed.

I knew the promise of money would break the ice.

"Well, what do you want from me?" Raven questioned.

"I need you to meet me tonight at eight o'clock in front of the post office on Ellamont Street. You know the one in Walbrook. I've got a hundred thousand for you. Please take it and do right by Treasure. It's obvious she loves you and looks up to you. She'll listen to you so make sure you guide her better than our mothers did us, okay? Use the money to get her in college or something."

"Keema, who's after you?"

"They've been following me all day, but don't worry about that. Just make sure you meet me. I've never done the right thing by Treasure. This is my last chance."

"I also have a letter for her. Please make sure she gets it. If something happens to me, I want her to know that I loved her. Raven, please meet me."

I made my voice sound as desperate as possible.

"Please, Raven," I pleaded. "Please do this."

"Alright," she finally said. "I'll be there."

"Thank you, Raven. You don't know how much this means to me. Be there at eight on the dot."

"Alright."

"And, Raven?"

"Yeah?"

"Make sure you're not being followed."

With that said, I hung up. As I drove, nearing the address for my interview, a smile graced my face as my mind thought about what would be awaiting Raven in front of that post office. The plan had worked.

As pissed off as I'd gotten Rios the night before, I'm sure he had special plans for me. I was sure he would probably make me face an even more gruesome death than the one he'd inflicted on Dollar. I couldn't blame him though. I'd want me dead, too. Rios was going to get his revenge tonight. The only problem was it wouldn't be me who'd feel his wrath.

It would be Raven.

I'd told Rios to meet me in front of the post office, but I had no intentions of being there myself. Raven would be there instead. It would be her who would pay for Peppi's murder, not me.

I pulled into the parking lot of the Waste Water Treatment Plant and simply wanted to throw up. The smell seemed unbearable. Someone must've died in the area or maybe some pipes had burst. Whatever the deal, it smelled horrible. I climbed out of the car and sashayed inside. After telling the secretary I had an appointment, she had me fill out an application; which I had *super* trouble doing. Besides welfare applications, I'd never filled out any others. Since I had absolutely no past job experience, I had no idea what to write down in the space on the application that asked for it. I also had no idea what to write down when it asked if I'd graduated from High School or if I'd ever done any volunteer work. Volunteer? Who the fuck would do that for free? A bitch was lost.

Finally, I handed the messy looking form back over to the secretary.

"Don't you smell that?" I asked her.

She looked at me crazily, obviously jealous.

I covered my nose and mouth with my hand as she sent me into the manager's office for the interview. I was nervous as hell and nauseated from the smell. When she shook hands with me, the palm of my hand was sweaty. Damn, that was embarrassing. After we made the proper introductions, she offered me a seat in front of her desk. As I sat down, it felt like my body was going to hyper ventilate. I definitely wasn't used to this.

With a smile, she said, "So, tell me about yourself, Ms. Newell."

I had no idea what to say. "Um, well, um, I...I...I," were the only words that seemed to spill from my mouth. No one had ever asked me that question before.

"What do you consider your strengths?"

"I can make a hell-of-a grilled cheese," I joked hoping to ease my nervousness.

She didn't laugh. She simply scanned my application some more.

Seeing my nervousness, she smiled and said, "Ms. Newell, it's okay. From looking at your application, I see you're new to this. Some of us join the work force a little later than others. Just loosen up. This type of job doesn't require a lot of previous skills since you'll be working in the building with the centrifuges."

"What's that?"

Her face froze. "Mrs. Kyle didn't tell you?"

"Tell me what?"

"Sweetie, we have the glorious job here of spinning water out of sludge so we can sell it as fertilizer to farms."

It didn't sound too bad, but her face told me differently. I wanted to ask more questions but that horrible smell had crawled up in my nose. "That smell is awful," I told her.

"Honey, that's the smell of sludge. You do know what that is, don't you?"

I shook my head back and forth while covering my nose again.

"It's human feces," she said matter-of-factly. "We turn

feces into fertilizer."

My blouse was drenched with sweat. I was unable to speak. Shit, who was I kidding? I was all the way up out of my league. There was no way I would work in a shit factory having the stench of shit on my body and clothes day after day.

I remembered what Mrs. Kyle said and thought about my kids. The thought gave little relief. I began to bite my fingernails and pat my foot on the floor nervously.

"Ms. Newell, are you okay?"

I got hot flashes. The room began to spin.

"You want some water?"

My stomach felt nauseous.

"Ms. Newell?"

"Oh no," I said to myself dreadfully just before I threw up everything in my stomach all over her desk. No wonder I stayed away from a legitimate 9 to 5 for so long. This lady wanted me to work around shit all day!

Aweeee, fuck that!

19

Just five minutes before eight o'clock, I sat impatiently in the car at the far end of the street. From where I was parked, the view of the isolated post office seemed perfect. I'd been sitting at the curb for the past twenty minutes smoking cigarette after cigarette checking out the area. Just as I suspected, not many cars passed since I'd been on stake-out. I drummed my fingers against the steering wheel and tapped my foot on the floor. Time was dragging too slowly.

The car was silent. I'd tried to listen to the radio, but turned it off. For some reason, I preferred to sit in total silence. I wanted to hear everything around me.

The late evening sun had gone down moments ago, leaving darkness behind in its footsteps. The overhead street lamps were the street's only illumination. From the driver's seat I watched intently every time I saw a car, waiting and expecting either Rios or Raven to arrive first.

I had no idea exactly how shit was going to go down. I didn't know if the Mexicans were going to kill Raven right in front of the post office or if they were going to snatch her up and take her somewhere else. In all honesty, I didn't care. I just wanted it done. Either way worked for me.

As I sat in the car, I couldn't believe that our relationship had come down to this. I couldn't believe that this is how it would end. We used to be so close. We used to be sisters. We shared secrets and so much more. We loved each other. But now all of it was going to come to a violent end. What we had between us was about to go all the way up in flames.

Damn, what a way to end a relationship.

My eyes dropped to the digital clock on the dashboard. The time had only changed by a minute. It was still four minutes until eight o'clock. Since I'd been sitting at the curb, my eyes had been watching the clock more times than I could count. Each time I'd look at it, only one or two minutes had passed, but I couldn't stop looking at it though. Just like biting my nails and chain smoking, it was being done out of nervousness. It was all I could do to pass the time, but it wasn't helping. Time was still dragging by at a snail's pace.

While waiting, I had also watched every parked car and the few that passed by. When I did see someone, I jumped from my seat and watched closely through the windshield, my fingers wrapped tightly around the steering wheel so hard it looked like my knuckles were going to rip through my skin. Each time, anticipation turned into disappointment as the driver or passenger hopped out to run up to the post office's mailbox to drop in a letter or package. Each time, my back would slam back into the seat in frustration.

I was leaning deeply into the leather of my seat when I finally noticed the Benz Coupe turn the corner in my rearview mirror. My heart took off like a runner from his starting block. I slouched down into the seat as the car came crawling slowly down the street towards me. I was scared to look at it as it passed by, but I did anyway. Inside were four Mexicans, no doubt ready for war. I rose up from my seat and watched them go by. The Benz approached the building slowly but didn't stop. As it cruised past, every person in the car scouted the area. My heart thudded against my chest as it headed to the opposite end of the street and turned the corner. Seconds later, it appeared again from the same corner. This time it made its way up the opposite direction. The occupants were still looking around. Once again, wearing scarves, skull caps, and hard looking shit. I slumped down into my seat, this time even lower than before. I definitely didn't want them to see me. As the car passed again I could hear them speaking in their language. I slowly turned my head and looked behind me to see them headed to the end of the street. Soon they disappeared.

I was now more nervous than before. The moment of truth was approaching. My hands trembled wildly as they gripped the steering wheel. The anticipation of what was coming became unbearable. Once again, my fingers drummed against the wheel. My body twisted and turned in my seat hoping for a view of Raven. Where the fuck was she? Had she decided to stand me up?

I leaned back into my seat and waited, sweating the entire time. Three more minutes inched by. They seemed like forever. Finally, a silver 535 BMW turned the corner behind me. Through the mirror I watched as it approached and then crawl at a slow speed. I slouched down into my seat and watched it as it got closer and closer. When it reached me, I noticed its windows were tinted too dark for me to see inside. I still watched it carefully, never blinking even once. When the car reached the post office building, it pulled to the curb. I leaned over the steering wheel and damn near pressed my nose to the windshield to get as good a look as possible. The BMW driver's door opened with me glaring in heavy anticipation. Raven finally stepped out.

"It's her," I said excitedly to myself. "It's her."

With five inch heels, the bitch also had on a pair of red, tight fitting jeans and a leopard print shirt. She made her way around the car's tail end and stepped up onto the sidewalk looking around. Quickly, I snatched my cell phone from my purse. I was so fearful that I dropped it on the floor. Still anxious, I pressed the digits of Rios' number into the keypad wrong. After two tries, I finally got it right. With the phone pressed against my ear and my eyes on Raven, I listened impatiently for Rios to answer.

"Come on, muthafucka," I whispered into the phone with each ring. "Come on, muthafucka, answer damn it."

After four rings Rios answered.

"I told you I was tired of running," I said. "I'm here. My heart doesn't pump Kool Aid, bitch. Just like I murdered your weak ass uncle, I'm ready to do the same to your ass."

"Oh, is that so?"

"Hell yeah! I'll kill all you son of a bitches! I'm out here in front of the post office, alone! Come get some, bitch! Come get some!"

The phone went dead.

I watched both Raven and my rearview at the same time. My eyes darted between both, never focusing on one for more than a few seconds. Finally, less than a half a minute from my call to Rios, the Benz bent the corner behind me. Once again I slouched down in my seat and watched as it shot by me. When it passed me completely, I sat up and leaned forward to watch the action

It was on!

The Benz pulled up in front of the building and skidded directly behind Raven's Beamer. All four doors opened at the same time. Out of each, hopped four of the most menacing look-ing muthafuckas I'd ever seen in my life. They were all young, dressed in Dickies, wife beaters, Cortez Nikes, and tatted up arms. One of them was tatted more than the others. He had them all over his face. That must've been Rios; I realized.

Each of their faces twisted into something far more than just anticipation of revenge. It was something more dark, more evil. In their hands they clutched the biggest guns I'd ever seen in my entire life.

Raven's eyes nearly bulged out of their sockets as they walked up on her. She backed up but had nowhere to go. Her back pressed stiffly against the wall.

I watched it all, refusing to turn away. Raven said some-thing quickly and frantically, but I was too far away to hear what it was. Rios said something in return as his henchmen stood beside him in silence with their guns pointed directly at Raven. She was terrified. Shit, even terrified was an understatement for how she looked as her eyes repeatedly surveyed all the guns pointed at her.

"Kill her, Rios," I said through the windshield, as if he could hear me. "Kill her ass. It's called karma."

Raven pleaded for her life.

"Come on, Rios," I urged. "Do her ass in. Do it now. I gotta get my family back."

Rios said something else to Raven angrily.

My eyes glanced in the rearview to make sure the cops weren't coming or anyone else for that matter. By the time I turned back around, I saw Raven attempting to escape. She dashed up the sidewalk. That's when shit got crazy. A white Toyota drove by and stopped after noticing the action. All four men opened fire. Their guns blazed brightly. The roar of the bullets loudly filled the streets, echoing off the walls of every building, some riddling the body of the Corolla which sent the car speeding off. I covered my face slightly as a few ripped into Raven's back. I grimaced slightly watching her body shake violently. It took forever, but she finally dropped to the pavement. As she lay squealing and regurgitating blood, her body was twitching. Refusing to show mercy, Rios quickly walked up on her, took aim, and squeezed the trigger. Several bullets spilled from his gun into her body, finishing her off. He then stood over her and spit on her dead body.

All four men immediately hopped back into the Benz and sped off. Within less than a few seconds, they'd disappeared. For a moment I stayed still, unsure of what to do. Even though I'd set it up, it was still hard to believe that Raven was dead. It was still hard to believe that she was gone. Finally, I stuck the key in the ignition, turned it and pulled away from the curb. Slowly, I passed the building and Raven's car. A short distance from her car, covered in blood, her face turned towards me. She'd died with her eyes open.

Damn.

As I slowly drove by, her eyes gave me chills because it seemed like they were right on me.

For a moment I felt terrible, but I realized it had to be done. Sorry to say but It was better her than me. Her dying was the only way I could think of to get MS-13 off my ass.

"Lord, please forgive me," I whispered and pulled away.

I had to get to the police station to file that missing person's report on Shane. He had me worried to death. I was truly ready to start a new life and finding Shane would be one of the first steps. I was going to put my family back together no matter what. I was going to make whatever sacrifices I needed to make in order to put us together and keep us together. From there, I was going to be the best mother in the world.

I was dead set on changing my life. It was time to make things right. It was time to make much better decisions. I was tired of the stress and problems in my life and was ready to make changes. Despite the fact that I'd thrown up on her, the manager at the Water Treatment Facility obviously understood my nervousness and hired me anyway. I now had a job. It wasn't the perfect one and didn't pay the type of money I was used to, but I was willing to make it work out. Plus, I was going to take full advantage of the help and resources Mrs. Kyle and the shelter were offering.

The only thing that could mess it all up was Frenchie. But as long as I kept things cool with him and did what he asked, hopefully everything would work out. Once that was done, the past would be completely behind me.

20

Mary J. Blige's song *Mr. Wrong* banged loudly from the stereo system in my living room as I worked the vacuum cleaner back and forth across the carpet. Occasionally, I took a sip of my Riesling as I cleaned the house. Once upon a time, I'd be blazing a fat ass blunt as I cleaned. Nowadays, though, I was trying to ease up off of that. As a matter of fact, my lungs and my system hadn't been graced with any weed smoke in weeks. It was definitely the longest I'd ever gone without smoking. I was truly focused on getting myself together. Besides, although, the factory I was working at wasn't paying a whole lot, they still piss tested their employees on a surprise basis. I wasn't trying to get caught up. I didn't want to lose the job. Mrs. Kyle had looked out for me and I was grateful to her for it. There was no way I was going to let her down.

Looking around the room, it felt weird to be back in my mother's old house. Since those MS-13 dudes had killed Raven thinking it was me, I felt much more comfortable coming back just to get myself together. As soon as the time and the money were right, I was moving the hell away from this entire city. I hadn't even seen that bitch Shy's anywhere around. Couldn't help but wonder if she'd moved away, too.

It had been three weeks since Raven's death. I missed her

and felt guilty for the betrayal, but realized there was nothing that could be done about it. Her life had to be lost in order for me to get on with mine. Since she'd died, I'd been working five days a week, helping out at the women's shelter, letting go of my bad habits, and doing everything CPS told me to do to get Deniro back. That was another reason why I'd left the weed alone. They were piss testing me, too. But I didn't mind. If anything, I felt proud to pee in that little cup. I felt proud and anxious to show them that I was willing to do whatever it took to prove I could change and that I could be a great mother.

Shane still hadn't been found. His absence had me breathless sometimes. I had come to grips with the fact that he could've been dead. Frenchie was going to undoubtedly kill me if that was the case. He'd been calling and calling me like crazy about his insurance pay-off. I didn't care. Shane's life meant more to me than mine. The selfish days of me thinking about my own well-being before the kids was over. What was best for them was what meant the most to me now.

After I'd filed the missing person's report, the cops told me they'd do everything they could to find him. It was now the first week in October and I'd been calling every morning for three weeks, hoping for some good news. It was always, "We haven't found him, but we're going to keep looking."

In a few more weeks I would be going in front of a judge to finally get the inheritance money. Mr. Hyde and I had met a few times. The only problem was that I had to get custody of Shane to make that happen. But as long as I kept my nose clean, it wouldn't be a problem. My case worker was cool. As long as I continued to keep things one hundred with her, she kept them one hundred with me. She let me know that she was going to recommend that I get Deniro back. Most likely, though, the white folks were going to be in my business for a while after that. They were going to want me to attend parenting classes and other types of workshops. They were going to be noseying around everything I did, but it didn't matter. I was clean these days and planned on staying that way. There would be nothing dirty for them to find.

Money was tight now. I wasn't used to that. Since I was no longer hustling and was now pretty much relying on my paycheck from the factory to pay the bills, my pockets were almost always broke, but I didn't care. I had a piece of mind now. That was more valuable to me than money. I wasn't even tripping on Frenchie keeping all his inheritance. Shit, he could have it. That would be less of a headache for me. I was going to be good with my kids. We'd manage. I figured I'd suck a dick every now and then if I had to, just to get by.

Mrs. Kyle had even got me to start going to church every Sunday. It was cool. At first, I thought for sure I wouldn't like it, but I turned out to be wrong. I loved it. Plus, most of the men there were *fine*! Sooner or later I'd snag me one of them. Maybe a deacon. I wasn't rushing it though. Right now, I was focused on me and my babies. Once I got that straight, then I could make room in our life for a man.

Just as Mary sang the last line of the song, a horn blew in front of the house. Turning off the vacuum, I peeped out of the living room curtain and saw Drake and Treasure in the driveway. Since Raven's death, I'd been consoling the both of them. At first, I thought that both Drake and Treasure had hooked up with Raven out of spite for me. A part of me still felt that way until it became clear how hard they took her passing. It was obvious they really had love for her. Damn, I felt guilty knowing that I was the person responsible for their pain, but it is what it is.

Putting the vacuum in the closet, I headed out the door and climbed in the back seat of the Range Rover, one of Drake's many whips. Drake greeted me, but Treasure who sat in the front proudly spat numbers and fees into her cell phone. I could tell the conversation was about her credit card hustle. As we pulled off, she finally hung up and told Drake she would need to make a stop across town later on.

"Hold tight. I told you I got shit to take care of first," Drake huffed.

"Okay, but time is money, my money."

Damn, she seemed so grown these days, speaking proper and confident.

"Hi, Treasure," I said softly.

She gave me a warm smile, which I was more than happy to receive and said, "Hey, what's up? Would've spoken when you first got in, but I had to get this business done."

These days we still weren't quite on good terms, but we were getting better, *a lot* better than before. She was my only daughter so whatever it took or however long it took, I was willing to do my part to make things right between us.

"Yeah," I agreed understandably. "Business won't handle itself."

"Isn't that the truth."

Wow, my baby seemed so mature. Although I was out the game, though, I couldn't help missing the days when we were side by side grinding.

"How exactly does your credit card hustle work anyway?" I asked from behind. I'd been curious about it but never really spoke up on it.

Treasure perked up immediately. She climbed onto her knees in her seat and turned to me, anxious to tell me as if she'd been waiting for me to ask. "It's easy," she explained. "Our hook up is this dude that Raven hooked us up with. Ole boy sells credit card numbers to us. And we sell 'em to people to use for a fee."

The hustle seemed easy enough.

"Clientele is growing every day," she added. "The guy I was just on the phone with is a new one. A friend of his told him about us. He wants to buy four numbers."

My eyebrows rose.

"Yeah," she said, seeing my reaction. "We've got a lot of 'em like him; dudes who like to buy in bulk."

"Your kinda niggas, Keema," Drake finally added.

"What's the money like?" I asked, ignoring his comment.

"Real good. We're pulling in about ten thousand a week. And that's on a slow week. Around the first of the month we

172

make even more."

Damn, a part of me wanted in.

"The great thing about it," Treasure added, "is the people who are taking the real penitentiary chances are the clientele, not us. They're the ones whose faces get caught on the cameras of the ATM machines."

I nodded.

"So, what's up? You down?" she asked.

"Treasure, you know I'm trying to leave that life behind. And I told your father you both need to stop all hustles before you get caught."

"Caught? Oh, hell nah, we ride or die."

I didn't approve of her talking crazy, like she'd be able to out-slick the law forever. Although, the reality was as long as she was in Drake's custody, there wasn't too much I could do or say. I definitely felt like he was a deadbeat for allowing her to do it and had let him know about it, but my words always went in one ear and right out the other.

"I see it in your eyes," she said bringing me out of my daze. "You know you wanna get this money."

Damn, she was right. I really did. The factory wasn't paying me too much.

Drake's eyes glanced at me through the overhead mirror. I wondered why he was so damn quiet.

As if knowing exactly what I thought, Treasure continued, "I know that factory ain't paying you what you deserve. You're just like me; you want and deserve the finer things in life."

I had to chuckle and shake my head at my baby's attempt to run game on me. She was right, though.

"I'm not saying get into it full time. I'm just saying try it out for a little bit. If you're not feeling it, cool. But if you are, it'll be just like old times; me and you side by side. Only now you'll work for me."

Thinking about it, I said, "If I do this, what exactly would you need me to do?"

"Nothing much. I'll teach you what you need to know."

It felt strange to be the pupil instead of the teacher, but I couldn't ignore the money. Damn, I didn't want to go back. God knows I didn't, but the money was so hard to ignore. Besides, I rationalized; Treasure could use someone to watch her back. Drake had been looking out for her so far. But shit, he'd been to jail because he didn't quite know how to watch his *own* ass. What should make me think he'd do a better job watching Treasure than me?

"She's right," Drake said. "It's a simple hustle. And we could definitely use you on our team. We can't trust anybody else."

"I'll think about it," I answered.

Treasure smiled and turned around in her seat to face the windshield.

"But if I do decide to do this," I added. "I'm not doing it for too long. It'll be just to save some money and get out."

Both Treasure and Drake glanced at each other with smiles.

Seeing their looks, I said, "I'm serious. It'll be just for a little while, if I do."

I put major enunciation on the word *if.*

"We understand," Drake said as he drove.

Within twenty minutes, we were passing through my old neighborhood. I hadn't been back since the whole Paco incident. I hadn't really found any need to. Not to mention, I didn't need niggas in my business. From what I was seeing now, nothing had changed. It was still the same bucket of piss it always was. Its corners were still crowded with dope boys and prostitutes. Loud music still played from open windows. Niggas still sat on porches turning up forty ounces and blazing blunts. It was just the way I'd remembered it.

Suddenly, the truck came to a stop at the light. From the backseat I looked out of my window as a young soldier who had his back to me stood on the corner making a transaction to a dusty looking man who was practically a skeleton. His dirty shirt and pants swallowed his frail frame while the young boy was dressed in crispy jeans, a white tee, and some new Jordans. My eyes dropped. I wondered if he had a father or had even met his father. Each thought made me shake my head, feeling sorry for him. He was probably going to go through a world of heartache just like I had before he would finally realize that hustling wasn't everything he'd hoped it would be.

When the light turned green and we pulled off, my eyes were still on the burly boy's back. Finally, as the crack head walked away satisfied with what he'd purchased and anxious to smoke it up, the young boy turned around counting a handful of money. I looked into his face. The sight of it made my mouth drop and my face grow flushed.

It was Shane!

"Stop the car!" I demanded.

"What?" Drake said, quickly glancing back at me in his rearview mirror.

"Stop the car!"

Treasure looked back at me.

"Why?" Drake asked.

"Just stop the damn car!" I screamed while reaching for the door handle. The car hadn't even come to a complete stop as I opened the door and hopped out into traffic.

"Keema, are you crazy? Stop wildin' out!" Drake shouted.

"What's wrong?" Treasure asked.

Ignoring both of them, I ran back towards the corner. As I did, Shane saw me. Without hesitation, he turned and ran. And in almost the blink of an eye, he'd darted around the next corner with me screaming his name.

21

I was laid out flat on my back in the bed with my thighs over Drake's solid and muscular shoulders while gripping his ears like handles. Moan after moan left my mouth as I rode his tongue wildly.

"Oh, shit, boy. Damn! Eat that shit!"

My clit was super swollen as I gyrated it repeatedly against his tongue as it slithered like a snake in and out of his mouth. It had been a long time since my pussy had been this wet. I wasn't quite sure if it was from my body's natural juices or Drake's saliva. All I knew was my shit was wetter than a water ride at an amusement park.

Drake moaned approvingly at the taste of my pussy. He sounded like he was eating a delicious full course meal as he gripped my hips and chewed me out, occasionally allowing his tongue to slip from my pussy to my asshole. Each time he did that, a loud squeal like a baby pig escaped from my mouth. My body squirmed and winced at how ticklish it felt, but a bitch wasn't about to tell him to stop. I loved it.

It had been a long time since my body had been pleasured this way. Shit, Lucky was who I'd been craving. He was who I wanted to marry. Even now, as Drake had me wanting to climb the fucking walls with his tongue skills, my heart and imagination was with Lucky. I visually imagined Lucky munching me out inside my head. I even wanted to yell out his name. My mouth wanted to scream it so badly but I had to fight it.

"Damn, you taste so good," Drake managed to say from downtown, despite how tightly I had his face pressed against my slit. I was trying to shove his whole damn face up in that shit. "Damn, girl," he muttered.

"Ahhhhhhhhhhh, yesssssss," I moaned.

Gripping his ears even harder and tighter, I pressed his face even further up in my nest. Fuck words. I knew my shit tasted good. I kept it clean. Besides, I'd sucked it off of plenty of dicks during sessions when they'd just come from out of me.

Drake's tongue skills were bananas. It was like he'd been eating pussy all his damn life. It was hard to believe he'd been in prison for the past several years. But I guess maybe eating pussy was like riding a bike. Once you learn how, you never ever forget.

Although I was truly wishing things between me and Lucky could have worked out, there was no hiding that I was beginning to fall for Drake. I still didn't quite know exactly how it happened. I had no intentions of being with Drake. Since Raven's murder, I'd been trying to help out, mainly for Treasure's sake. The goal was to patch things up with her so I began to come around a lot more, just wanting to be a part of her life. By doing that, me and Drake began to grow closer.

At first, I only wanted his money, but seeing him so hurt over Raven gave me compassion for him. He was truly broken up over her, so I began to drop by his spot more often; cleaning, cooking, and even giving Treasure some pointers on her hustle, despite the fact that I disapproved of it. I never got involved like they asked, but since I couldn't stop her, I wanted to make sure she at least did it right.

Visits began to turn into me spending nights, mainly because Drake would tell me that I didn't have to go home certain nights. It had gotten to the point where more time was spent at their spot than my own.

I had to admit, despite him condoning Treasure being in these streets, Drake was sweet. He had no problem spending money on me without me even asking him. If I needed to keep an appointment, he always took me. Even after a long day of grinding, he would find time to call me to see if I wanted him to stop off at my favorite Chinese restaurant and grab me something to eat. During times when I wasn't at his house, he would call to see how I was doing. He basically seemed like a different nigga from the one he was before he went to the pen.

Eventually, I began to develop feelings for him. They weren't as intense as they were for Lucky. But nevertheless, they were there and growing. It surprised me, but I just decided to let nature take its course. I'd told myself that I was done with street niggas, but for some reason my heart decided to let Drake in. From there, my pussy decided to let him in, too.

I had to admit, though, it also felt good to be a family, or as close to a family as possible. Me, him and Treasure went to the movies together. We went shopping together in between their runs. We were really like a real family. I'd yearned for that. I always wanted that. Now that I was getting it, I didn't want to let it go.

"Oh, God!" I screamed as my body began to tremble from the upcoming orgasm.

Drake began to munch on me like a cavity creep.

"Oh God, Drake!" I yelled even louder.

His tongue went deeper.

"Shit, Drake, I'm cumming!" I screamed as my thick juices gushed out of me and into his mouth.

Drake pulled out from between my thighs, kissed me and headed to the bathroom. As for me, my clit was still pulsating. My energy was drained. All I could do was turn on my side, lock my legs together tightly, and rest. My body didn't want to move from that position or spot.

Moments later, my cell phone rang from the nightstand. Recognizing Mrs. Kyle's ringtone, I answered reluctantly. Guilt would've come over me if I'd ignored her call. She was still like my mother. I still had so much love for her.

"Keema?"

"Yeah, what's up, Mrs. Kyle?"

"I don't know, Keema. Maybe *you* can tell *me*. I just got a call from your job."

My eyes rolled inside my head. I knew what was coming.

"They said you haven't been to work in two weeks." She paused. "Keema, I had to call in a favor to get you that job. I know the job isn't much and that it doesn't pay the type of money you're used to. But nonetheless, it's a start. What's going on?"

"Mrs. Kyle, I'm sorry, but I just haven't been able to focus on work right now. I've been trying my hardest to find Shane."

That was true, partially. Since seeing him out on the block a few weeks ago, I'd been going back and forth to my old hood looking for him daily. Drake had even put out the word that he had a ten thousand dollar reward for anyone who had information that would lead to Shane's whereabouts.

"Oh my," Mrs. Kyle said worriedly. "Have you had any luck?"

"Nothing so far."

"The police don't have anything?"

"Nope."

They really didn't. Shit, I seriously doubted they were even looking for him. Obviously, he wasn't some little white kid from the suburbs. Missing black kids, especially teens, weren't too much of a priority for Baltimore PD.

"Well, Keema, I sincerely hope you find him. In fact, child, I *know* you'll find him. I can feel it. God's a good God. I can feel in my heart that he's keeping Shane safe."

Her words warmed me. As usual, Mrs. Kyle always knew what to say to ease my pain and worry.

"So, where have you been staying? Are you back at your mother's old house?"

"Yeah." I loved Mrs. Kyle, but she didn't need to know

anything about Drake.

"Maybe I'll come see you soon," she replied. "How's everything going with CPS?"

"It's okay. I wish they would let me see Deniro more, though."

"I've got a few connections down there. I'll make a call for you. I'm pretty sure I can get you in to see him tomorrow."

My body arose from the bed in excitement. "Are you sure, Mrs. Kyle?"

"Yeah, don't worry. I'll get you in."

"Mrs. Kyle, you're a life saver."

She chuckled. "I wouldn't say all that. I do my best. But anyway, I'm also going to call your job and let them know what's up. I'll smooth things over with them."

"Thank you so much."

"Don't worry. You just find Shane, okay?"

"Alright."

"And soon as you do, bring him by the shelter so I can meet him, okay?"

"I got cha."

We hung up.

As usual, Mrs. Kyle was on my side. People like her were very rare. That was why, although I was happy to be able to see Deniro tomorrow, I felt guilty. Mrs. Kyle had done so much for me. She'd seen in me something special that I couldn't see in myself. She was truly priceless. I appreciated it all, but I hadn't expected Drake to get into my system.

As I lay in the bed, I looked at the diamond studded David Yurman watch on my wrist he'd spent six thousand dollars on. I hadn't even asked for it. He just did it. He'd been doing so much of that lately. And I couldn't help starting to fall for him. My thoughts were interrupted by the ringing of my cell phone again. Looking at the screen, I saw Frenchie's name.

"Shit," I whispered dreadfully, but knew letting his call go unanswered was not an option. He was probably parked outside. My heart pounded against my chest.

"Hello?" I answered as if I didn't know it was him.

"Bitch, don't 'Hello' me," he said. "How's shit going with the money? You get with the attorney yet?"

After swallowing a lump in my throat, I answered. "Everything's good," although I knew it was a lie. Without Shane, I had a problem.

"Are you sure?"

"Yes."

"So, how long will it be before the money is in your hands? My patience is wearing."

"Soon."

"How soon?" he inquired.

"I'm not sure. Shit, you know how white folks are. They're talking about tons of paper work."

"Keema, don't bullshit me."

"I'm not. I swear I'm not."

"If I find out you are, you're a dead bitch."

Those words made my heart sink.

"The next time I call, I better hear a specific date as to when you'll have my damn money. You understand? Or it's lights out."

"Got it."

"Tell Shane I said to call me tomorrow after four o'clock. I think it's time he knows I'm alive."

"I will."

CLICK!

My body trembled. Hearing his voice and threats had me terrified once again. I had to find Shane. And quickly. The court date for the money flashed in my head, but without Shane by my side, I couldn't get the money.

Too nervous to stay in bed, I got up, put on a robe, and headed to the kitchen. Damn, my life was complicated. As I reached the kitchen, my phone went off again.

"Fuck!" I said, still on edge about what Frenchie had just told me. My eyes dropped to the phone's screen. I didn't recognize the number. But I answered anyway.

182

"Yeah, what?" My voice was filled with attitude.

"Keema?" the caller asked.

"Yeah, who wanna know?"

"This Stormy."

I hadn't recognized her voice at first. "Stormy, I'm kind of busy right now," I said, not really in the mood for conversation.

"Why haven't you gotten in touch with my homegirl?" she asked, ignoring what I'd just said.

"Stormy, I've been busy."

She chuckled. "I thought you was a hustla, nigga."

"I am, but lately I've been trying to…"

"Keema, I don't care what you've been *trying* to do. When I gave you my homegirl's number, I opened up my world to you. I don't do that for just any bitch."

"Stormy, look…"

"Nah, Keema, *you* look. I need you to get with homegirl ASAP and get that little enterprise we talked about off the ground. I need that extra cheese coming in."

"Stormy, I ain't fucking around with that shit no more."

"What do you mean?"

"I mean I left that shit behind."

"Keema, I need you to get that money. Fuck that change of heart shit. You owe me."

I looked at the phone like it was human and had gone crazy before I responded. "I *owe* you?"

"Hell yeah, bitch!"

"How? I never made you any promises."

"Bitch, when you didn't kill that hoe up in here after I gave you that shank, all these bitches up in here thought you were weak. They all thought you were a snitch. It was me who kept them off your ass. If it wasn't for me, you'd be dead."

"Whatever, Stormy. I would've brought it to any of them bitches if they would've stepped to me."

"They woulda ate your ass alive, Keema. You wouldn't have seen it coming. I was the one who stopped it. Now, I need

183

you to return the favor."

"What part of 'I'm Out' don't you understand, Stormy? I'm finished with that shit. Don't call me any more!"

"Keema…"

I hung up before she could say another word. With the phone in my hand, I leaned backwards against the counter in thought. With both her voice in my head and Frenchie's, I realized my past was calling me back. I didn't want to answer it. I hated it. If anything, all I wanted to do was get the Frenchie situation finished and move on. I wanted to see where this Drake situation could go. Could me and him really work out? Could me, him, and Treasure, Deniro and Shane really be a family? I wondered heavily. But for some strange reason, despite me wanting and needing to leave my grinding days behind me, something was urging me to call Stormy's homegirl. Drake had two extra bedrooms in the house.

22

Mrs. Kyle came through just like she said she would. She got me in to visit Deniro. The morning was bright, warm, and sunny as I sat on the grass in my Peace Love World sweat suit underneath a tree. Around me, throughout the CPS outdoor visiting area were dozens of other parents and children. Laughter and chatter came from all directions. While Treasure sat beside me, Deniro sat in front of us wearing a pair of jeans, a Polo shirt, and a pair of Lebron James sneakers. I was so glad he was able to take his clothes with him when Drake first sent him away. The last thing I wanted was for my baby to look like a bum.

"When am I coming home?" Deniro asked pitifully. "I hate it here. When are you getting me out?"

"Real soon," I promised him. "I'm working on it right now."

He dropped his eyes to the ground in disappointment. Obviously, he was ready to come home instantly. Placing a hand underneath his chin, I raised his face gently until our eyes met. "It'll be real soon, baby. I promise."

Deniro still didn't look too reassured. If anything, it looked like he didn't even believe me. It broke my heart to see the look on his face. I felt so ashamed knowing that I was the cause of it. If I'd been the mother I was supposed to be all along, he'd be at home with his family where he belonged. I'd caused all of this. I felt guilty and shameful all at the same time.

Seeing the disappointed look on her brother's face, Treasure grabbed his hand. "Hey, look at me," she told him firmly.

He looked her directly in her eyes.

With a warm smile, she told him, "I promise you *myself* that you're coming home."

The two were silent for a moment, only their eyes vibing with one another.

A moment later, his face brightened.

Seeing the change in his face and hearing the emphasis that Treasure had placed on the word *myself* made me feel bad. I wasn't sure if she'd said it to be smart. And silently it hurt me to know my son had more faith in his sister than his own mother. My words were supposed to be enough for him. I couldn't help feeling a little jealous.

"You sure?" Deniro asked happily.

"When have I ever let you down?" she responded.

When your ass allowed Drake to send him here, I thought as the two hugged each other.

Seeing that I was hurt and trying to hide it, Drake placed a hand on my shoulder and said, "Hey, Deniro, we got you somethin', lil man." He extended his hand to offer the bag from Toys R Us.

Buying my baby something was the least Drake's ass could do since this was his entire fault. I often wondered if he felt bad or not.

Deniro's smile faded quickly. He looked at the bag skeptically. His face even twisted up slightly. Obviously since Drake didn't let him stay at his house, he wasn't too quick to trust Drake or his gifts. He made no moves towards the bag at all. He wanted no parts of it.

"It's okay," I told Deniro. "There's something in there from all of us".

He still wasn't convinced. Instead, he glanced at Treasure. She nodded to him. It was only then that he took the bag.

Once again, it kind of annoyed me that he seemed to be following Treasure's word more than mine. At first I wondered if she
was doing it to be sneaky, but I realized that for all these years it
had been Treasure he'd always been close to. When I left her at
home alone with the other kids, it was Treasure who was in
charge. It had always been that way. I guess, in a way, she
seemed more of a mother to him than me, but despite rationaliza-
tion, it still hurt.

Deniro opened the bag and pulled out a new PSP and
three games. His face lit up. "Wowwwwww," he said. "Thanks!"

From a distance my caseworker watched our interaction
from a bench. Every now and then she wrote something down in
her notebook.

Deniro couldn't take his eyes off his new games.

"We weren't sure which ones you wanted," I told him. "I
hope you like them."

He nodded wildly. "I love them."

Seeing his happiness made me smile.

"Can I have a hug?" I asked, truly needing to feel him in
my arms. It had felt like forever since the last time I'd held him.

Deniro rushed into my arms.

I closed my eyes as I squeezed him. My nostrils took in
his smell. My heartbeat synchronized itself with his. My arms
and body didn't want to turn him loose. They held him tightly.
Being without him had been torment. His absence was something I hoped I wouldn't have to endure for too much longer. I
needed my baby with me. I needed my new life to start.

"I love you," I whispered into his ear. "Do you know
that?"

He nodded.

Once we separated, I took his face softly into my hands,
for the first time in a long time realizing just how much he
looked like me. If I were his age, people would've believed we
were twins.

"No, baby," I whispered to him. "I mean, *really* love you,
Deniro. Do you know that?"

187

I meant those words now more than I'd ever meant them before. Of course, I'd told him I loved him millions of times before.

"Do you love me, baby?" I asked, desperately needing him to tell me that he did. Everything inside me needed to hear it.

Deniro smiled. "I do mommy," he told me.

I'd never heard words more beautiful and had never seen a smile more bright. I felt like the luckiest woman in the world.

Drake's cell phone suddenly rung. "What's up?" he answered.

A second of silence.

"You sure?" he finally asked into the phone and walked away from us.

Something about the call seemed strange. Since I'd been coming around to mend our relationship, he never treated a call like it was private. He knew I wasn't into any illegal shit, so he never felt the need to keep anything secret. I'd heard it all. He'd discussed shit in detail as if I wasn't even there. What was so different about this call?

My eyes followed his back as he walked away, still talking. When he was a safe distance away, he stopped and glanced at us. Seeing that I was looking at him, he quickly turned his back again and continued with his conversation.

"I've been wanting this one for a long time," Deniro said happily, talking about one of his games.

My eyes were still on Drake's back.

"You hear me, Mommy?" Deniro asked.

"Huh?" I took one last glance at Drake then gave my attention back to my son.

"I've been wanting this one," Deniro said, waving his game towards me.

I smiled. "I'm glad you like it."

He began to tear it open.

"So, do you have any friends here?" I asked.

"Nah."

188

"Why not?"

"I don't trust them," Deniro answered.

"Why? Do they steal from you?"

He shook his head as he began to tear open another game.

"Do they talk about you?"

"Nope."

"Then why don't you like them?"

"Because they're broke." The look on his face as he said those words was as if he'd just swallowed a lemon.

I frowned with confusion. "What do you mean?"

"They don't wear nice sneakers. They don't keep their hair cut. Their clothes are ugly."

He said it all as if each of the children around him were *beneath* him and his standards. It made me feel bad to hear him talk like that because I knew I was the one who'd instilled that in him. I'd always taught him and Treasure that a human being didn't deserve respect if they didn't wear name brand clothes and shoes. I'd taught them that their clothes and the price of their clothes was what made them important.

"Deniro, just because they don't wear nice clothes doesn't mean you can't trust them. You have to judge people by how they treat you, not by how they dress."

"I guess," he said, shrugging my words off as if they didn't mean anything.

"Deniro, I'm serious. Promise me you'll judge people by the way they treat you, not by what they wear or how much money they have," I said.

"Okay."

"Promise?"

"Promise."

I smiled. The last thing I wanted now in life was for Deniro to pick up my bad habits. He deserved more than that. He had his whole life ahead of him. I didn't want him to fuck it all up by thinking as ignorantly as I had.

The visit went on for twenty more minutes. Time had flown. When it was over, we each hugged Deniro. It broke my heart to have to leave him behind. My eyes grew glossy as I kissed him on the cheek. A tear fell and I wiped it away.

"You promise me you're gonna get me out of here soon?" he asked me.

"I put it on my life, baby, I promise."

This time, instead of looking at his sister, he took *my* word for it and smiled. Seeing that smile made my day.

The caseworker called for someone to get Deniro. When he was taken away, she said, "I have good news for you, Keema."

"What is it?"

"They've set a date for your hearing to get Deniro."

"Really?" I asked excitedly.

She nodded. "It'll be this Friday. I know it's short notice, but…"

"No, that's perfect, actually. Do you think anything will stop me from getting him back?"

"No," she said. "You've been meeting all your requirements and attending your programs. I'll be recommending he be placed back in your custody."

"I can't believe this."

"Can you be at the court house by eleven? Your case will be called by noon," she informed.

"Absolutely," I told her. "Thank you so much."

"You're welcome," she said, hugging me. "See you then."

As me, Drake, and Treasure headed out of the building and into the parking lot, my cell phone rang. Glancing at the screen, I couldn't believe who it was. It was the attorney for the inheritance case. I answered quickly.

"Ms. Newell?" he asked.

"Yes, this is me."

"Hey, I just wanted to let you know that the insurance company is finally ready to give you your money."

I stopped dead in my tracks at the sound of those words. Drake and Treasure stopped also. They looked at me, trying to figure out what was going on.

190

"Are you serious?" I asked Mr. Hyde, not able to truly believe it. The insurance company had been taking me through so much damn bullshit over the past several months that it was difficult to believe it had all finally come to an end.

"Are you *really* serious?" I asked again.

"Yes, they're finally ready. Can you be in my office around four o'clock on Friday?"

"Of course I can."

"Alright, I'll call you before then so we can talk over a few things. From there, we'll be ready to go."

"Great. Talk to you then."

The two of us hung up.

"What's up?" Drake asked. "What was that all about?"

Too excited to answer him, I realized everything was working out perfectly. There really was a God. I'd changed my life around and he was now really and truly blessing me for it. Mrs. Kyle had been right.

The only thing that was still up in the air was the Shane situation. I still hadn't found him. He was still out here in the streets somewhere. But something inside me told me everything would be alright. I just had to keep doing what I needed to do to get my life back on track and to put my family back together. As long as I did that, God would handle the rest.

With Treasure and Drake still looking at me, I dialed Frenchie's number.

"Bitch, I'm busy so you'd better have some good news," he said, evidently recognizing my ring tone.

"The attorney just called," I told him.

"And?"

"It's on for Friday afternoon at his office."

"You sure?"

"Yeah," I assured.

"What time?"

"Four o'clock."

"Bet. Let me talk to Shane," he said out of the blue.

"I'd completely forgotten that he wanted to talk to him

191

today.

"Ahhhh….he's…"

"Baby, come back to bed," a female voice came from his background.

Everything around me went silent. The sound of that voice made me press my ear tightly to the phone. I'd recognized it. Immediately, I heard some sort of shuffling noise come from Frenchie's end and his entire background went silent for a moment as if he'd quickly covered the receiver.

"Hello?" I asked.

No answer.

"Hello?" I asked again, wanting to hear that background voice again much more than Frenchie's. I knew that voice anywhere. I definitely recognized it. "Hello?" I called again.

"Yeah," Frenchie finally answered. "Tell Shane I'll call him a little later. And make sure you're at that lawyer's office on Friday."

"Frenchie, who was that? I…"

The phone went dead.

With the phone in my hand, I could only stand in the center of the parking lot, unable to speak. That female's voice stayed on my mind and in my ears. Was that really *her*, I wondered? Why would *she* be with him?

"Keema, what's up?" Drake asked.

"What's going on?" Treasure questioned, too.

I couldn't answer neither of them. All I could do was stand there and wonder why *Shy* was with Frenchie.

23

The sun shone brightly through the bedroom's curtains as I woke up to Drake's pleasant smile. He was sitting beside me on the bed with a tray in his hand that held a huge breakfast; eggs, sausage, grits, biscuits and toast. A light steam arose from the meal and slithered its way towards the ceiling. This nigga hooked me the fuck up!

"Mornin', beautiful," he said, before leaning to kiss me on the lips. I could taste peppermint on his tongue.

Drake was still in the streets and still thuggish, but obviously the time spent in prison had truly taught him how to treat a lady. It had definitely educated him on the value of a good woman.

"Morning," I returned with a smile of my own. Letting my eyes drop to the food, I asked, "What's the occasion?"

He kissed me again. "Today's special."

I watched him carefully. "What do you mean?"

"I'm kinda takin' a huge step with you today."

"What are you talking about?" I sat up in the bed and pressed my back against the headboard.

Drake placed the tray of food on my lap and sat a tall glass of ice cold orange juice on the nightstand. He then took my hand into his own and said, "Keema, over these past few weeks, you've been a Godsend."

Our eyes were locked on each other's. Neither of us even blinked. I, myself, hung onto his every word.

"I thought I loved Raven more than you," he continued, "but you came back into my life and proved me wrong."

Damn, I wanted to cry.

"You didn't have to do those things, Keema. I know. Before I went to prison, I was a bastard for the way I treated you. So, I definitely didn't deserve for you to come into my home and make me whole again."

I couldn't hold back. The first tear fell.

Softly wiping my tear away, Drake continued, "Baby, I'm sorry for the heartache I've caused you. I'm sorry for it all."

Another tear fell.

"I want to make it all better. I want to take care of you for the rest of your life. I mean that. Diamonds, cars, maids, massages…the whole nine." He squeezed my hand. "That's why today is special."

As if it were possible, I listened even more closely to his words.

"I've never been able to trust anyone. But today, I'm changin' that. I'm trustin' *you*."

I was now lost in his eyes and words.

"Keema, I'm takin' you to the bank today so I can put your name on my account."

"Are you serious, Drake?" I asked in disbelief. I was just as happy right now as I would've been if he'd proposed marriage. I'd been a little worried lately from all his secret phone conversations, but now I knew that it was all business.

"I'm *more* than serious, baby. If anything ever happens to me, I want you and Treasure to be taken care of. In order to do that, I now understand that I have to give you the key to everything that's mine."

More tears fell.

"I love you, Keema. I love you with all my heart."

"I love you, too, Drake."

I really meant those words. To know that he trusted me sent an overwhelming feeling of love across my heart, body and soul even stronger than I'd ever imagined or felt before. I, of all people, knew just how hard it was to trust someone. I'd trusted and had been trusted. I'd betrayed and had been betrayed. So, I definitely knew that trust, real trust, only came with real love.

"How much is in the bank?"

"Only ninety thousand," he said. "But I have another three hundred thousand stashed away in that storage unit. I also have a few other hundred thousand tied up in the streets."

Wow, I thought to myself. It was like I'd hit the lottery. Tomorrow was Friday. I'd be going to get both Deniro and the inheritance money. But although, Frenchie had made it clear I wouldn't receive a penny of the inheritance, I'd just come up on several hundred thousand just from my man, Drake.

Everything was now working in my favor; everything except the Shane factor. I had no idea what was going on with him, but at least he was alive and walking the streets. I kept my head up, believing I would find him. The plan was to go back to that same neighborhood and search the blocks, taking old pictures of Shane with me.

Suddenly, my phone rang. Someone was calling from a restricted number. Usually, I didn't answer restricted calls, but for some reason I chose to answer this one.

"Hello?"

No one responded. All I could hear coming from the background was passing traffic.

"Hello?" I said again.

Still no response.

I was going to hang up, but something in my heart told me who it might be. "Shane?" I questioned.

There was still no response. I could see Drake becoming worried as he sat by my side, ready to help me in any way needed.

I knew it was him. "Baby, you don't have to say anything," I told him. "I'm just glad that you're okay. I miss you though. We all miss you."

I got silent and listened, hoping he would respond, but still only got silence.

"Shane," I finally continued. "I owe you a million apologies. I owe you a million kisses and hugs. I wasn't the mother I should've been. I understand that now and I admit it."

The words were my heart itself crying out to him.

"But, baby," I told him. "I'm ready to make things right. "Tell me where you are so I can come and get you."

I desperately hoped he would respond, but he didn't. Instead, the line went dead. My heart was broken but now, with the news from Drake, I had nothing but faith that Shane would be back in my arms by the end of the day.

Everything was going to work out.

"Go ahead and eat your breakfast," Drake told me, kissing me softly on the forehead. "We're gonna head to the bank later on."

Damn, I felt like the luckiest woman in the world right now.

An hour later, me and Drake walked out of the house and climbed into his truck. I felt so proud to be his woman. As I leaned back into the soft leather, the front door of the house opened. Treasure stepped out and made her way down the steps toward us. Seconds later, she was in the back seat. I looked over at Drake, wondering why Treasure was going on a trip that was supposed to be meant for only me and him.

Maybe it was the selfish side of me, but the trip signified that I was back on top. I was the queen of the castle once again. Yes, Treasure had played her position properly and she'd been a valuable soldier, still at the end of the day, I was the true HBIC. I was the queen of his growing empire.

Seeing the look on my face, Drake said, "Don't worry. It's nothin'. She just has to take care of somethin'."

He kissed me on the cheek, turned on the engine, and pulled from the curb. As we drove, I thought about my life and my decisions. This moment seemed like a turning point. It, along with tomorrow's day in court, was the moment when the entire past would be placed behind me.

I glanced at Drake thinking about what our wedding day would be like. I imagined him in a custom made tux and myself in a beautiful, designer Badgley Mischka gown with a long train trailing behind it. I pictured us getting married on the beach in Turks & Caicos as the sun set behind us. It was beautiful and strangely the mellow music in the Range matched my thoughts for most of the ride.

One block away from the bank, Drake shocked me when he pulled the truck to the curb. I looked around at the buildings and wondered why he was stopping. Treasure then hopped out of the truck without saying anything.

"Hold it down, baby girl," Drake told her as she closed the door.

"I got cha," she returned.

Drake pulled away.

I sat straight up. "What does she have to handle? And where is she going?"

"Somethin' important," he told me.

The answer was too short for me. There wasn't any information attached to it as if it was secretive. That was strange. I didn't quite like it, but I let it go since I was on my way to sign my name on the dotted line. Co-account holder on ninety grand sounded good to me. I sat back again thinking about how I would ask Drake to buy me a Birkin bag as soon as we left. So many thoughts about my new life with him shot through my mind. A moment later, we pulled directly in front of TD bank. The two of us parked out front and walked inside like a loving couple. We stood in a line of only two people. When I turned to Drake, I noticed him glancing around nervously. It made me feel strange because his glancing became more fretful by the minute.

I grabbed his hand and smiled. "What's wrong, baby?" I

asked. "You nervous about putting me on the account, huh? You getting cold feet?"

Drake stared at me, but didn't respond right away.

The look he had was the strangest and coldest I'd ever seen him give me. Suddenly, he pulled a gun from underneath his shirt and shoved it flat against my chest.

"Let's get to it, Keema," he said aggressively.

Grabbing the gun, I gasped, "Drake, what the hell are you talking about?" My eyes had grown to the size of watermelons.

He pulled another gun from behind his back. "What the fuck do you think I'm talkin' about, nigga? We're robbin' this bitch!"

The other two people in line turned to us.

"Get the fuck down on the floor!" Drake ordered them.

They did as they were told without hesitating, fear shown on their faces.

I was frozen.

Mortified.

Unable to speak.

I kept gawking at Drake as he turned into some crazed maniac.

"Get your fuckin' hands up!" he ordered the two tellers. "Make any sudden moves and I'll blow your heads off!"

The room began spinning.

"Keema!" Drake called out to me. "Hold me down! Aim the gun at them muthafuckas!"

My heart was pounding. "Drake, what- what- what… the hell are you talking about? I didn't come here for this!"

He quickly pressed up on me. While keeping his gun pointed at the tellers and his eyes on them also, he whispered viciously to me, "It's close to a million dollars in this fuckin' bank. Let's get to it, bitch!"

His eyes were wide and wild looking.

"You're gonna help me steal it," he told me.

"Drake, I didn't ask to be a part of this."

"Fuck all that. Trent's outside watchin' the front door.

We're gonna split the money three ways.

"Trent?" I asked in surprise.

"Yeah," he returned, while still making sure to keep an eye on both tellers.

My body shook uncontrollably. I didn't want to go to prison. "Drake, I don't want any parts of this. I don't want to be in it."

"Well, you're in it anyway! Now move!"

"Drake, look, I…"

"Bitch," he spewed in a loud and angry whisper. "You're in it whether you want to be or not. If you try to back out, you're a dead bitch. The same way you had Raven killed."

Those final words scared me to death. I had no choice in the matter. How in the hell did he know?

"Now let's get this fuckin' money!" he yelled and dashed over the two people lying on the floor in front of us to the counter. "You!" he screamed at one of the tellers. "Give me all the fuckin' money now!"

Tears began to fall from her eyes. "I have children," she pleaded. "Please don't kill me."

"Fuck your damn children! Give me all the money!" Drake yelled.

I was still frozen as tears dripped slowly from my eyes. I had no idea what to do. I clearly didn't want to go to jail or die trying to escape when we were done. I couldn't help but wonder if this is what all of those secret phone conversations were about.

I'd clearly been tricked.

Hoodwinked.

Bamboozled.

"Bitch, don't just stand there like a statue!" he shouted at me. "Come watch this other hoe!"

I was still too scared to move.

"Now! Keema, now!" he demanded.

Fuck! He'd said my name. I walked over nervously and held my gun to the other teller's face. When her eyes connected with mine I felt like vomiting. Something told me I wouldn't make it out alive.

Soon, Drake hopped over the counter. Seconds later, he and the teller he had his gun trained on were in the bank safe filling up bags.

"Hurry the fuck up!" Drake ordered.

My hand was shivering so badly that I almost dropped the gun. *How the fuck did I get myself into this one*, I wondered. My eyes darted back and forth from the teller to the safe over and over again. I also turned my head a couple times toward the front doors to see if the cops were coming. Shit, I was expecting them to be there. I was expecting guns blazing. Damn, I wished with all my heart I could be anywhere but here.

As he stood over the teller in the safe, Drake pulled out a small walkie-talkie. He pressed a button on the side of it and said, "How things lookin' out there, baby girl?"

"So far, so good," Treasure returned. "No cops."

As if I couldn't be any more shocked, hearing Treasure's voice over the walkie-talkie weighed down on my shoulders like a ton of bricks. Drake had included our own daughter in this shit. I couldn't believe it. Wrapping my mind around that one was nearly impossible.

Drake truly hadn't changed. He was still the same sneaky ass bastard he was before he went to prison. He hadn't learned a damn thing. Now, he wanted to take both me and his own baby back to prison with him.

My mind scrambled in countless directions. There were so many thoughts flowing through it. I had no idea what to do. The situation was happening so fast. God, I just wanted all of this to be over.

Finally, Drake made his way out of the safe with a huge, black bag in his hand. "Get your ass in the safe with your girl," he ordered the teller I was guarding.

With tears in her eyes and her hands raised in pitiful defense, she did as she was told. As soon as she was inside, Drake shut the door.

"See how easy that shit was?" he asked me, smiling and

sweating all at the same time.

For a moment I could only stare at him, unable to believe how nonchalant the situation seemed to him. Here we were standing in the middle of the bank we'd just robbed with no ski masks, and he's sitting here talking about how easy it was. He was fucking nuts!

Seeing that he'd dropped his gun at his side, I was tempted to raise mine and kill him. He'd just destroyed my life. But just as I was about to raise the gun, Treasure's voice came over his walkie talkie.

"It's the cops!" she yelled.

"Awee shit!" Drake commented the moment the bomb-shell had been dropped on us.

"They're coming down the street right now!" she screamed "One...two...three cars! Get out of there!"

"Damn it!" Drake yelled in a rage. "You dumb bitch!" he screamed at me. "You let the teller push the button!"

"What?" I asked, just as stunned as he was.

"You were supposed to watch her!"

"I was! I never saw her push a button!"

"Fuck!" he hollered. "We gotta get out of here!"

With those words said, he dashed across the tiled floor towards the front glass doors. Not knowing what else to do, I followed. In the blink of an eye we were out the door charging toward the Range. But just as quickly as we reached it, a squad car came speeding down the street. It spun out a short distance away from us. Immediately, two cops jumped out and screamed, "Freeze!"

"Fuck that," Drake told me, "I ain't going back to prison."

He dropped the bag, raised his gun and squeezed the trigger at the cops. Both cops took cover behind their cars and returned fire. It was like something I'd seen only in movies. The moment had me totally frozen in one spot. I had no idea if I should duck or run. My first thought was to act like a pedestrian until Drake fucked that up.

"Here!" Drake shouted to me over the gunfire. He tossed me the bag of money and pointed across the street.

I looked across the street to see Trent sitting in a grey Lexus watching the action. After seeing Drake toss me the bag, he screamed, "Go!"

The sounds of more approaching sirens began to fall over the street.

"Run!" Drake demanded.

"Come the fuck on!" Trent shouted stepping out of his car. Panic could be seen in his eyes.

I was still too petrified to move.

"Go!" Drake shouted again, while still letting off shots at the cop.

My mind kept taking me back to how I almost died in Arizona. I was petrified and could only glare at Drake shooting like a maniac at war. Then suddenly, something so insane happened it stopped me in my tracks. A bullet entered the center of Drake's forehead. Immediately after, the back of his skull exploded right in the middle of the street, sending blood and brain fragments splashing onto the ground behind him. His body fell backwards into his own blood.

I screamed as his body fell hitting the ground hard. For a moment, I could only stare at him. He was lying there on his back with his eyes staring up into the sky.

"Drake!" I screamed!

He didn't answer.

He couldn't answer.

He was dead.

"Come the fuck on, Keema!" Trent hollered. "Let's go!"

He then stepped closer into the street and began to fire off shots at the cops attempting to give me cover.

Finally, I came out of my daze and ran like crazy, ducking and dodging bullets along the way. After releasing several more shots, Trent hopped into the driver's seat and jetted off as soon as I had one foot in the car. I was a nervous wreck until my eyes spotted Treasure. All feelings escaped me. I was now numb. My baby was jetting toward the car, running into a war zone, with bullets still flying.

"We've got to go back for Treasure!" I screamed uncontrollably as we raced away from the scene.

"We can't!" Trent yelled back.

"Fuck that!" I told him, refusing to leave my baby behind. I grabbed the steering wheel wildly, causing us to swerve.

Trent shoved me to the side forcefully and regained control of the car. "We can't go back!" he hollered. "That area is swarming with cops right now!"

"But Treasure is back there!"

"She's going to be alright!"

"No, she won't! We've got to go back!"

"Yes, she will! She knows what to do!"

"What do you mean?"

"We've been planning this shit for weeks, Keema! She knows what to do! She'll be okay! Trust me. We'll get up with her later!"

My eyes bulged then closed. I fell back into my seat, breathless. A heart attack was on the way.

24

I found myself pacing the floor of Drake's living room relentlessly. It was a wonder I hadn't walked a damn hole in the floor. My feet and body had a mind of their own. They wouldn't stop letting me pace even if I'd wanted to. Shit, I must've walked from one end of the room to the other over and over again at least a hundred times in just the past hour.

Nervously, I placed the cigarette to my lips and inhaled deeply. The smoke hadn't been in my lungs for a full second before I was exhaling. I repeated the process damn near every couple seconds hoping Treasure would show up, or at least call. By smoking one cigarette after another I'd gone through an entire pack in just an hour and a half. I was now on my second pack. Just like the one before it, it didn't stand a chance.

My eyes were swollen and red. There were heavy bags underneath them and tears fell from them more and more. I couldn't help it. All I could do was cry. All I could do was let them fall down my cheeks and drop to the floor like raindrops as I repeatedly hugged myself for comfort.

"Damn, Keema," Trent said from the couch while smoking a cigarette himself, and watching TV. "Calm down. Shit's gonna be alright."

He'd been with me since yesterday.

"Fuck you!" I shouted angrily at him. "Don't tell me

things are gonna be alright!"

I was more than pissed. I was still super- heated that he and Drake had gotten my daughter involved in this shit. They were grown ass men! How could they involve a child in a muthafuckin' bank robbery? How? I mean, who the hell does that?

It was seven o'clock and the local morning news was coming on as I paced. I hadn't slept a wink the night before, not a brief second. I couldn't. Shit, I couldn't even lay down for more than a few minutes. The entire house felt like it was too small, like it was closing in on me. All I could think about was Treasure.

I'd called her cell at least fifty times since the very moment we'd fled the bank scene. Treasure never answered. All I got was her answering service, causing me to leave message after message for her. She never responded to any of them though. I'd also sent her countless texts begging her to call me, but still never got a response. The shit was driving me absolutely crazy. Why wasn't she answering her phone or returning my messages? Something was definitely wrong. The possibilities of what could possibly be keeping her from responding to my calls had me terrified for her. My first thought was that she'd gotten locked up. I was so scared that I dropped to my knees a couple of times and prayed harder to God than I'd ever prayed before in my entire life.

What a damn day today was turning out to be. It was Friday. It was the day when everything in my life was supposed to finally change for the better. I was supposed to get Deniro from court at twelve. Then I was supposed to finally get the inheritance money at four. It was all finally going to work out. But, instead, everything had turned into a damn nightmare.

"Top story this morning," a newscaster said from the television. "A violent bank robbery yesterday afternoon on Eastern Avenue in Essex, Maryland left three people dead, two wounded and a community mourning."

I finally stopped pacing at the sound of those words. My

feet stood in one spot as my eyes stared at the television screen. On it was the white, male news caster talking into a microphone. Behind him was the bank, which was now surrounded by yellow cautionary tape and a bunch of nosey people in the area.

The news caster began to go into detail about yesterday's events. Trent leaned in closer from the couch. Both me and him were focused on the screen. Nothing else existed around us.

"The three people killed in the robbery are suspected to be the perpetrators," the man stated. "The police aren't releasing the names of the deceased until their families have been notified.

My hand covered my mouth. My eyes grew wide with worry. Was one of those three Treasure? Was my daughter dead?

"Oh God," I said as more tears began to pour. It suddenly hit me that she *had* to have been one of the three dead bodies. That was why she wasn't answering her phone. That was why she wasn't returning my messages. The police would've called me by now if she'd been locked up.

"She's dead!" I screamed, dropping to my knees. "Oh my God! She's dead!"

Hours later, I found myself standing up in a daze. Almost like a zombie. My mood in the courtroom was somber. I'd spent most of it silent and staring off into space. It was supposed to be a joyous occasion, instead, it seemed dark.

"We still expect you to keep all appointments and complete all programs," the judge said to me as I stood at the podium.

"Yes, sir," I said politely.

"Good luck," he said.

"Thank you," I returned.

And just like that, Deniro had been returned to my custody. My child rushed into my arms and I held him as tightly as I could, never wanting to let him go.

"I love you," I leaned and whispered into his ear. "I love

you so much."

"I love you, too," he told me.

When we finally let each other go, he asked, "Where's Treasure?"

Hearing that question made my knees weak. It made my eyes well up again. I couldn't answer him. All I could do was take him by the hand, throw on my sunglasses and get out of the courtroom before the tears started to fall again. He deserved to know what had happened to his sister. He deserved to know she was dead. But I couldn't bear to tell him.

Deniro and I headed outside and hopped in the car headed toward Pikesville. By the time we stopped and had lunch, it was close to four when we arrived which gave me a chance to call Mrs. Kyle to let her know what was going on with Treasure. Of course she jumped right in ready to help me. She told me she'd make some calls and get back to me. Finally, Mr. Hyde's secretary told me to have a seat and that he'd be with me shortly. As we sat in the plush leather seats, I was in a complete daze thinking about Treasure. I'd called every hospital in Baltimore to see if she'd been taken to any of them. Each said no. That hadn't consoled me though. It didn't prove that she was alive. I also went as far as to call the morgue. They gave me the same answer the hospitals did.

As I sat in the lobby, the stress and worry was getting to me. My nerves were bad and my heart was broken. I was even seeing glimpses of Drake's face, his last moments on this earth. I kept seeing him lying out with his eyes open. The sight and memory was sending shivers down my spine and making my stomach nauseous. I needed a cigarette badly. I reached into my purse, pulled one out and was getting ready to light it when the secretary said, "I'm sorry, ma'am but there's no smoking in here."

"Why not?" I asked angrily.

"It's the law, ma'am. You're welcome to go outside and smoke though."

"Shit," I said underneath my breath. The last thing I felt

like doing was going all the way outside. Finally, Mr. Hyde came out of his office.

Mr. Hyde was about in his early forties and white as snow. His hairline was receding and he was dressed in a navy blue suit and Ferragamo shoes. He invited me and Deniro back to his office in a speedily manner. Once inside, we all took a seat.

"So, the process is finally over," Mr. Hyde informed.

I didn't say anything. I was too drained to speak. I just wanted to get the shit over with, give Frenchie his money, and figure out where to go from there.

"I know you're glad," he continued.

Knowing he was trying to be polite, I still wasn't in the mood for small talk. "Mr. Hyde, can we please get this over with?" I asked softly.

"Oh, quite certainly.

"Thank you."

"As I said when we spoke on the phone this morning, the payment is for five hundred and fifty thousand dollars." He opened up a long vanilla folder on his desk and began to ruffle through some papers.

This morning, I thought to myself with a question mark. We hadn't spoken this morning. "We didn't speak this morning, Mr. Hyde," I told him with confidence. "You must have me mixed up with one of your other clients."

He looked at me puzzled, but with an uncomfortable smile. "No, I'm quite sure we spoke. I told you that I couldn't give you all of the specifics over the phone."

I leaned forward in my chair and looked at him like he was crazy. "Mr. Hyde, you and I didn't talk this morning." My words were more pointed this time.

He chuckled nervously. "Yes, ma'am, we did."

He was starting to piss me off. What was he trying to pull? I knew for a damn fact that I hadn't spoken to him this morning.

"Look, Mr. Hyde," I told him angrily. "I don't know what

you're talking about. It wasn't me you spoke to this morning."

Mr. Hyde looked more puzzled. "Someone called me this morning saying they were you."

"What?"

"Yes, they said they were you, Keema Newell."

"What did they want?"

"They were asking questions about the case."

"And what did you tell them?"

"I told them that I couldn't give that information over the phone."

Even Deniro was now puzzled. Even he was smart enough to smell bullshit. He looked at me and said, "Something's weird."

"Mr. Hyde, that wasn't me you spoke to this morning. I'm sure of it. But I'd really like to get this done, so I can get some business handled."

"Of course. I understand. Where are the other children?"

"In school," I lied.

He looked nervous again. "I really need them to be present."

I was losing patience. "Look, Mr. Hyde, they're in school and I really have things I need to do. Can we please get this over with? I've already waited for almost a year for this money."

He smiled. "You're right. It has been a tedious process."

I nodded.

"I'm not supposed to do this without the children present, but alright," he said and pulled paperwork from his folder.

I spent ten minutes reading paper after paper and signing my signature to every single sheet. When I finally finished, he told me a check for five hundred fifty thousand dollars would be mailed to my house by Express Mail. He also told me all the other assets would have to be liquidated. He kept asking me if I wanted to sell the inherited properties or keep them.

"Sell it," I finally said. I wanted no parts of Frenchie's bullshit.

"No problem."

His phone rang interrupting us.

"Excuse me for one moment," he said and then answered his phone. After a brief moment a weird look spread across his face. He looked at me. Several moments later he took the phone away from his ear, covered the receiver, and whispered, "Ms. Newell, it's the person who called this morning. It's the same person."

"Let me hear her voice, damn it," I demanded. Whoever this bitch was, I wanted to know.

Mr. Hyde put the call on speaker and carried on with the conversation. "So, what is it that you want to do, Ms. Newell?"

When the caller's voice spoke again, not only did I recognize the voice, Deniro did also. He looked at me and whispered, "Ma, that's Shy."

"Shhhhhhhhh," I told him, placing a finger to my lips.

I then leaned back into my chair and remembered the last time I'd spoken to Frenchie. It really was Shy that I'd heard in the background that day. What the fuck was going on? Why were they now both in cahoots? Obviously, they had some kind of game going on.

That was it!

I'd had it!

I was fed up with the fucking games. I was fed up with the lies. I was fed up with people betraying me. I threw my purse over my shoulder, got to my feet, and snatched up my copies of all the paperwork I'd signed.

Mr. Hyde told Shy he'd have to call her back later. He still wanted to know what that was all about. My shrug proved that I didn't know and didn't care either. A short moment later me and Deniro were headed out the door. It was time to put an end to it all. Frenchie and Shy were going to get their money. They were definitely going to get it…

And a whole lot more!

25

It seemed as if time stood still even though another day had gone by. My mind and body remained in shambles. There still had been no info about Treasure. I'd been watching the news and had even gone out to get the paper the first thing this morning. None of them had anything on her. I'd also been to every single police station and hospital within a fifty mile radius of the bank robbery. I hadn't told them that she'd been involved in the robbery. I just showed them a picture and asked if she'd been admitted or locked up. They each said no, but I was still far from relieved.

I'd become an absolute wreck. My appetite was gone. I couldn't eat anything. When I tried, nothing seemed to stay down. I'd throw up immediately. It was like I was fucking bulimic. I'd already lost ten pounds in just two days and it was showing. My skinny jeans were getting slightly baggier. My eyes were beginning to sink into my skull like a crack head. They stayed blood shot and swollen from all the crying I was doing and I didn't have the motivation to put on makeup. The combination had me looking fucked up and aged beyond my years.

Cigarette after cigarette still got blazed. Glass after glass of wine had been guzzled. Tear after tear fell. I had totally fallen into a depression that wouldn't turn me lose. My daughter was most likely dead and there was nothing I could do about it. Her death was even possibly my fault. It was me who had introduced her to a life devoted to getting money. It was me who had made her feel as if she should be down to do just about anything for a fast buck. Now she'd paid for it with her life.

Over and over, in my mind I saw her lying on some cold steel slab somewhere in a white room with a toe tag dangling from her foot. I saw the coroner slicing her open and digging inside her body during the autopsy. The sight broke my heart.

"Oh, God, what have I done?" I whispered as I sat on the couch with my head resting in my hand. In my other hand was a glass of Ciroc. Beside me, on the arm of the couch my cigarette sat in an ash tray. A stream of gray smoke slithered from its lit tip towards the ceiling.

Suddenly, a loud crash came from the kitchen. Something had fallen to the floor and broken, but even that didn't even jolt me.

"Ma," Deniro said, coming out of the kitchen.

I stayed in my daze.

"I was trying to reach something and broke a glass."

Just clean it up," I said emotionless.

"Can I have some pizza?"

I didn't answer.

"Ma," he said.

"Huh?"

"Can I have the rest of that pizza in the kitchen?"

"It's old, but do whatever."

Ignoring the glass he'd broken, Deniro rushed into the kitchen and came back out eating the two day old pizza. When he was done, he turned on the television and plopped down on the floor in front of it. The volume was sky high. A moment later, he turned on his Nintendo Wii, pulled out a fake guitar jumped up and began to play one of his games. It was that Guitar Hero game that I hated.

"Ma, come play with me," Deniro said excitedly over the loud wailing of his guitar.

I began to massage my temples.

"Ma!" he called louder.

"I don't feel like it right now, baby. And please turn that game down."

Ignoring me, he left the volume up and continued to play the game. The music was making my head hurt.

"I said turn it down."

Deniro kept right on as if he hadn't heard me. It was obvious that being in CPS had done more harm this time. Deniro always listened to me, but now he'd started to challenge my authority…something I'm sure he'd picked up from those bad ass kids.

"I wish Shane was here!" he yelled. "He'd play it with me. Ma, where's Shane anyway?"

I massaged my temples harder. I hadn't told Deniro about Shane or Treasure and had no idea when I would. The old Keema would've jumped up and slapped the shit out of Deniro, but I had to learn to be a better mother. Just as I was about to sit him down for a talk my cell phone rang.

Recognizing the ringtone as Lucky's, I answered and placed a finger in one of my ears to block out the guitar coming from the television.

"Have you heard anything?" Lucky asked immediately.

I'd called him yesterday and told him about Treasure. He was worried immediately and was going to make plans to get back to Baltimore as soon as possible.

"No," I said.

"Are you sure?"

"Yes."

"You sure you've checked all the hospitals?" he asked.

"Yes."

"Well, someone has to know something, Keema. People don't just vanish into thin air."

"I know, Lucky. But I don't know what else to do."

Tears began to fall from my eyes again.

"Fuck!" he screamed into the phone. "I can't believe this

215

shit, Keema! I can't believe a fuckin' father would involve his daughter in damn bank robbery!"

More guilt fell upon my shoulders.

"He's lucky the cops killed him! If they hadn't, I would've killed him my damn self!"

"Lucky, I feel so terrible." I broke all the way down again with Deniro stopping his craziness only for a second to watch me. He then started up the noise again. "It's all my fault."

"No, Keema, it's not your fault. You didn't know what that sorry son of a bitch had up his sleeve."

His words still didn't make me feel any better. With more tears streaming, I dropped my face into my hand.

"Keema, everything's going to be alright," he promised. "You've got to be strong. You've got to for Deniro."

I cried harder. My world seemed over.

Then suddenly the front door opened.

With my face buried, I had no desire to lift it.

The loud guitars from the television stopped abruptly.

"Treasure!" Deniro screamed.

I couldn't have heard him correctly. My head rose from my hand. A moment later my mouth dropped to the floor.

"Keema?" Lucky asked from the phone.

In total shock at what and who I was seeing, the phone fell from my hand to the floor. In front of me, Treasure was hugging her brother. "Treasure!" I instantly jumped up from the couch and ran across the room.

Oddly, my daughter had a very nonchalant look on her face.

With a mixture of anger, worry and joy, my hand reached behind me and came around hard landing on Treasure's face. "Where the hell have you been? I've been worried sick about your ass!"

She didn't say anything. She simply stared at me while holding her face. Within a brief second she was in my arms. I'd yanked her hand, wrapping my arms around her tightly.

"Don't you *ever* do that to me again!" My arms were

squeezing her snugly.

She still didn't say anything.

"I missed you, Treasure," Deniro blurted out.

She finally smiled. "I missed you, too, Deniro."

"Treasure, I thought you were dead," I told her. Suddenly, I released my arms and stepped back to inspect her for any gunshot wounds. "Are you okay?" I asked as my eyes quickly traveled from her head to her feet. "Are you hurt?"

"I'm good."

"You're good? Girl, I thought you'd been shot by the cops. Why didn't you call me?"

"For what?" she asked snidely. "You left me for dead."

"Treasure, what do you mean?"

"Exactly what I said. You left me." Her tone and eyes were filled with spite.

"I tried to come back for you, but Trent said you knew what to do in that situation. He said that y'all had planned for it."

"Whatever," she said, shrugging it off and rolling her eyes. "I'm a ride or die chick about mines. I found my own way up out of all that and have been handling business ever since. Every mother ain't maternal. What's a girl to do?"

"What the fuck is that supposed to mean? I've taken care of you your whole life and now you acting like I haven't been a good mother?"

She shrugged again.

"I shouldn't have left you with your father, Treasure. That was my mistake."

Before I could finish my sentence I could see water well up in her eyes.

"Aweee, baby, so you know about your father?" I asked sympathetically, ready to take her in my arms again if she broke down about it. "Baby, I'm so sorry about Drake. I know you and him were getting close and making up for all that time he'd spent in prison."

She rolled her eyes again. "Are you serious?"

I didn't know what she meant.

217

"The game is chess, not checkers," she told me heading into the kitchen and opening the refrigerator.

I followed, leaving Deniro in the living room. "Treasure, what are you talking about?"

Before she could answer, I could hear Lucky's ringtone going off on my phone again. But he would just have to wait. I needed answers from my daughter.

"Daddy was a deadbeat, a sperm donor. That's all. He was never really there for me," Treasure said.

"But, I thought you loved him?"

"Yeah, just enough to get that money from the storage unit."

I stared at her, eyes bulging, wondering how she could be so cold and vindictive. I'd created a monster. I kept glaring into her stone-looking face.

"I was playing him the whole time," Treasure continued after grabbing two slices of bread and some deli meat from the pack. "It was all an act."

I didn't know what to say. I didn't know who I felt worse for; her or Drake. The more I thought about it, the more I felt bad for Drake. He'd died thinking his daughter loved him.

"Did you go get the money yet?" she asked taking a bite from her sloppy looking sandwich.

"What money?"

"The money in the storage unit, dad's stash."

I hadn't even thought about that money. So much had gone on that I'd forgotten all about it. I didn't want it anyway. It was blood money, bad luck.

"No, I didn't," I told her. "I haven't even thought about it."

She looked at me skeptically as if she didn't believe a word I'd just said. "Uh huh," she mumbled then suddenly turned to jog upstairs.

"Where are you going?" I followed quickly and rested my arm on the railing at the bottom of the steps.

She ignored me and disappeared when she reached the

top of the stairs. A few seconds later she appeared again and came jogging back down to the living room. When she was in front of me, she was holding a key and a small piece of paper.

"What's that?"

"It's the storage key and the code to the lock." She had a wicked smile on her face.

I never knew Drake even kept the key to the storage in the house. I'd never seen it. "Treasure, where'd you get that?"

"Don't worry about it," she said, headed for the door. "Come on. Let's roll."

We pulled up at the storage company in my Camero several minutes later. As we came to a stop, Treasure looked in the side mirror again. She'd done it over a dozen times, since we'd left the house.

I looked behind us to see what she was looking for. Deniro did also from the back seat. "Treasure, you've been watching that mirror since we left home," I said. "Who are you looking for?"

"There was a strange car sitting outside the house when I first got home, so I'm on the look-out. You gotta have all eyes and ears peeled open," she warned.

"What car?"

"A black Impala. I've seen it a few times before. Something about it gives me the creeps. I don't trust it."

Realizing it was Frenchie's car she'd seen, I quickly glanced around but didn't see it. She didn't know anything about Frenchie. I hadn't told her or Drake about him. It was time to tell her at least a little about him now, though.

"Treasure, the money from Frenchie's inheritance finally came through."

"What?" she said, her eyes growing big.

"Yeah."

"Well, where is it?"

"It hasn't arrived yet. They're mailing it."

"How much is it for?" she questioned.

"Five hundred stacks."

"Wowwwwww."

I nodded.

"Look, Treasure, it's time to leave this life behind. There's no future in it."

"What do you mean?"

"I mean, when the check gets here, we're hopping on a plane and leaving B-More forever. We're never coming back."

I meant it. Fuck Frenchie! I was going to take his money and start a whole new life with just me and my kids.

"Are you serious?" she asked, still wide eyed.

"Yeah, baby, I'm serious."

She turned to stare out the window, her mind probably calculating where we would go.

"Treasure, that's not all. Baby, I've got something else to tell you."

"What is it?" she asked, turning to look at me again.

"Frenchie isn't dead."

She looked at me like I'd lost my mind. "What?"

"I know it sounds crazy, but it's true. That's who is behind the wheel of that black Impala you've been seeing."

Her mouth dropped.

Reluctantly I went on. "Treasure, me and your aunt Imani double crossed him. Now, he wants all of the inheritance money or he's going to kill me."

Treasure had no idea what to say.

"Shy's involved with him now, too."

She looked at me even more strangely. "How do you know that?"

"I heard her in the background during a phone call with him one time. I also heard her again yesterday at the attorney's office. She'd been calling my attorney posing as me to get info on the inheritance money."

"Are you sure?"

I nodded.

"I heard her, too, Treasure," Deniro cosigned from the backseat.

Treasure leaned back into her seat for a moment, letting the outrageous sounding story sink in. The car was silent for several moments. Finally, she said, "Shy needs to be dealt with. You can't just keep letting people punk you."

"Treasure, I'm done with that life. When I leave with that check that'll be payback enough."

"Well, I don't agree. I say we body her ass. And running is not an option," Treasure replied.

"What?" I really had created a monster.

"You can't run."

"Why can't I?"

"Every time you try to run from someone, they catch you. They always do," Treasure said.

She was right. I ran from Paco and he eventually found me. I ran from Dupree's murder, but Rick eventually figured it out. I even ran from Frenchie's murder and now he found me.

"For half a million dollars there's no way Frenchie isn't going to look for you. For that type of money he'll hunt you until you drop."

I sighed, leaning back into my own seat. Damn, she was right. There was no way he'd let five hundred thousand disappear. "So, what do you suggest?" I asked her, feeling weird that I was now asking my child for advice.

"You face him head on," Treasure said as if I should've known the answer.

"How?"

"We'll figure it out. But for now, let's get this money."

Minutes later we were headed past dozens of rows of storage units. The lot was like a labyrinth. Eventually we reached a unit located in the back of the lot.

"This is it," Treasure said.

I'd remembered that Drake said there was a couple hundred thousand inside. Anticipation began to fill me. If things didn't work out quite as planned with Frenchie's money, the money inside the storage would still give me and my babies a decent down payment on a new life.

Treasure placed the key in the pad lock and turned it. She then bent down and raised the orange bay door. The unit was empty except for a small steel box sitting in the center of the floor. Treasure immediately walked inside, knelt in front of the box and began to turn the combination lock dangling from it as she looked at the code written on the small piece of paper in her hand while me and Deniro stood over her. When she finally got the box unlocked all of us expected to see several stacks of money. Instead, when she opened the box, there was only four stacks. Wrapped around the center of each stack was a strip that read $20,000. Altogether there was only eighty grand.

"Damn," Treasure said. "I thought there was more."

"Me too."

I was disappointed, but kept quiet.

"Drake made trips here regularly to get money," Treasure continued. "He must've run through it all. That's why he needed to rob that bank."

I nodded in agreement.

Treasure grabbed the money, and attempted to slip it into her purse until I cleared my throat. Immediately, she handed it over and closed the box. Shortly after, the three of us headed out of the unit. Once outside my heart stopped at who was standing there waiting for us…

It was Trent.

I dropped my purse at the sight of him standing there with a gun pointed at us. Treasure and Deniro stopped, too.

Cocking the gun, Trent spat loudly, "Give it to me!"

Quickly, I stepped in front of Treasure and Deniro. If bullets flew, I needed to be the one to die, not my babies. "Give you what?" I asked.

"The money, bitch! Don't play with me! Give it up now!"

"Okay, okay, you can have it," I told him, wanting to defuse the situation. "It's in my purse."

"Get it!" he yelled.

"Don't give that nigga shit!" Deniro shouted.

"Shut up, Deniro," I told him, shocked that he would even talk that way. I knelt down, pulled the money from my purse and extended it to him. "Just take it and go," I muttered."

Trent snatched it from my hand and looked at it like it had shit stuck to it. "What's this?" he asked sharply.

"The money."

"Bitch, don't play with me! This is only eighty stacks! Where's the rest?"

"Hell if I know. That's all that was here! I swear."

Trent shook his head. "No it's not!"

"Yes, it is!" I yelled back.

"Fuck it! I'm done with the game! I'm just gonna kill you and see for myself!"

I reached behind myself to push my kids behind my back. My body tensed, preparing for the gunshot, preparing for pain, preparing to die. My eyes closed. In my mind and heart, I hoped God would look out for my kids once I was dead.

Then it happened.

The gunshot sounded like a canon.

I thought I was dead.

Everything went silent.

I couldn't even feel the pain.

For several moments I was scared to open my eyes. Finally I did. Surprisingly, I was still alive and breathing. It was Trent who was dead. He was lying on his stomach in blood. His brains were scattered around him looking like spaghetti. Slowly my eyes rose from his dead body to see Frenchie's gruesome face standing a few feet away with his .45 pointed directly at me. He'd obviously followed us there.

"Trying to hold out on me, Keema?" he asked smiling.

I was too shaken by the situation to say anything.

"It doesn't matter if it's eighty thousand or eight *hundred* thousand. What's yours is mine. Any and everything you ever get belongs to me."

223

I still couldn't speak.

Boldly, as if not scared of dying, Treasure stepped out from behind me and eyed Frenchie with the most evil look I'd ever seen grace her face.

26

My eyes were fixed on the street and traffic ahead of me, but my mind was focused on a million other things as I drove the U-Haul truck. Staying in Baltimore or even Maryland for too much longer was not an option at all. Mr. Hyde informed me yesterday that the inheritance money had been mailed out overnight yesterday morning. By it being express mail, I would get it today. It had been six days since I'd signed the paperwork in his office. Since then, I'd been stalking the mailbox like a welfare recipient on the first of the month.

I was absolutely done with not only Baltimore, but the fast city life, period. B-More and cities like it were filled with far too many guns, violence and death for me. Out here someone was always dying before their time. Someone was always out to cut your throat.

Once upon a time I'd worn my love for my city like a badge of honor. I was proud to be a B-More bitch. I represented. Those days were over now. I'd grown out of that ignorance. I'd finally realized my kids and I deserved better.

Ms. Kyle schooled me on Hampton, Virginia. She told me that she had family back there and went to visit every summer. She loved it. The city was smaller than Baltimore and much safer. It was also real laid back and country. That all sounded beautiful to me. I was sold. As soon as the inheritance money got here, that's where me and my kids were headed. We wouldn't waste a single second. We were hitting the highway immediately, and of course I wasn't giving Frenchie and Shy one red cent.

Ms. Kyle and I had been talking on the phone a lot over the past several days. She'd been giving me so much advice about life and living. I hadn't told her about the deaths of Drake or Trent. I hadn't told her about the robbery. I felt no need to, but I was in dire need of her motherly counseling. She told me to keep my head up, keep my faith in God and to keep pressing forward.

I was always inspired by Ms. Kyle. God, how I wished she was my mother. She was just as sweet of a person as she could be and I loved her for it. She told me that when I moved to Hampton, she wanted us to stay in touch so she could visit me next summer when she went down there to visit her family.

With urging from Mrs. Kyle, I'd planned on going back to school to get my GED. From there, I would get myself in a community college and study business. I would totally throw myself into my education, accepting nothing short of success.

Becoming a mother that my children could be proud of was my motivation. It was now what I lived for. I was sick and tired of them seeing me this way. I was sick and tired of them seeing me struggle. All of that had to stop. It had to come to an end. Besides, I'd brought them so close to their own deaths several days ago outside that damn storage place. That shit worked on my nerves and my conscience ever since. If Trent or Frenchie had killed them, it would've been all my fault. I would've burned in hell for it.

Thank God all Frenchie wanted that day was the money. He took the eighty grand. He also took the few hundred dollars I had in my purse. The nigga was merciless. But I would rather he take my money than my life and the life of my children.

"I'm not going," Treasure said from the far end of the passenger seat, breaking me out of my thoughts.

"What?" I asked, jerking the U-Haul slightly.

"I'm not going," she repeated.

226

"Treasure, we already discussed this. Baltimore is not safe for us."

"So, we're just supposed to run like cowards?"

"I ain't no coward," Deniro said, sitting between us. "I'll kill Frenchie's ass."

"Watch your mouth," I told him.

"He put a gun in your face, Ma. I'm gonna murk his ass."

Immediately Deniro pretended to shoot multiple times into thin air.

"Deniro, don't talk like that," I demanded.

"Well, he's right," Treasure cosigned with a mean scowl. "We should fight fire with fire."

"Treasure, that's not going to solve anything. When you live by the gun, you die by the gun."

Treasure rolled her eyes then mumbled something under her breath.

"Treasure, aren't you tired of losing the people you love? Over this bullshit, we've lost Imani, Dupree, Cash, and your grandmother. Damn it, Treasure. When is enough for you?"

She pursed her lips, obviously not feeling anything I was saying.

"Huh, Treasure? When will you get tired of this?" I asked.

"Whatever, I'm still not leaving. I get too much money out here in these B-More streets."

I shook my head at her ignorance.

"I'm not leaving you."

"You'll be fine without me," she shot back.

"No, I won't."

"Yes, you will. You'll get over me just like you got over Cash."

Treasure's last statement was purposely meant to sting and it had found its mark. I looked at her, pulling over to the side of the road. Her comment made me unable to even think clearly.

"It's true," she continued. "You'll have another child and get another welfare check. Kids are expendable to you."

"Treasure, honey, how could you say that to me?"

She rolled her eyes again. "Unnnnn, huh."

"Look," I told her. "I'm not perfect. I'm not the perfect mother. I've made mistakes. But I'll be damned if I'll repeat those mistakes. Treasure, I love you, Shane, Deniro and Cash equally. None of you are expendable or replaceable. You're all my heart. And I'll die before I lose any more of you."

She continued to ignore me.

"You may not believe me, Treasure, but it's true. And I know you think you're grown. But contrary to belief, you're not. You're still under eighteen. So, until you turn eighteen, you're my responsibility. And you're going to Hampton whether you want to or not."

Suddenly, my cell phone started to ring. Recognizing the ringtone, I knew it was Lucky calling once again. After briefly talking to him the day before just to let him know Treasure was okay, I'd been ignoring his calls ever since. Not that I had anything against him, but for once I didn't want anyone to interrupt my family time or try to talk me out of moving to Virginia. For once, I wanted to take charge of my family without any outside judgments or opinions. Surprisingly, Treasure wasn't answering his calls either. One minute she loved him, the next minute she had an attitude. Her ass was so bipolar.

Quickly, I pulled back into traffic. The inside of the U-Haul was silent for the rest of the drive. Finally, we reached my house. It was strange seeing someone sitting on the front porch with his head down. Fretfully, I attempted to catch a glimpse of the person's face, but a fitted baseball cap shielded my view.

"Who is that?" Deniro asked loudly.

I was kind of skeptical about turning off the truck's engine; unsure about who the stranger was on the porch. Shit had been too hectic lately for me to trust strangers. Finally the stranger raised his head.

"Oh my God," I gasped, seeing the face I'd been dreaming about and missing for what seemed like decades.

"Shane!" Deniro screamed with excitement as he damn

near bowled over Treasure to get out of the truck.

I almost tripped over my feet to get out myself. Quickly, we all ran up on him like the police on attack. The four of us hugged, tightly. "Boy, look at you," I told him admirably as I inspected him from head to toe and then began ripping off question after question to him about where he'd been and what he'd been doing.

Shane had changed. His build was still large, but it had become more solid and chiseled like he'd been working out. His clothes were no longer sloppy on him. They were now clean, name brand, and expensive. His sneakers were spotless and his hair was neatly cut.

"Been okay," he said to me.

"Are you sure? Where have you been?" I looked at him again. Wherever he'd been, someone had taken good care of him.

Instead of responding, Shane just stared at me.

"Boy, you had me worried sick," I said.

"Sorry, Keema. Shane is sorry, Keema. Sorry, Keema," he kept repeating.

"Don't worry. What matters is that you're back. But why didn't you call me? Why didn't you let me know you were okay?"

"Shane called you," he responded.

I shook my head. "No, Shane, you didn't call me."

"Shane called."

Just when I was about to disagree, I suddenly thought back to the strange phone call I got that day when no one said a word. I guess my assumptions were true. It was Shane who'd called. "Why didn't you say anything when I answered?"

Again, Shane just glared at me, then began to rapidly move his fingers back and forth. I looked down to see an envelope in his hand. "What's that?"

"The man left it for Keema. He left it for Keema," Shane said, offering it to me.

My eyes perked up. It was the money!

229

I snatched the envelope, ripped it open and took out the check.

"Is that it?" Treasure asked.

Smiling, I looked at her and said, "Yeah, baby, it sure is."

Shane sat back down on the steps.

"So, what's next?" Treasure asked.

"We get in here, get our stuff packed in the truck, and hit the highway."

Treasure wasn't too happy about that. Her face showed it.

Ignoring us, Shane began to rock back and forth. "Shy gon' kill you," he said.

He caught me off guard with those words. He'd caught all of us off guard. We each looked at him.

"Gon' split your head down to the white meat," he continued. But instead of looking at me, he was looking off into the distance, glassy eyed.

I looked at him with a puzzled look. "Shane, what are you saying?" I asked. "What are you talking about? Who told you that?"

"Keema killed Trent," he began to say. "Keema killed Trent," he repeated.

All three of us were definitely caught off guard by that one. How did he know about Trent? Someone had obviously told him that for him to repeat it. Treasure, Deniro and I glanced at each other and then back at Shane.

"Shane, baby, how do you know about that?" I asked him. "How do you know about Trent?"

He didn't answer. He just kept rocking back and forth.

"Shane, where have you been?" Treasure asked.

He didn't speak.

"Boy, you hear me talking to you!" she screamed at him.

"Stop yelling at him," I told her and knelt in front of him. "Shane," I said softly, touching his thigh and looking into his eyes. Shane stopped rocking back and forth and looked at me. Giving him a smile, I asked, "Baby, where have you been? Who have you been living with?"

"With Frenchie," he said. "Yeah, living with Frenchie."

Frenchie, I thought. "What do you mean?"

He smiled proudly, poked his chest out and said, "He's my boss man."

"Your boss man? What do you do for him?" I questioned.

"Frenchie my boss man. I work for him. I'm a soldier. I get money, Keema. I get money. A soldier. Yeah...a soldier." Shane reached into his pocket and pulled out a fat wad of hundred dollar bills. "See, Keema. I get money."

"I see," I told him. "Baby, what did you mean about Shy wanting to kill me?"

"I...I...I heard her. She said it." Shane moved his fingers rapidly. "She lives with us. She's my new mommy!"

Hearing those words made me jump to my feet. Treasure and Deniro watched me as I began to pace back and forth.

"That ratchet ass bitch!" I screamed. "That dirty bitch!"

"I told you," Treasure spat, stroking the rage inside me. "I told you. We can't leave yet. That bitch has been plotting against you. Are you going to let her get away with that? I say it's time for get back!"

"I had her in my house! I had her around my kids! And this is how she does me?" I asked no one in particular.

"We need to pay her back, mommy," Deniro said.

"Fuck!" I yelled angrily and in frustration.

I had the check. I had it in my hand. All I had to do now was hop on the highway. That was all. But the old Keema was telling me to get revenge and retaliation. It was telling me not to walk away. The bitch had my baby calling her his new momma!

"Damn it!" I yelled.

Every time I seemed to be out the game, something always pulled me back in. Something always kept a hold of me. I was letting my anger and need for revenge make this time no different. I just could not allow that third rate ass bitch to think she'd gotten the best of me. I just couldn't. She had to pay for crossing me.

Suddenly, I stopped pacing back and forth and looked

around the block quickly. Shy and Frenchie could've been nearby. Sending Shane could've been a set up. Were they near? Were they watching me? What did they have planned? Obviously they had *something* planned for me. What exactly was it?

I finally realized something…

Frenchie wasn't going to allow me to live.

Once Frenchie got the money, he was going to kill me. I no longer doubted it. Once he got what he wanted, he wouldn't need me anymore. He'd probably kill my kids too so there would be no one left to tell what had happened. With all of us out of the picture, he could take the money and disappear once again.

Remembering Shane saying, "Keema killed Trent," I also realized they were possibly trying to frame me. They were probably somehow going to make me go down for Trent's murder.

Shit, I was in the dark. They had so much on me, but I had no idea where they were going to come at me. If I ran with the money, Frenchie would most likely hunt me down. He'd even possibly kill my kids if he couldn't get his hand on me. If I gave him the money, he was still going to kill me. I was in a no win situation.

"Let's go," I said and headed to the U-Haul.

"Where are we going?" Treasure asked. "I thought we were gonna put all our stuff in the truck."

"Don't worry about it. Just come on. There's no time. You too, Shane, let's go."

We all piled into the cramped truck moving as fast as possible. As soon as we were inside, I backed out of the driveway and headed up the street. As soon as we reached the end of the street, I made a quick left.

"Ma," Treasure said, looking in her side view mirror.

Guess I was no longer Keema anymore.

"What?"

"That black Impala is behind us."

I quickly looked in my own side view mirror. Treasure was right. Frenchie was right behind us. Running was now definitely not an option. Someone was getting ready to die.

232

27

My foot slammed down onto the gas pedal viciously. "Put your seatbelts on!" I screamed to my children.

Since there weren't enough seatbelts to go around, Shane put on his and grabbed hold of his brother and sister.

The U-Haul truck jerked and gained speed eventually, but it struggled to do so. The speedometer's limit was 120 mph's and I was determined to milk it for as much as I could get out of it. The engine revved and roared, but struggled to even reach eighty.

"God, watch over me and my kids," I whispered as my hands gripped the steering wheel like my life depended on it.

Shit, in all actuality, my life and the lives of my kids *were* depending on it. Obviously, Frenchie knew I had the check. If he caught me, I didn't doubt he'd kill me on the spot.

Looking in the side view mirror, I could see the Impala dead on my ass, and also saw Ms. Kyle pulling onto my street as I barged down the block past her. Our eyes connected and I knew from the frightened expression that she knew we were in trouble. I tried to mouth my desire for her to go away yet my heart told me she'd attempt to help me.

"Stay away from me," I shouted as I kept driving past her.

The truck was up to ninety mph, but was no match for

Frenchie's car. Obviously, the truck wasn't built for the pressure I was putting on it right now. Not to mention, it was an older model. It had nearly two hundred thousand miles on it already. Most likely it had moved countless families and had hit the highway thousands upon thousands of times. The Impala, on the other hand, was a beast. It was chasing us down like a lion chasing down its prey. Repeatedly I swerved the truck to keep Frenchie from riding up alongside of us, nearly clipping his front bumper a couple of times. Each time, he fell back while the truck violently rocked off balance.

"Go faster!" Treasure screamed as she looked in her side view mirror.

"I am!" I belted. "I'm going as fast as this raggedy piece of shit will take us!"

Within moments, we were off of the side streets and skidding sharply onto a busy street. Cars slammed on their breaks, swerved and even crashed into each other to avoid us. Horns and car alarms went off loudly as I slammed on the gas once again.

"You crazy bitch!" someone screamed from one of the cars I'd left behind.

My heart ran sprints with no rest. My adrenaline did the same. Over and over I kept looking in my side view, hoping I'd lost Frenchie. It was a no go, though. Each time, the Impala was right there, refusing to allow me out of its sight, let alone escape.

Constantly my hand slammed against the horn, trying to get cars to clear the way for me. On the side streets I had clear straightaways. Now, there were cars and pedestrians everywhere, causing me to slow up, and swerve in and out of traffic to keep from hitting anyone. Where were the fucking police when I needed them?

"Move!" I screamed. "Get out my damn way!"

Buildings, cars, and people whizzed by my window quickly as the truck darted and dipped through traffic like a bat out of hell. I could see us getting closer to the intersection so I told the kids, "Hold on!"

We all saw traffic crossing.

The kids ducked.

I panicked.

Instead of slowing down, I slammed the gas pedal to the floor, terrified of the consequences. The light was green as we quickly approached it. With a quick prayer, I got closer and closer.

"Shit, shit, shit, shit," I kept repeating over and over again as we raced toward the crossing trail of cars like the nose of a falling plane approaching the ground.

Too late to turn back, we flew through the traffic causing cars to skid. Just like the last intersection, several cars crashed. With no time to worry about the damage, my foot remained on the gas pedal, thankful to be alive.

Street after street continued to whiz by us. Continuously, I whipped and weaved, refusing to let Frenchie catch us. Once again, I looked in my side view. This time, what I saw horrified me even more than the life threatening chase itself. Frenchie was now holding a gun out of his window.

CLAP!

The first shot went off.

I ducked slightly, while still gripping the steering wheel and also keeping my eyes on the road ahead of me. The truck jerked as I lost control for a brief second. Immediately, I re-gained control and stayed the course. I wasn't ready to die.

More shots rang out. The next rang even louder. The back driver's side tire exploded as the bullet ripped through it.

"No!" I screamed.

Shards of rubber flew and sparks began to fly from the rim as it sharply tore into the street top. Although my foot was still on the gas pedal, the truck began to lose some of its speed, then it began to wobble.

"No!" I screamed again.

As more and more streets whizzed by, the truck became difficult to control. Once again I looked into my side view mirror. This time the Impala was now coming up along my side.

"Shit!" I yelled.

Before I could react, Frenchie swerved the Impala against the side of the truck causing it to rock side to side. I grabbed the steering wheel even more desperately than before, trying to keep control.

The children screamed.

When I finally regained control of the U-Haul, it didn't do much good. As soon as I straightened it out, the Impala slammed against its side once again, this time much harder than before. Keeping control this time was impossible. The truck ran up onto the curb.

"Get down!" I shouted to the kids.

They each ducked.

Realizing I had no other choice, I slammed on the brakes. The truck's hulking frame skidded to the right and spun out. Quickly, I reached beside Shane and unbuckled his seat belt.

"Get out!" I yelled. "Get out now!"

Each of my protégés jumped out with me right behind them. Seeing Frenchie's Impala spin out ahead of us, I grabbed my kids and darted into traffic.

"Help me!" I screamed at the top my lungs while waving my arms wildly. "Please, somebody help me!"

The tires of the Impala screeched as it headed back towards us. Seeing the car coming, I grabbed the kids and ran back up on the sidewalk, not knowing what else to do. Moments later, the Impala swerved across traffic and closed in on us in no time.

"He's going to kill me!" I screamed. "Someone help me! He's going to kill me and my kids!"

Passerby's looked, but no one stopped.

The Impala shot up onto the curb in front of us and skidded to a stop. Its driver's side door swung open and Frenchie leapt out with a gun in his hand.

"Please, Frenchie," I stepped in front of the kids and gathered them behind me. "Please don't do this!"

Without a word said, Frenchie made his way toward us, not caring about the countless passing witnesses. His menacing eyes never strayed from mine.

"Don't do this!" I pleaded again.

Frenchie finally reached me and snatched a hold of my neck.

"Get off of her!" my kids demanded.

Shane stepped out from behind me and took a step toward Frenchie.

"Get your ass back, lil nigga!" Frenchie ordered, aiming the gun in his face.

Shane had no choice but to back off.

"Frenchie, please," I said. "You can have the check. It's in my purse. Just please don't kill me."

"Don't kill you?" he repeated as if I had no right to beg for my life. His grip around my neck grew tighter. "Don't kill you?"

"Please don't."

"Fuck you!" he hollered into my face. "Fuck your life!"

I was scared to death.

"Just like your ass didn't have mercy on my life, I ain't havin' mercy on yours, bitch!"

"Frenchie, I swear I'm sorry for what I did to you. I really am."

"Oh, is that right?" he responded.

"Yes, Frenchie. I mean it."

"Are you sorry for what you did to my brother's, too?"

I fell silent.

"Yeah, bitch, I know about what you did," he said.

I had no idea what to say. How did he know?

"You should be more careful about who you allow into your circle, Keema. Not everyone around you is your friend or even your family," Frenchie spoke.

"What are you talking about?"

"Your own daughter gave your sneaky ass up. She takes after you. For a few dollars, she told me everything."

"You're a liar!" Treasure screamed at him from behind me. "I didn't tell you anything! You sucka-ass nigga!"

I didn't know what to believe. The last thing I wanted to

237

believe was that my own daughter had sold me out like that, but in all honesty, Treasure had changed. Treasure's track record had grown shaky lately. Money had her hard up to get it.

Frenchie laughed. "Like mother, like daughter," he said snidely.

"You're a damn liar!" Treasure screamed again, this time boldly taking a step toward him.

With the pistol still in hand, Frenchie suddenly back-handed Treasure to the concrete. "Lil bitch, stay in your place! Don't you ever run up on me again!"

Treasure sat on the ground dazed and holding the side of her face as blood ran from her bottom lip.

Suddenly, a car came to a stop beside us. Mrs. Kyle leapt out of it. Shit! She'd still managed to catch up after all of our crazy driving. I had no time to beg her to go away. Next thing I knew, a Honda Crosstour raced up on us, too. I recognized the car immediately as Shy hopped out. I had no idea what was going on as both headed towards me. My eye caught a glimpse across the passing traffic at someone standing across the street talking on their cell phone as they watched us. With all my heart, I hoped they were calling the police.

"Oh, God, Mrs. Kyle said," as she approached with a ter-rified look on her face. "Keema!"

"Stay back, you old bitch!" Frenchie ordered. "Or I'll blast your ass out here, too!"

Mrs. Kyle stayed at a distance, but pleaded for my life Cars slowed in the street as their drivers and passengers watched the action.

"Kill her ass!" Shy urged Frenchie as she stood behind him. "Kill that bitch! She always thought she was the shit. The bitch looks down on everybody."

Everything was happening so fast.

Every voice seemed so loud

Sirens began to appear from the distance.

"The cops are coming, baby," Shy said to Frenchie. "Kill her now!"

"Don't do it!" Mrs. Kyle begged. "Please, don't do this!"

"Come here, Shane!" Shy said. "Come here, baby!"

Shane didn't move. He stayed behind me.

"It's okay, baby. Come here," Shy continued.

He still didn't move.

The sirens grew louder and nearer.

Out of the blue, Shy pulled a gun of her own; a .32, which didn't mean shit compared to Frenchie's .45. "Shane, come here!" she demanded again, this time much more force-fully.

Shane still remained behind me.

"Nigga, don't you hear me talking to you? I said come here!" Shy ordered.

"Leave him alone!" both Treasure and Deniro yelled.

"Shut the fuck up!" Shy said as she raised the gun and pointed it at them.

"Please put the guns down!" Mrs. Kyle pleaded. "It does-n't have to be like this. These are children out here!"

"Shy," I said, my throat still trapped underneath Frenchie's grip. "If you hurt my children, I'll kill you! Bitch, I swear to fucking God I'll kill you!"

"Keema, you're already dead. Your life has always been shit, doing nothing, going nowhere. Just a life of scamming. Kill her, Frenchie, baby!" Shy yelled.

The sirens were growing closer, yet I couldn't see them. Apparently, Frenchie wasn't afraid of them coming either.

"How could you do this to me, Shy? I always treated you like a sister, like family."

"Bitch, you never cared about me. You always treated me like a damn flunkie."

I didn't speak. She was right. I'd always had more respect for Raven than her. Although I had love for her, she's always seemed a little slow to me.

"You never thought I was smart enough to be on your level. But what your ass didn't realize was that I was smart enough to watch and learn from you. Your ass taught me to get

239

down as hard as necessary for the money."

I watched her finish her words over Frenchie's shoulder as flashing lights could be seen from my peripheral vision.

"So of course, when Frenchie offered me a chance to get *real* money and get back at your ass, I took it," Shy bragged.

"You snake ass bitch," I said, hoping her dumb ass would keep talking so the cops would shoot her ass down.

Shy smiled. "Don't be mad, Keema. It's just karma, baby. Your ass is just finally getting back what you gave for so long. It has all caught up with you."

People had gathered across the street to be nosey, but no one attempted to get involved or offer any kind of help. With the sight of so many guns, no one wanted to get too close.

Mrs. Kyle was now crying and praying.

"Shoot her, baby," Shy told Frenchie once again. "Quick, let's go!" she added after spotting the first police car just two hundred yards away.

"Grab her purse," Frenchie told her after laying eyes on the police car speeding towards us. "The check is in there."

With her gun pointed at me, Shy stepped from behind Frenchie and snatched my purse from my shoulder. She stepped back immediately. Frenchie did the same, while still keeping the gun and both eyes trained on me.

All I could do was stand still. With so much going on around me, so many people watching, I felt utterly alone. My ears had blocked the entire world out. All I could focus on was the moment and the gun.

"This is for my brothers," Frenchie said as he cocked the gun.

My body stiffened at the sound.

Frenchie's finger locked around the trigger.

Instead of closing my eyes, I watched. My eyes never blinked. They never strayed as even my entire life began to pass before them.

CLAP!!! CLAP!!! CLAP!!!

The gun spat off three shots, each tearing into me and

knocking me backwards. Seconds later, I was lying flat on the ground staring up at the sky. Screams came from everywhere as my kids and Mrs. Kyle rushed to me.

Frenchie and Shy dashed to the Impala, hopped inside and sped off just as the one police officer jumped out of the cruiser with his gun drawn. His ass was a day late, and a dollar short. Where the fuck was his back-up?

"Mommy!" my kids screamed as they each knelt beside me.

"Dear God," Mrs. Kyle whispered as she took my hand into her own.

Blood poured from my body and began to pool around me.

Onlookers who were once too scared to come near me were now rushing towards me from all directions, including the first officer on the scene. Cars finally stopped and pulled to the curb.

Treasure pointed her finger. "Go after him! He went that way!" she yelled to the officer as he spoke into the little radio on his shoulder.

"Baby, hold on," Mrs. Kyle pleaded desperately to me as she held my hand tightly. Tears fell from her eyes.

"Mommy, I didn't sell you out," Treasure said with tears rolling down her cheeks. "I swear I didn't. Please don't go."

"Mommy, we love you," Deniro said, crying. "Hold on, mommy."

Shane remained silent. His eyes were filled with tears.

"Child, you hold on," Mrs. Kyle said again. "Help is coming."

Suddenly the sirens were blaring much louder than before. They'd finally reached me. Tons of police officers and EMS jumped from squad cars and an ambulance. They rushed toward me. Something told me it was too late though. Shy was right. All my dirt had finally caught up to me. I raised my eyes to Mrs. Kyle.

"Please take care of my babies," I said. "They're all I

got."

> With those words said, everything went black and silent. Karma had finally gotten me.

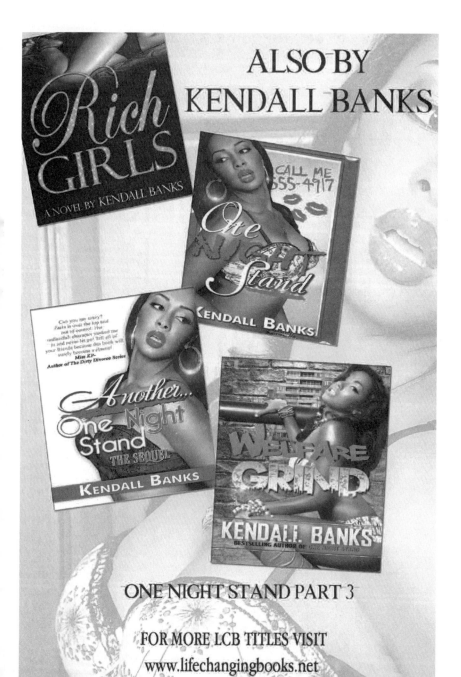

MAIL TO:
PO Box 423
Brandywine, MD 20613
301-362-6508

FAX TO:
301-579-9913

ORDER FORM

| Date: | Phone: |
| Email: | |

| Ship to: |
| Address: |
| City & State: | Zip: |

Make all money orders and cashiers checks payable to: **Life Changing Books**

Qty.	ISBN	Title	Release Date	Price
	0-9741394-2-4	Bruised by Azarel	Jul-05	$ 15.00
	0-9741394-7-5	Bruised 2: The Ultimate Revenge by Azarel	Oct-06	$ 15.00
	0-9741394-3-2	Secrets of a Housewife by J. Tremble	Feb-06	$ 15.00
	0-9741394-6-7	The Millionaire Mistress by Tiphani	Nov-06	$ 15.00
	1-934230-99-5	More Secrets More Lies by J. Tremble	Feb-07	$ 15.00
	1-934230-95-2	A Private Affair by Mike Warren	May-07	$ 15.00
	1-934230-96-0	Flexin & Sexin Volume 1	Jun-07	$ 15.00
	1-934230-89-8	Still a Mistress by Tiphani	Nov-07	$ 15.00
	1-934230-91-X	Daddy's House by Azarel	Nov-07	$ 15.00
	1-934230-88-X	Naughty Little Angel by J. Tremble	Feb-08	$ 15.00
	1-934230820	Rich Girls by Kendall Banks	Oct-08	$ 15.00
	1-934230839	Expensive Taste by Tiphani	Nov-08	$ 15.00
	1-934230782	Brooklyn Brothel by C. Stecko	Jan-09	$ 15.00
	1-934230669	Good Girl Gone bad by Danette Majette	Mar-09	$ 15.00
	1-934230804	From Hood to Hollywood by Sasha Raye	Mar-09	$ 15.00
	1-934230707	Sweet Swagger by Mike Warren	Jun-09	$ 15.00
	1-934230677	Carbon Copy by Azarel	Jul-09	$ 15.00
	1-934230723	Millionaire Mistress 3 by Tiphani	Nov-09	$ 15.00
	1-934230715	A Woman Scorned by Ericka Williams	Nov-09	$ 15.00
	1-934230685	My Man Her Son by J. Tremble	Feb-10	$ 15.00
	1-924230731	Love Heist by Jackie D.	Mar-10	$ 15.00
	1-934230812	Flexin & Sexin Volume 2	Apr-10	$ 15.00
	1-934230748	The Dirty Divorce by Miss KP	May-10	$ 15.00
	1-934230758	Chedda Boyz by CJ Hudson	Jul-10	$ 15.00
	1-934230766	Snitch by VegasClarke	Oct-10	$ 15.00
	1-934230693	Money Maker by Tonya Ridley	Oct-10	$ 15.00
	1-934230774	The Dirty Divorce Part 2 by Miss KP	Nov-10	$ 15.00
	1-934230170	The Available Wife by Carla Pennington	Jan-11	$ 15.00
	1-934230774	One Night Stand by Kendall Banks	Feb-11	$ 15.00
	1-934230278	Bitter by Danette Majette	Feb-11	$ 15.00
	1-934230299	Married to a Balla by Jackie D.	May-11	$ 15.00
	1-934230308	The Dirty Divorce Part 3 by Miss KP	Jun-11	$ 15.00
	1-934230316	Next Door Nympho By CJ Hudson	Jun-11	$ 15.00
	1-934230286	Bedroom Gangsta by J. Tremble	Sep-11	$ 15.00
	1-934230340	Another One Night Stand by Kendall Banks	Oct-11	$ 15.00
	1-934230359	The Available Wife Part 2 by Carla Pennington	Nov-11	$ 15.00
	1-934230332	Wealthy & Wicked by Chris Renee	Jan-12	$ 15.00
	1-934230375	Life After a Balla by Jackie D.	Mar-12	$ 15.00
	1-934230251	V.I.P. by Azarel	Apr-12	$ 15.00
	1-934230383	Welfare Grind by Kendall Banks	May-12	$ 15.00
			Total for Books	$

Shipping Charges (add $4.95 for 1-4 books*) $

Total Enclosed (add lines) $

* Prison Orders- Please allow up to three (3) weeks for delivery.

Please Note: We are not held responsible for returned prison orders. Make sure the facility will receive books before ordering.

*Shipping and Handling of 5-10 books is $6.95, please contact us if your order is more than 10 books.
(301)362-6508